The Menagerie

A Zoo Story

By

J. D. Porter

Copyright © 2012 by J. D. Porter. All rights reserved.

This is a work of fiction. All of the characters, organizations, and events portrayed in this novel are either products of this author's imagination or used fictitiously.

Part 1

1

Friday, September 2nd, 2011

Silence covered the monkey house like a shroud in the pre-dawn darkness. Sonny, the male chimpanzee, lay quietly on his bench with his brown eyes open and alert. This would be his only quiet time of the day. He listened to the hum of a fan and the tapping of rain on the roof as the pungent aroma of yesterday's rotting fruit and last night's feces and urine filled his broad nostrils. Sonny was small for an adult male chimpanzee, at ninety pounds, but he was still many times stronger than the strongest man. His dark fur was flecked with gray, making him appear even older than his twenty years. He was a handsome, muscular animal who appeared to be flawless, but who carried many scars on the inside. Years of captivity had changed some of his instinctive chimpanzee behavior to fit his environment. He used threat displays, for example, many times more each day than he would in the wild. He masturbated frequently, whereas in the wild, self-stimulation might only occur under extreme stress or anxiety. In a wild troop of chimpanzees an alpha male like Sonny would have dominated every other animal in his group. Sonny, however, directed so much aggression at zoo visitors that he neglected to keep his own troop in line. He was stronger than any of the others, but he was pushed around by nearly everyone, especially his mate, Simba.

Simba shifted onto her back as she slumbered on the next bench. She was much older than Sonny and this, coupled with the fact that she was unusually large for a female chimpanzee, allowed her to dominate her world. She was not attractive, even by chimp standards. She was large, but without the muscle mass of a male, and her lower lip hung down when she was relaxed, showing her lower gums. Her personality was confident and assertive. In the wild, she would have been beaten into submission by the powerful males, but at the Dotson Park Zoo she was queen.

Jana was the most peaceful animal in the group. Perhaps this was because she was only ten years old and she was born at the zoo. Her parents were both dead, so she had no protectors, but with her mild playful personality, she fit in well. She had an attractive, light colored, heart shaped face and she was popular with the other chimps and with the public. Young Jack was also born at the zoo to Simba and Sonny. At five years, he was small for his age and his huge ears stuck out the side of his head. Jack was not very smart but was unusually determined and persistent. It was not hard to imagine Jack succeeding as leader someday.

Sonny idly watched as Jana arose, moved slowly around the cage and sat at the door. He knew she would check the padlock on the front of the cage. He also knew it was locked, because he had watched the zookeeper lock it the night before. The loud click the lock made when she pulled on it startled him. He sat up immediately. The lock had come open.

"Boss, we have a problem." exclaimed Fred Williamson as he charged into the Dotson Park Zoo construction office.

Lyman Denton looked up in mild annoyance and covered the mouthpiece of the phone.

"The rain last night uncovered a body." Fred continued breathlessly.

"I'll call you back," Lyman said into the phone. "Where?" he asked.

"Just before the hook up to the old elephant house."

"Are you sure it's a human body? They used to bury animals around here, you know."

"Oh, it's a person, all right, you'd better come see."

Lyman Denton had been with Dooley Construction Company for seventeen years, the last eight as a construction site superintendent. He was accustomed to problems like these. Usually, when his crew found a body it meant an archeological site and it resulted in long delays by slow, methodical people with little shovels and whisk brooms. He didn't need those kinds of problems now. He debated on what to do as he and Fred walked over to the site.

Lyman and Fred had worked together for over fifteen years. They were an unlikely pair. Fred was tall, muscular and slow moving. Lyman, nearly a foot shorter, was slender and had sandy hair and skin like old leather. Fred supervised all the laborers on the job and had risen as high in the ranks of this company as he ever would – or ever wanted to. They made a good team, had dealt with many problems in the past, and would work through this crisis together.

The trench for the zoo's new sewer main was four feet deep and three feet wide, except where the rain had widened it to nearly five feet in places. The $470,000 project would replace sewer pipes that were over fifty years old. It would create a sanitary sewer system and a storm sewer system where only one system had been. The first phase, the sanitary system, was bringing in an eight inch line off the sewer main that ran down Riverview Road. They had a lot of pipe to lay and they had made good progress in their first two weeks, but all that was about to change.

"Here it is." said Fred as they leaned over the side of the trench. Lyman looked down and a lump came into his throat. The dirty, white skeleton of a human hand did not look like the other ancient grave sites he had seen. This looked like a more recent burial. This was not a job for an archeologist. He headed back to his trailer to call the police.

Chelsea Johns wasn't happy working in the children's zoo, but she would have to be content there for now. She wanted to work with large mammals - the elephants, the rhinos, and the apes. She looked carefully at herself in the mirror as she got ready for work. She was twenty two years old and she knew she could do the work of most men. Her long, red hair was a tousled mop, but would soon be tied up in a careful, tight bun. Strong shoulders and biceps, a narrow waist, and sturdy legs, "I could kick the shit out of most of those guys," she said to herself in the mirror. Her round, freckled face and large, green eyes stared back from the mirror. She was an attractive, even beautiful, lady who cared little for men at this point in her life.

An hour later she was driving down Riverview Road in the rain, heading for the zoo. This was the end of her first week on the job, the last day of her six day run, her Friday, and it promised to be the most interesting day yet. It was sheep dipping day. She wondered how they would dip their little herd. The sheep she had seen dipped on the farm were herded into a corral and forced down a narrow chute containing a trough for the sheep to swim through. No such area existed at the zoo. She wheeled her ten year old Honda Accord through the gate and found a parking place between two pick-up trucks.

"Morning," said Billy Scales as she walked past the tiny kitchen on her way to the break room, "Coffee's on". Billy was one of her fellow keepers and was always first to arrive in the morning. He had been raised on a dairy farm and was conditioned to being awake before dawn. He was not only awake but cheerful, something Chelsea found difficult in the morning.

A few minutes later John Bullard walked in and headed to the coffee without a word. His morning disposition was the opposite of Billy's and even a new keeper like Chelsea knew to stay out of John's way in the morning.

"Asa and Clarence here yet?" asked John quietly. He was referring to lead keeper, Asa Wright, and Mammal Department supervisor, Clarence Watts.

"No," said Billy.

"Figures," grunted John. They both knew that neither Clarence nor Asa was very reliable and that, even though this was sheep dipping day, they would probably be late. They all carried their coffee to the dining room table that sat in what was once the living room. The building that housed the staff break room was built in the late 1940's as a residence for the zoo director. It replaced the one that had burned down a few years before. Zoo directors had not lived in it for years, and it made a perfect place for staff to take their breaks and eat their lunches. No one spoke as they sipped their coffee. Even Billy was quiet.

Billy Scales had been up since 5 am. He was up that early every morning milking cows on the dairy farm where he lived. He was a short man of average build and, though not handsome by any measure, his engaging personality made him a pleasure to be around. He was not married and probably never would be. His whole life revolved around working at the zoo and working at the dairy. If he did take any time off, he was fishing or hunting. He was a country boy who had just turned thirty-five, and he was one of the most competent keepers at the zoo.

Chelsea stole a look at John Bullard and marveled at the contrast. John was tall, about six feet two inches, a powerfully built black man who generally had little to say. He could work hard if he needed to, but seldom did. He was in his mid-fifties and had worked at the zoo nearly thirty years. The only things that he and Billy had in common was their lack of education, both had a GED instead of a high school diploma, and their superb instincts at working around animals.

"Why do we need to dip the sheep", asked Chelsea.

"Ticks, mostly", said Billy.

A once-a-year dipping was the best prevention against the sheep tick. This tiny external parasite is not a true tick, but actually a wingless fly that can be found wherever sheep are raised. They burrow into the wool of sheep and attach themselves to the skin, sucking blood and spreading disease. The treatment is to completely submerge each animal in a vat of insecticide, usually Lindane.

The click of the time clock broke the silence and all heads turned to confirm the time. As they stood, the door opened and their supervisors rushed into the room to punch their cards in the time clock before it went to 8:01.

Half an hour later, all of the mammal keepers were assembled in the sheep pen at the children's zoo. Jake trotted down the fence-line as the zookeepers moved in behind him. When he got to the corner the line of people closed in behind him and he was trapped. Jake was the largest of the sheep in the children's zoo and the last one to be dipped. As the big ram reached the corner of the corral, he turned to face his pursuers. He was afraid and had no intention of giving up without a fight.

As the keepers closed in, they crouched low, stretched out their arms, and moved slowly to cut off Jake's avenues of escape. They were wet, dirty and smelled like the phenol-based sheep dip they had been splashed with. The line of people stretched from fence to fence, with Chelsea standing next to one fence and Clarence Watts next to the other. All of the experienced keepers knew that Jake would most likely run along the fence line to try his escape rather than charge at the group. They also knew how easy it was to force an animal to make a move away from you just by stepping toward it. So when Clarence Watts stepped forward, they all knew that he was trying to send Jake down the other fence line toward the only female zookeeper in the group. John was next to Chelsea, but he was too slow to reach Jake before the animal scooted by. He figured they had lost him and would have to start over and he could not believe his eyes when he turned to give chase. Chelsea had thrown herself on Jake and was being dragged across the pen as she clung to his back. Asa and Billy had an easy time catching the big ram by the horns and dragging him over to the horse trough to be dipped.

John offered his hand to Chelsea as she sat in the mud. "Nice job", he said as he pulled her up. He knew she was in for a rough time working here and wondered why she didn't find herself a good man and get married so she could stay home and raise children.

They all left Chelsea to clean up the equipment, since this was her area. Everyone had to change clothes and get to their own areas. By now, they were two hours behind. It was going to be a long day.

"I see you still don't know how to coil a hose", said John as he leaned on the fence.

"What do you mean?" asked Chelsea.

John ambled over to where Chelsea was standing and, without a word, took the hose as she offered it. "The secret is in the twist with the fingers", he said.

Coiling a hose is an art and Chelsea knew she was watching a master at work. John held the hose in both hands and slid his right hand as far down the hose as he could reach. While his left hand steadied the hose, he brought his right hand back to where the coil would be on the ground. He twisted the hose forward with his wrist and fingers as he laid it down and it just seemed to fall into a neat coil. In a few long, smooth strokes He was finished. The hose lay in a perfect coil with the nozzle pointed to the center. "See you at lunch", John grunted as he headed for the elephant house.

Don Laskey stared out the window at the zoo. A soft rain made the sidewalks glisten with moisture in the gray morning light. The muddy boots on the tray by the door attested to the fact that, as usual, he had already been to the construction site.

"Coffee, Mr. Laskey?" asked Wilma Watson. She stood in the doorway holding two Styrofoam cups of coffee, one with milk and sugar for her, and one black for her boss. She didn't always bring him coffee, but she knew he could use it this morning.

"Thanks, Wilma."

"Did you see the body when you were out there?" she asked.

"No, they had it covered up."

He took the cup and they stood looking at the gloomy, gray morning. G. Donald Laskey had been director of the Dotson Park Zoo for twenty two years. He was tall, thin, and in good shape for a man of fifty three. His once blond hair was mostly gray. He had probably been a handsome man when younger, but his face was deeply lined from years of stress and worry. He had the look of a weary, troubled man, and his deep, bass voice often contributed to his air of gloom.

"The mayor's office called, and so did that Wilson Jackson from Channel 8 News," said Wilma.

Laskey walked back to his desk, seeming to ignore her remark, and she left. His office was large and well appointed. The wall to the right of the door was lined with book shelves and the wall opposite was a bank of windows that stretched the length of the wall and from four feet above the floor to the ceiling. A grizzly bear skin, complete with head, hung on the wall behind his desk. The fourth wall was covered with photographs and certificates. The desk was oak, and sturdy, the chair was leather, and large. Two pretentious wing-backed chairs stood in front of the desk and a zebra skin rug covered the floor. Visitors were immediately drawn to look around at the many knick knacks and souvenirs that cluttered every available space. One could not help but notice that most were bears of all shapes and sizes – bears of wood, stone, glass, ceramic, and even plastic. The occupant of this office was clearly obsessed with bears, probably as a result of being mauled by one over forty years ago.

The American black bear had been chained to a post outside the back door of a tavern near his home. Twelve year old Donnie Laskey and three of his friends were taunting it and poking it with sticks when Donnie decided to show off. He dropped his stick and rushed forward to slap the bear on top of the head, but bears were quicker than he realized. It grabbed his hand in its mouth and shook him like a rag doll. Only the owner's arrival saved him from worse than a mangled hand and a horrible gash on the face.

Laskey flexed his left hand as the memory of that day flashed into his mind.

"Wilma."

"Yes, Mr. Laskey," said Wilma from her desk in the next room.

"Tell Susan I need to see her when she gets in."

"Need to see me about what?" asked Susan Daniels as she stuck her smiling face in the door. "What's going on over by the elephant house?" she became more serious as she walked into the office.

"The construction crew found human remains in one of their trenches."

"Good Lord," she exclaimed. "What does that mean for us?"

"I don't know yet."

As the zoo's manager of marketing and public relations, she had to be worried about the impact on public perception. She wrote an imaginary headline in her mind – *Dead Bodies Uncovered at the Zoo*. She closed the door and walked to one of the chairs. She was a former television news anchor who was eased out of her spot by fading looks. She had only been at the zoo for a little over a year, but Don was pleased with her grasp of the complexity of zoo marketing.

"Have you talked to that author?" asked Don.

"Yes," she replied. "He'll do it for five thousand plus ten per cent of the sales."

"Ten per cent?" Don said. "That's ridiculous. Offer him three. Are you sure he's good?"

The zoo's centennial anniversary was next year and Susan had been negotiating with local author and historian, Amos Morris. He was to write a history book on the zoo and help with the production of a thirty minute television show, as well.

"He's good," Susan said with confidence. "You know we're not going to sell that many books. They are mostly going for promotional give-aways."

"We'll see," said Don, unconvinced. "Just get this deal wrapped up. I want this guy digging into his research before the people who lived through our history are dead."

"Cause of death was trauma to the head," said Cyril Bagston confidently. He was new to the coroner's office and hadn't seen all that many bodies, but there was no doubt about the cause of death in this case.

Detective John Stokes didn't really want to hear this. He already had too many murders on his case load, but as a homicide detective, he didn't have much of a choice.

"What kind of trauma?" asked the detective.

"Hard to say, body's been there a long time."

"How long?" He asked as his patience started to wear thin.

"Hard to say."

"Don't give me that crap. Just tell me how and when this person died!"

Cyril didn't mind policemen all that much, but this one irritated him. The detective sitting across his desk was a young, good looking hot shot in his mid-twenties. He was climbing the ladder and probably anxious to make a name for himself any way he could. Cyril, on the other hand, was small, thin, and efficient. He hated doing other peoples' jobs for them. He read from his report in a monotone.

"Male Caucasian; five feet, four inches tall; approximate age at death, 60 years; Cause of death, severe trauma to the head (his head was crushed – looks like he was run over by a truck); Time of death," he paused, "about fifty to eighty years ago."

"Great," grumbled Detective Stokes. "He died fifty years ago and we're not even sure if it was an accident or a homicide."

"He was buried at the zoo, for cryin' out loud. Why wouldn't you suspect foul play?" exclaimed Cyril.

"So, you think he was run over by a truck," said Stokes, ignoring Cyril's outburst.

"Not necessarily. The skull was compressed laterally by some tremendous force. It could have been run over, squeezed in some type of machinery, or had something heavy dropped on it."

"All right," said the detective as he rubbed his chin thoughtfully. "We'll investigate this as a possible homicide. What can you give me on I.D.?"

"Nothing," snapped Cyril. "There were no dental records back then. You'll have to start with zoo personnel records. See if the zoo reported anyone dead or missing in the twenties or thirties."

Billy Scales put up the hood of his yellow rain slicker as the rain started falling again. Catching sheep had made him tired and, most importantly, had made him late in starting his routine at the monkey house. He walked briskly, carrying a bucket of produce he had picked up from the commissary. As he approached the door of the monkey house, he shifted the bucket to his left hand and unhooked the keys that were clipped to his belt. He turned the key and leaned into the heavy wooden door, which was suddenly jerked inward, causing him to fall into the hallway. He was aware of a dark shape rushing out into the rain soaked morning. Before he could stir his body to action, his mind knew that Sonny, the adult male chimpanzee, had somehow escaped.

Chelsea heard the whistle as she was emptying the last of the sheep dip from the water trough. It sounded like a referee's whistle at a sporting event and it was coming from the direction of the monkey house. She was new to the zoo and had not heard that sound before, but her recent training had taught her that the whistle all the zookeepers carried with their keys was to be used in case of an emergency. She started for the monkey house at a trot.

As she rounded the corner of Monkey Island, she stopped suddenly. Before her, about fifty yards away, stood seven men in bright yellow rain slickers. She thought they were all looking at her until she saw the dark shape moving between them. It was a chimpanzee, and it was moving her way. She fought the overwhelming urge to run. In fact, if all those men had not been watching, she probably would have.

"Sonny's going to tear her head off, if she doesn't get out of his way", said Billy as he started to move forward.

"Wait", said John Bullard. "He's stopping. Let's wait and see what he does".

The frightened chimp stood in the middle of the pathway leaning on his knuckles. He didn't like the rain, he didn't like the people dressed in these strange hooded costumes, and he didn't like being away from his group. He looked around for shelter and spied an open door. Maybe it would be a dry, safe place to rest.

When the chimp moved, Chelsea stepped back as if to run. She quickly realized, however, that he was not coming straight for her but was angling off to her right. She reluctantly stood her ground.

"Where is he going?" whispered John to no one in particular.

"That girl had better get out of his way", said Billy quietly.

"He's headed for the bathroom", said John as they both started to move forward.

Chelsea saw the chimp moving faster as he approached his destination, the open door of the public rest room. Fortunately, the zoo was empty on this rainy Friday morning and the rest room was vacant. She could see the other keepers moving cautiously toward the rest room and she knew they could not reach it in time to close the door behind him. She would have to do the job.

Billy and John stopped and watched in amazement. This was action that could not be taught. It was pure instinct. The young woman, who had only been on the job for about a week, moved in behind the adult male chimpanzee. She angled around so she would be behind the door and somewhat protected. As she moved near the small block building, she unhooked the keys from her belt and selected the one for the rest room door. Time seemed to stand still as she stood behind the door and the chimp sat inside in the darkness. Billy and John were too far away to be of any help. With the rain muffling any sound, she slowly slid her key into the lock and then bent down to lift the doorstop. In one fluid motion she pushed the door closed with her right shoulder and twisted the key with her left hand. Sonny hit the door with a powerful bang and let out a piercing scream, but it was too late. His moment of freedom was over.

2

Detective Stokes plodded over the muddy ground. The rain had stopped and evidence had surely all washed away, but he found it helpful to return to murder scenes, even when there is nothing new to see. It helped him visualize what might have happened. It was almost like being a psychic, and his fellow officers teased him about his methods.

There was something mysterious, even primal, about the zoo in the early morning. The animals were waking up, moving around, and starting the cacophony that pierces the air on every still, quiet morning. Stokes stared at the hole where the body had been found. The sides were still moist, and an inch or so of water filled each tiny depression at the bottom. The yellow plastic ribbon that identified this as a crime scene sagged to the ground in places.

The rays of the rising sun warmed his back as Stokes squatted and slowly looked over the scene. A few feet to his left was the old elephant barn, which had housed the elephants and hippos. It was an imposing building that had been built in the 1930's, sometime around the time the murder had been committed. He wondered if that would prove to be significant.

"How did you get in here?" asked a curious voice from behind him.

Stokes was startled and stood up quickly as he reached for his badge. "It's all right", he said, "I'm investigating the body that was found here."

Tom Watson eyed the detective suspiciously. Tom had been a volunteer at the zoo for as long as anyone could remember, and was well known for the stories he liked to tell about the zoo's history. He normally had the zoo to himself at this hour, but he also recognized a potential audience for some of his stories.

"Oh, I've seen bodies here before." Tom began. "It was back in '56 when we found that homeless man propped up against the fence along Riverview. Dead as a door nail, he was. I ..."

"What about this body?" Stokes interrupted. "Do you know anything about the body that was buried here?"

"Well, no." Tom hated to admit.

"Do you know any stories about people back in the 1920's or 30's?"

"Sure. I can take you back to the first animal at the zoo, a black bear. He was confiscated from a man by the name of Henry Koch who used him in a wrestling bear act. Bear killed a guy in a bar-fight so they took him and gave him to the city to start a zoo. Old Koch was quite a character. Real mean. Always in some type of trouble. Had one leg. Supposedly had the other leg cut off after the bear mauled him. He hung around the zoo for years after that."

"When was all that?" Stokes almost hated to ask.

"That would have been 1911 and 1912, when the zoo started."

"What about later? Do you know any stories from the '20's or 30's?"

"Well," thought Tom. "Calvin Griffith, the first zoo director, would have been turning the zoo over to James Malone in the '30's. Calvin's son, Buddy was around then, too. Quite an elephant man, he was. Only one who could handle Bwana."

"Bwana?"

"The zoo's first elephant. A real tough customer, the elephant, I mean. The circus gave him to the zoo after he put a few of their guys out of action. Buddy had a knack for handling him. He'd do anything Buddy said. Bwana killed a guy here, too. Hey, maybe that's your body. He killed one of his keepers on Easter weekend, 1937. I have the newspaper clipping"

Stokes wrote all this down. He wondered if the injuries were consistent with what an elephant would have done. But if it was in the newspaper, they wouldn't have buried him here on the grounds – or would they?

"Who's that," asked Stokes nodding to a woman walking away from them toward the children's zoo.

"That's Chelsea Johns," Tom said. "She's a zookeeper."

"Nice," Stokes said under his breath. He watched her for a moment and turned back to old Tom. "So, you don't know who this body might be?"

"No." Tom hated to admit. "But those were tough times back then. Rough customers worked at the zoo. Not like today with all these biologists with their degrees and their good intentions. That body could be one of twenty or thirty people who worked here or just hung out here."

"I'm only interested in this one," replied Stokes. "Thanks for the information."

Stokes headed through the mud back to his car. Suddenly he turned back to Tom, "Could I get a look at some of your old clippings sometime?"

Sonny rubbed the spot on his rump where the dart had hit him. Those tranquilizer darts pack a wallop at close range and, if his skin weren't so black, he would have quite a bruise to show. He had not thought much about his escape overnight, but he knew he was not anxious to try that again. It had been a frightening experience. He was glad to be home.

This cage at the Dotson Park Zoo was the only home Sonny could remember. He had been captured as an infant, lived for a time with a white family in West Africa, and been sent across the ocean in a crate. All that had taken place nearly fifteen years ago. He was five years old when he came to the zoo. His past was a distant memory that had faded into oblivion. Simba, his cage mate, had been at the zoo slightly longer than Sonny and she was also wild caught. Fifteen years is a long time to live in one cage, but when that is all you know, it isn't so bad. He had plenty to eat, good company, and a safe, dry place to sleep.

The door to the hallway opened with a creak and in walked zookeeper Billy Scales, more cautious than a few days ago. Sonny felt compelled to greet his friend by going through his regular display routine. He rose to stand up-right with his clenched fists at his side. He swayed from one foot to the other while a low pant-hoot rose from deep inside, "OOO…ooo, OOO…ooo". As the hoots became louder, he banged a metal plate that was attached to his bars with the back of his right hand, and stamped his feet on the concrete floor. He suddenly lunged at the bars on the front of his cage, slamming into them with hands and feet at the same time. His hoots had screamed to a crescendo. He then sat in the front corner of his cage and picked at the fur on the back of his left arm, as if nothing had happened. The entire performance had been a mixture of dominance and aggression, colored by the excitement of seeing a friendly face.

Billy had watched the whole thing with amusement. "Hey, Sonny" he crooned. He knew the display was friendly because when Sonny was truly angry, the display lasted longer, his hair bristled, and he threw whatever items happened to be at hand. This usually meant that Sonny's own feces came spraying into the hallway with deadly accuracy.

Billy began the morning routine by greeting each animal and offering a treat. For the females and the young male, Jack, the treat was a peeled banana that had been dipped in peanut butter. Sonny usually got that, too. Once in a while, however, Billy lit up a cigarette and gave it to Sonny. Sonny had picked up the habit years ago and really loved to smoke. He took the cigarette, always an unfiltered one in case Sonny decided the tobacco was better eaten than smoked, and moved to a back corner of the cage. There he sat with his back to the wall and puffed away with utter contentment.

Once Billy got that bit of business out of the way, he started his cleaning routine. He unlocked the iron bar that connected to the sliding door between the cages and slid it closed. Once the shift door was safely locked, he unlocked the iron barred gate on the front of the cage next to Sonny's and climbed inside. The monkey house was laid out like many animal houses that were built in the 1950's. A long, wide public hallway was lined on both sides by animal cages. The concrete floor of the cages was elevated thirty two inches above the public floor for better viewing, and a decorative wrought iron guard rail kept the visitors from getting too near the animals. The sturdy stainless steel bars that formed the front and sides of the cages were an inch in diameter and the walls were lined with ceramic tiles, giving the cages the look of a public bathroom. The cage floors sloped to the front so water and urine ran to a gutter that ran the length of the building. The heavy, orange rubber hose that Billy pulled into the cage had a brass nozzle that forced the water out in a small, powerful stream.

Billy was soon into his morning routine. He hosed the piles of fecal material, orange peels, and other remnants of yesterday's feed out the front of the cage. When the cage had been thoroughly hosed down, he threw a small plastic packet the size of a tea bag into his bucket and filled it with water. The water dissolved the plastic and released a powerful quaternary ammonia detergent into the solution. Billy scrubbed the cage from top to bottom. It was mindless work and he had a bunch of cages to do, so he wasn't really concentrating on what was happening around him. He suddenly realized he was getting soaked. Water was pouring over him from somewhere. It didn't take him long to realize what had happened. Sonny had gotten hold of his hose again and was having great fun hosing Billy, the other chimps, and any other animals he could reach. Billy was not amused. It was going to be a long day.

"I see the crime-scene tape is still up," Fred said as he pulled off his boots at the door of the construction trailer. "Does that mean we are still shut down?"

"Yep," replied Lyman without looking up from his newspaper.

Fred poured himself a cup of coffee and grabbed the sports section from the desk. He only worked half-days on Saturday and the atmosphere was much more laid back on the weekends. It was the day he and Lyman planned the week ahead.

"Did they say how long they'll be?"

"Just a day or two," said Lyman. "But they won't start till Tuesday because of the Holiday weekend."

Fred scanned the baseball scores and sipped his coffee. "These zoo jobs are a bitch. Nothin's ever straight forward."

"Yeah, but it's the first time we've found a dead body," said Lyman. "Dead *human* body at least."

"You right about that."

Dooley Construction had done most of the construction at the zoo in recent years, and the team of Lyman Denton and Fred Williamson had been here since the Monkey Island project in 1973. That was followed by the large area called *Into Africa* in 1989. *Into Africa* had taken up about ten acres of the zoo and was what the zoo people called an immersion exhibit, because the separation between public space and animal space was blurred.

The visitor was immersed into the simulation of a wild habitat. Then came a series of smaller projects that were done by smaller contractors. Dooley was brought back to handle the Tropics building in 1996. This gigantic combination greenhouse and animal habitat took nearly two years and cost just over fifteen million dollars. The last project they oversaw was the animal hospital in 2005. They had done hospitals and doctor's offices, so the technical aspect of this one was pretty straight forward, except for all the cages in the attached building. Now they were laying in new sewer lines in preparation for some secret project – something the zoo people were very excited about.

The elephant yard wasn't as muddy as some parts of the zoo. The elephants had packed the soil so hard that the rain either ran off or gathered in puddles. Tommy Ross maneuvered his wheelbarrow around one of those puddles as he steered to another pile of yesterday's droppings. He stopped next to a soggy pile of dung and deftly used his five-tined pitchfork to toss the pile into the wheelbarrow. He paused to look around.

"I don't see why we need a new elephant area," he said loudly.

"You don't think the elephants need more space?" called Salvatore Martinez from across the yard. Sal was raking wet hay from yesterday's feed into a pile so they could pick it up.

They had had this conversation a thousand times, but there wasn't much else they had in common to talk about. Sal was one of the few Latinos on staff and Tommy was what might politely be called a red-neck. They were the Saturday elephant crew. The elephant manager, Sam Kest, was off.

"I don't see what for," replied Tommy. "All they do is stand around all day and eat hay."

"Elephants in the wild walk for miles every day in search of food," said Sal, wasting his breath.

"Right. So if we turn them loose on three acres, they'll wander in circles all day," said Tommy. "And if something happens out there, we won't be allowed to go in with them to do anything about it."

They had had this conversation, as well. They had been forced to switch to a new method of handling elephants last year by the zoo's management team. It was called 'protected contact' and it meant that any contact they had with the elephants was done from behind a barrier. The elephants had to be trained to do things voluntarily. Sam had not been in favor of the change and he had indoctrinated his new keeper, Tommy, into his way of thinking. Sal liked the new system. He understood the reasoning for it, especially after two fatal accidents at other zoos last year. He didn't care to become the next statistic.

"They're starting to pip," said Betty Willis sticking her head in the door of the kitchen.

Janice Fredricks looked up from her diet preparation in the bird house kitchen. "That's great," she said without enthusiasm. "Congratulations."

Betty had been watching the nest of black swans for nearly a month. She had worried about raccoons raiding the nest, the parents abandoning the nest, and reaching the end of the incubation period only to discover that the eggs were infertile. All of these had been the result of previous nesting efforts by this pair. This time, it appeared that success might be in the offing. It would a first-hatching for the Dotson Park Zoo. But today was not the day for Janice to get excited about anything. Her divorce had become final yesterday and she was not looking forward to being single again or to raising her six year old daughter alone.

"Ann's off sick," Janice continued. "We're going to need to double up today."

Betty exhaled slowly and looked at Janice. "You OK?" she asked finally.

Janice didn't look up and didn't say anything. She simply nodded yes. They both knew why the third keeper in the bird house was not present. Ann Gordon was the reason for Janice's divorce. She was the other woman in her husband's affair. Now, Janice, the curator of birds, had to supervise the woman who broke up her marriage and who would likely end up marrying her ex-husband. It was going to be a long winter in the bird house.

3

Eldene Simpson hated her job in personnel. She would hate any job. She would rather be home watching the soaps, but the city personnel office wasn't a bad place to work, especially for someone like Eldene who had no ambition.

"I'm Detective John Stokes." He said flashing his badge. "I need to look through some of your old personnel records."

"Personnel records are confidential," quipped Eldene. "You'll need a warrant."

"Look," he said, "These are from the 1920's and 1930's, I don't need a warrant for stuff that old."

"All of our records are confidential," she said with authority. She knew she was on shaky ground, but she was enjoying her position of temporary authority over this policeman. "Oh well," she said, softening, "I guess if they're that old I could let you see what you can find. They'll be down in the basement. Follow me."

The shelves in the basement reached nearly to the ceiling. She pointed out the boxes and he hauled them down. There were no tables and there was barely enough room to turn around, so Stokes would have to work on the floor in the aisle. He was used to rough conditions and he had the patience that was reserved for saints and policemen. He lifted the lid on the first box, sneezed, and began his investigation.

"Good morning, Ralph," Don Laskey said into the phone. He paused to listen to Ralph Polaski's reply.

"How did you know about that already? That's why I called you." He paused again.

"How did she find out about it so soon? What else did she say?"

Ralph Polaski was president of the board of directors of the Dotson Park Zoological Society. He was a big, amiable man who was vice president of First National Bank. He was slow talking, slow moving, and slow acting. Not a very effective leader, but well connected in the community. He already knew about the discovery of a body on zoo grounds because one of the other board members had called him. Joanne Newman, a prominent local socialite and member of the Dotson clan, was even better connected than he was. She thought the discovery of a body at the zoo might hurt the zoo's image as a family place. That thought had not occurred to Ralph.

"Ralph, here's what I'm going to do. I need to call the mayor's office and then the press. They may call you for a statement from the Board, so you'll need to go along with this. As soon as the police confirm that they are investigating the discovery of a body, I'm going to release a statement that confirms that a body has been found. I'm going to suggest that, since it was found near the zoo's perimeter fence, it was probably dumped in here from the outside. I'm going to try to down play any connection to the zoo. This might even turn into a positive. We can certainly use some publicity to get people out here, even if it is a little bit on the gruesome side." Laskey paused to hear Ralph's reply.

"You will be out here for today's announcement, won't you?" Don asked.

"Good, I knew I could count on you, Ralph. And I'll also see you tonight at the board meeting." Don hung up the phone.

Don knew he could count on Ralph because Ralph didn't really think on his own. Ralph liked to be led, which made him a perfect society president as far as Don was concerned. Joanne Newman, on the other hand, was trouble. He would need to work hard to keep her in her place.

"Is everyone here?" Don asked.

"Everyone but Fox News," Susan replied. ""They're always late, but they'll be here. We have the other TV stations and the newspaper people with their photographers. It's after two, so we need to get started."

Don Laskey moved up to the podium and tapped the microphone in front of him to make sure it was turned on. The small, elevated platform had been set up in front of the elephant exhibit and in addition to the podium and microphone he shared the stage with an easel that was covered by a white sheet.

"Good afternoon," he began, "and welcome to the Dotson Park Zoo. We are here today to announce the development of a new exhibit that will revolutionize the art of keeping animals in zoos. As most of you know, this zoo has long prided itself on being at the cutting edge of zoo technology. We were among the first to develop zoogeographic exhibits that grouped a variety of species into clusters of exhibits based on where they are found in nature. We were among the first zoos to envelop their visitors in spaces that were similar to the animal habitats – a concept known in the business as immersion. The animal hospital we opened in 2005 is state-of-the-art, with equipment that many human hospitals would be proud of. Now we are ready to embark on our next great adventure."

He paused dramatically to allow Susan to move into position and, together, they carefully removed the covering on the artist's rendering.

"Ladies and gentlemen," he said with a flourish, "I give you *Primates and Pachyderms*. For the first time in any zoo in the world, we are going to create a space that will allow chimpanzees and elephants to live together."

When the murmuring died down, he continued. "We already have both new exhibit spaces under development and, since they are side-by-side, we have decided to allow these two species to cohabit a common space."

A hand in the audience shot up and the questions began. Are they found together in the wild? Yes. Won't the elephants try to kill the chimps? No, we don't think so. Why hasn't this been tried before? We don't know. When will it open? In time for our Centennial anniversary, next June. Tell us about the dead body that was found here last week.

"That's a police matter," said Don evasively. "I can't really comment on that. It was probably just a homeless person who decided to pass away here at the zoo. That's all the time we have. Thank you for coming out today"

The crack of the gavel filled the room and everyone around the table looked up from their dinner and became silent.

"I call this meeting to order," said Ralph Polaski. He finally had a quorum of six board members, with the sixth being Betty Bexley, who had just arrived and was taking her seat. Ralph looked around the table at his fellow board members – Betty, the wife of a wealthy cardiologist, Ivan Robson, the owner of a modest hardware store, Rodrick Olsen, a stock broker, Sam Wilson, from the mayor's office, and Evelyn Woodson, the director of the local humane society. Absent were attorney Milton Wagner, accountant Oren Gifford, and Joanne Newman. Also present were zoo staff members Don Laskey and Susan Daniels. Wilma Watson served as recording secretary.

After he dispensed with the formalities of approving last month's minutes and the finance report, Ralph brought up the first real order of business.

"Next on the agenda is the zoo director's report, Don."

The sound of his name brought Laskey back to the present and he suddenly realized that all eyes were on him.

"As you heard in the financial report," he began, "we will be facing some significant challenges over the next few months. Revenue is down with all the rainy weekends and expenses are a little higher than expected. If the City cuts our subsidy, as they have threatened, we will be in very bad shape financially."

"I've heard there is talk of cutting *all* of our support," said Rodrick.

Sam Wilson looked uncomfortable, but managed to smile as he said, "I really don't think this is the time or place to speculate on that. We are working hard to keep all programs in place, but with the State budget crisis, everyone is feeling the pinch."

"What about the dead body they found in the zoo last week?" asked Betty. "Is that going to affect our bottom line?"

"No," said Don. "The police are investigating but it shouldn't have any effect on our operations."

"Body?" asked Evelyn. "What body?"

Don turned to Susan Daniels who stood and explained what they knew about last week's discovery. She downplayed its significance and shifted the focus onto the new exhibit that was announced that afternoon.

"It has been a long time since we opened a major, new exhibit," said Don, picking up the positive direction. "The last big project we did was the animal hospital, which was necessary for our operation but not attractive to the public. You have to go all the way back to the Tropics Building in '96."

"The idea of putting elephants and chimpanzees together is a little troublesome to me," said Evelyn. "That might be a stressful environment for both species."

"It should also be an enriching environment for both species," Don countered.

Evelyn folded her arms and did not respond. She was clearly not persuaded.

"Stress and enrichment won't mean much if the City cuts our funding," said Rodrick. "That's thirty per cent of our budget. How will we make up that shortfall?"

The meeting degenerated into multiple conversations and Ralph looked a little lost. He glanced at Don for guidance and Don dragged his forefinger across his throat in a sign that meant 'cut'.

"This meeting is adjourned," shouted Ralph as he banged his gavel.

"Well," said Tommy Ross. "If it isn't the Chimp Whisperer."

Chelsea smiled weakly as everyone laughed. The zoo crew was gathered at Mario's Pizzeria across the street from the zoo. It was something they did on special occasions and on Fridays after work. Chelsea was not a regular, but she had to stop-in once in a while in order to be social. They had pulled two large tables together and were well into their beer. Chelsea threw eight dollars into the middle of the table and poured beer into the only clean glass she saw.

"So, how did you do it?" Tommy continued. "Did you whisper in his ear?"

"She showed him a little leg," said Sam Kest. "'Come on in the bathroom, big boy. Let me show you what I've got for you'."

Few people knew about the chimp escape because it had not been released to the media, but the zookeepers knew. They also knew that Chelsea had responded well in a crisis. They all admired what she had done, but the elephant crew couldn't let her know that. She was forced to sit between Sam and Tommy because that was the only spot left. Clarence Watts was across the table talking earnestly to Dr. Salinda Donaldson, one of the zoo veterinarians. Janice Fredericks was talking to veterinary technician, Eve Stewart, who both acknowledged Chelsea's arrival with a wave and a smile.

"What did you boys think about Laskey's big announcement today," Chelsea asked. "Elephants and chimps together?"

"Bull shit," said Sam. "Total bull shit."

"The elephants are going to stomp the shit out of those monkeys," Tommy continued. "And all we're going to be able to do is stand there and watch."

"Billy thinks it might work," Chelsea said. "He says the chimps will be able to stay away from the elephants and they'll eventually figure out how to coexist."

"Billy Scales should stick to milking cows," said Tommy as he took a bite of pizza. "He don't know shit about elephants."

Chelsea opened her mouth to respond, but the horrified look on Janice Fredericks' face caught her attention. She turned toward the door and saw Janice's ex-husband and her employee, Ann Gordon, coming in. This was no accident. Ann knew they were gathering at Mario's and, even though they went to their own table, they were there to make Janice uncomfortable. Before she turned back to the table, another person entering the door caught her eye. It was that good looking policeman who had been working on the construction site at the zoo. He smiled at her and moved to the bar without a backward glance. He probably did not see the puzzled look on her face. She had never seen him in here before and she wondered why he had showed up on this particular night.

4

Dotson Lane was marked by a city street sign, but heavy iron gates made it obvious that the public was not invited. The entry to the Dotson compound was located a mile and a half up the Tecumseh River, south of the zoo on Riverview Road. The big house over-looked the river like Washington's Mount Vernon, but it was no longer the only home on the estate. Several homes had gone up over the years for various family members making it less like an estate and more like an up-scale neighborhood.

"An Amos Morris to see you, sir." announced Simon, the butler.

"Thank you, Simon. Show him in." James Dotson was a man who was obviously comfortable with his station in life. His erect bearing and regal air made him seem taller than he really was. His hair was white, but if you knew he was nearly to his eighty fifth birthday you would be surprised at how young he looked. He was one of those people who could fill a room with his presence, and he liked it that way. His younger sister, Sally, was the same way and she probably used her position better than he did. They formed an intimidating pair as they rose to greet their visitor.

"I'm James Dotson. This is my sister, Sally Dotson."

"I'm Amos Morris. Thank you for taking the time to see me."

"Always a pleasure to help the zoo." said James, forcing a smile. "Please, have a seat," he said, motioning to the large chair next to the door. James and Sally sat together on the small sofa across the coffee table. "What can we do for you?" James asked.

The room was smaller than Amos had expected. Perhaps it was the dark walnut paneling that made it seem so. A floor-to-ceiling window overlooked the wide lawn that led down a gentle slope to the river. Dark green carpeting and worn leather furniture made this a very comfortable room to sit in. Amos would really need to concentrate to keep his mind from straying from the business at hand.

"I have been hired to write a book on the history of the Dotson Park Zoo," he began. "It is expected to be out next year, in time for the centennial celebration of the zoo's opening."

As Amos laid out the materials on the coffee table, the doorbell rang and Simon's footsteps rushed by the room. Amos presented an old master plan from the 1930's, a few grainy black and white photos from the 1920's, and a sample history book he had done for the local garden club.

"I am so sorry to be late," said Susan Daniels after she was announced. She offered no excuse.

Amos glanced her way and continued. "Your family's involvement will be featured prominently, beginning with the donation of the land for the zoo and concluding with your generous donation of funds for the Dotson Animal Care Center."

"Will the book look like that?" James said pointing to the book on the table.

"Similar," Amos replied. "It will depend on how much money we raise."

"We need three sponsors at ten thousand each to make this possible," said Susan.

"Who else have you talked to?" asked Sally.

"You're the first," Susan replied. "But Ralph Polaski is sure he can get First National Bank and we intend to talk with Joanne's husband. We don't expect any problems finding the money to do this. We just thought you would like to be first onboard."

Joanne Newman was the youngest of the three Dotson siblings, the children of Buckley and Raven Dotson. It was common knowledge that their grandfather was born on the property and their great grandfather had donated the land for a park.

"We also need help with materials," said Amos.

"What kind of materials?" asked Sally. "We can't have you poking through our personal papers."

"No, nothing like that," Amos replied quickly. "I just need to interview each of you and I would appreciate any access I can have to old photographs and documents that we might use in the book."

Sally was an imposing figure, just like her brother. She had the same pointed angular features and close set eyes that seemed to characterize the Dotson clan. She was, Amos estimated, a few years younger than her brother, but seemed to be his equal in every other way. Amos didn't do well with forceful women. He wasn't sure he liked Sally Dotson.

James stood and locked eyes with his sister before turning to look out the window. He paused for a moment and said without turning, "We're in. We will cover all of the costs. But," he said turning back to his guests, "we want full editorial rights."

"We can't do that," Amos said.

"Yes we can," said Susan quickly.

"Not as long as I'm the author of this book," Amos turned to face her.

All eyes were on the unassuming, little man. They were surprised at the force of his objection.

"I will be able to back up everything I write with source material," he continued. "I want to write a true story based on all of my research."

James glanced at his sister and turned back to the window. He knew this story would be told whether his family liked it or not. "All right," he said finally. His sister rose to protest but he silenced her with a raised hand. "Let's begin now," he glanced at the two women, "in my study." He signaled that this meeting was over.

"Simon," James said as they passed through the door, "bring some coffee to my study."

Susan was standing at the front door shaking Sally Dotson's hand when she heard James say before he closed the study door, "The story begins in November of 1911."

Part 2

5

Saturday, November 18th, 1911

Calvin Griffith was a master at keeping things alive – both plants and animals – so it was a cruel irony that his wife had died so young. He had taken great pains to ensure that the small beech tree he had just transplanted from the woods across the creek would someday shade his wife's grave. Rachael had been gone nearly two years, but he still came to talk to her every day. He was a tall man who pretty well filled out his bib overalls. He had lived on this property for all of his thirty-eight years, abandoned by his parents and raised by Mama Ellie Mae, a colored maid on the estate. He grew up as a yard boy. Although Calvin always had a place to live and plenty to eat, he never really fit in – not with the colored people with whom he lived and certainly not with the whites, who considered him little more than a servant. His only friend had been one of the Dotson boys.

The best thing that ever happened to him was the arrival of Rachael Krauss. Her family had emigrated from Germany and farmed a parcel of property further out of town. Calvin had seen her riding past the estate and he occasionally talked to her at barn raisings and church picnics.

Theirs had been a passionate courtship and a loving marriage. When the influenza epidemic of 1909 took her, his grief was profound. He rarely spoke now, even to his kids, but somehow they'd all survived. He threw himself into the care of the estate, grateful for the kindness of old Cyrus Dotson, who had arranged a small salary and a permanent place to live and raise his children.

With the tree planted and a prayer said, he stuffed his cigar back in his mouth and raised his head toward the creek and the river beyond. The estate covered nearly a hundred acres stretching from the road to the river, and included what was once an impressive house right in the middle of the property.

"I still say it's too far out of town for a park," Rollo Wilson said, as he gazed over the property from his wagon seat.

Rollo was a thin, ferret-like man with a long nose protruding from an already pointed face. As the city's director of parks, he should have been happy about adding a second park to his department, but all he could think about was how long it would take him to come out here to check on things. He couldn't imagine anyone from the city ever coming to this remote area, and these country people wouldn't know what to do with a park.

"That's true, but look at those houses springing up," replied R. C. Crofton, waving his arm to the left. "We may be fourteen miles from downtown, but the town is moving this way."

Mayor Crofton was a visionary. He was a large man, some would say fat. A big cigar jutted from his permanently smiling mouth and his right hand shot out to shake every hand that came near. R.C. was ambitious for himself and for his city. He wanted this land for a park. He knew of another parcel that would make a proper course for the sport of golf. He even dreamed of someday building a zoological park.

"I just can't believe Cyrus Dotson gave this to the city," mused Rollo. "Why would he do that?"

"He knew his no-good sons would ruin it," R. C. explained. "Too bad they get to keep the house."

R. C. studied the Dotson home. It was set back on the property, halfway between the road and the river, at the end of a straight, tree-lined driveway. The house Cyrus Dotson had built after the war was an unsightly mix of turrets, towers, and chimneys. Its wooden walls were a faded gray. One end of the wide front porch had collapsed, lending an air of decay to the whole place.

As if to confirm the old man's assessment of his sons, his youngest boy, Cyril, had turned the house into a bar called Dotson's Emporium. The other son, Cecil, had moved out west and hadn't been seen in these parts for years. Everyone knew that if it weren't for their man, Calvin, the estate grounds would be falling apart just like the house. As it was, the dilapidated house looked as out of place on the beautiful lawn as a pig at a Bar-B-Q.

"I told you we shouldn't be playin' this close to the road," Raven Griffith hissed, as she and her brother walked quickly across the field.

"Where else are we gonna to play?" Buddy shot back. "Pa won't let us play back by the house."

Raven didn't answer. They stopped at the edge of the road, looked at the lumpy baseball lying in the dust, and then peered up at the wagon they had just hit. Buddy was a year older than Raven at seventeen, and they were about as different as a brother and sister could be. He was tall and sturdy, some would say pudgy. She was slender, with penetrating light gray eyes and thick dark hair worn in a single braid, reaching almost to her waist. He was confident, cocky, and somewhat lazy. She was shy, quiet, and insecure.

The horses fidgeted and the driver jerked sharply on the reins. He was a hard looking man, with curly black hair, dark deep-set eyes, and beard stubble that was several days old. Tying the reins to the wagon brake pole, he swung his legs over the side and paused, allowing the kids to notice that one leg was actually a piece of wood. He hopped nimbly to the ground and briefly glared at them. He was thick, solid and not much taller than Buddy. His cheek bulged with a plug of tobacco and he spat a stream of brown juice into the dust with a "phitt".

The horses lurched and the wagon rocked from side to side, emitting a low but distinct growl. Raven and Buddy glanced at each other and looked back at the wagon. Under the layers of dust and road grime, they could make out the letters *B. B. Wilson, Undertaker*. A narrow window, framed with a chipped gold-leaf design, ran the length of its side. As the kids stepped back for a better look, they saw the beady eyes of an animal peering back at them.

"Sorry we hit your wagon," Raven offered, as she bent to pick up the ball.

With ball retrieved and apologies offered, Buddy and Raven took a step backward, turned toward the field, and returned to their game. The man stared into the distance. He never said a word.

"A bear," shrieked a child's voice. "He's got a bear!"

The children stopped their game and turned toward the undertaker's wagon, which had pulled off the road. Calvin couldn't believe his ears, as he hurried across the field. The mayor stared in bug-eyed astonishment, holding tight to the reins and struggling to contain his rearing, frightened horse.

A man with a wooden leg stood next to the wagon with a large black bear on a leash, like some great dog. The leash was a rope, attached to a heavy chain collar. As the man looked around, the bear peed in the road. It didn't lift its leg like a male dog or squat like a female, but just stood there, letting the pee splash on the fur of its back legs. The man and the bear were equally menacing in their indifference, as a crowd slowly gathered. It seemed they had done this before, arriving in a town and immediately becoming the center of attention.

6

The immense black bear stood calmly in the shade. He was tied to the old oak tree with a long rope fastened to his neck chain, ignoring the scrawny, shirtless man who faced him in a crouched, fighting stance. The sun hung in the cloudless afternoon sky on an uncommonly mild winter day. A Christmas wreath banged against the door of the bar, as another patron came out to join the restless crowd. People closed in, forming a circle around the bear and his opponent, making it difficult for the children to see.

"Come on," Buddy said, as he turned away from the action. "Let's go up there."

He bounded up the steps and moved to the porch rail, with Al and Raven beside him. The Dotson boys, nineteen-year-old Simpson and eighteen-year-old Buckley, were on the porch, too.

The bear's tiny black eyes showed no expression. His teeth glistened through his partially open mouth, as a small spot of puss oozed from an open sore under his jaw.

The bear's opponent was Jacob Zelienski, a Polish immigrant, who badly needed the two-dollar prize for pinning the bear. He had come to this country with nothing and still had nothing. His wife took in laundry to supplement the meager living he made as a handyman. His daughter was born with a deformed foot and had to walk with a crutch. His house had just burned down. Bad luck covered him like dust on a donkey.

With his wife and daughter looking on and the crowd growing restless, Jacob moved deliberately toward the bear. The bear took notice. His head came up, he backed up a step, and his upper lip puckered out. Jacob put his hand out toward the bear to test its reaction. Nothing. He pushed the bear's head down and the bear opened his mouth with a half-hearted lunge at Jacob's hand. Zelienski was a good boxer. Most people in the crowd had seen him fight. He had large, quick hands that had surprised many an opponent.

Since the object was to pin the bear to the ground, Jacob decided to jump on the bear's back and push it to the ground. He stepped to his left and quickly rushed the animal. Gripping tightly around the bear's chest, he pulled sideways with all his might. The animal hardly moved and seemed to take no notice. The crowd shouted encouragement.

"Grab his back legs."

"C'mon Zalienski, hit him between the eyes."

"Bite him on the nose."

Cyril Dotson moved through the crowd with slips of paper in one hand and dollar bills in the other.

"Last chance," he said. "The house takes the bear. Who wants a dollar on Zelienski?"

"What's the pot?" asked a man as he dug into his pocket.

"We're up to forty nine dollars. Let's make it an even fifty."

The man handed over a bill and Cyril had him write his name on a slip of paper.

"That's it," Cyril shouted above the crowd. "Pot's closed at fifty dollars."

He turned his attention to the porch and motioned for his boys to come down. They bounded down the steps, thinking they were to be in on the action, but were disappointed to be sent up to the end of the driveway to watch out for the law.

Cyril thumbed the wad of bills. The one-legged man had told him the bear would look docile, but when Koch gave the signal the bear would end it quickly. Cyril looked around the crowd and spotted Koch directly across the open ground. He wanted to catch Koch's eye and let him know he could signal the bear, but he was talking to someone.

"What's in it for me?" Henry Koch asked the smartly dressed man standing next to him.

"Two hundred," said James Purtle, without looking at the scruffy little man.

Koch spat and scratched at his stubbled chin. That was a lot of money for a drifter. He eyed Purtle and wondered what the game was.

"Why me?"

"Why not?" he replied. "You look like you can handle it".

"Why do you want me to do it?"

"That's none of your business. Do you want the money or not?"

Koch didn't like being talked to like that. He toyed with telling this dandy to stick it up his ass, but two hundred dollars was too much to turn down.

Jacob pushed and pulled without much result. He was clearly no match for the bear. His wife had told him to avoid danger by staying away from the head, but he felt bolder now. He decided the head was the key. He slipped his arm around the bear's neck and pulled up on its chin, to flip it over. As Jacob grabbed the sore spot on its lower jaw, the bear became enraged, turning quickly, and flipping the man to the ground with a roar. The bear pinned Jacob with its front paws and bit down. He shook the man like a rag-doll. He had bitten deep into Zelienski's neck and when he pulled out, his teeth ripped out the wind pipe and artery. Blood squirted into the air and began to pool in the dirt. The blood-splattered bear looked as casual as if nothing had happened.

Everyone stepped back, as ladies screamed and Mrs. Zelienski fainted. The kids on the porch couldn't see what was happening on the ground, but they clearly heard a man's voice pronounce that Jacob Zelienski was dead.

A murmur ran through the crowd as everyone backed up.

"The son of a bitch killed him," exclaimed one man.

"I'll get my gun," said another.

"Hold on," Calvin Griffith ordered, as he strode to the center of the crowd. "There's been enough killin' here."

"Get that bear out of here," he said quietly to Henry Koch, who had been reeling in the bear's rope leash.

"Mason," Calvin called to the man who wanted to get his gun, "go call the sheriff. The rest of you go back inside or go home."

"What are you going to tell the sheriff?" asked Cyril after he covered the body.

"The truth," Calvin replied.

They stood looking over the covered the body. Blood had soaked through the yellow-flowered bed sheet giving it an almost festive look.

"I never meant this to happen, you know," Cyril muttered.

"Well, it did," said Cal as he looked around.

The crowd had dispersed. Most had gone back inside to continue drinking. The swiftness of the savage attack had shocked Cyril, and now he would have to deal with the sheriff. Bear fighting wasn't against the law, but a man had been killed. Someone would need to answer for that.

7

New Year's Eve 1911

The cold hit Raven in the face like a wet towel. It almost took her breath away. The house hadn't felt that warm when she was inside but, compared to the frigid temperature outside, the wood stove was working just fine. She hadn't dressed to be outside for long, so she'd need to hurry. The heavy wooden bowl she cradled in her hands held the scraps from dinner, and she wanted to get them to the bear before they froze into a solid mass.

Zeke, the bear, had been tied up behind the big house for weeks and Henry Koch showed no sign of going anywhere. The sheriff hadn't charged him over the death of Jacob Zelienski, nor had he tried to punish the bear. He simply ordered a stop to the wrestling matches and confiscated the bear. Koch had taken a job cleaning up around the bar and lived in the loft above the barn. Everyone called him "Coke" and he told anyone who would listen that he'd lost his leg to a bear bite that wouldn't heal. He'd shot the bear and raised her cub to be his companion. He got along with most everyone, but he still had an air of menace about him. He was like a dog that wags his tail while he watches you out of the corner of his eye. He'll bite you if you get too close.

The bear never showed any meanness to anyone. Even killing Jacob Zelienski had seemed an accident. Raven and Buddy took turns feeding him and cleaning up his poop. Now, with the temperature always around freezing, the cleaning was easy. His turds were frozen solid and they had no smell.

The resting bear raised his head, as the young girl approached. She could see his breath in the fading daylight. He had large ears, small eyes and no visible tail. His fur was shiny black, except for the brown on his muzzle between the eyes and nose. She poured the contents of the bowl on the ground and quickly stepped out of range, as the bear ambled to the pile. He seemed to relish the green beans, mashed potatoes and meat scraps as he lapped, sucked and chewed noisily. Bears in the wild will eat just about anything, so this combination of meat and vegetables was good for him. The cold air wrapped Raven in its embrace, tickling the hairs on her bare legs and stinging the inside of her nose.

Visiting the bear was the only time she felt happy. She'd just finished another Christmas with few presents, little joy, and no ma – just a brash, loud brother and a stern, unhappy pa. They lived in a small house that people affectionately called a cottage, next to a barn and behind the old mansion that had been turned into a bar. It was as if they were servants. Life in their little cottage was an austere existence, without laughter, and it made her angry. Why did her ma have to die and leave her to cook and clean for two men? It just wasn't fair.

Rachael Krauss had not been a particularly tender and loving mother to Raven. In fact, most people remembered her for her looks, especially her blue eyes and fair hair. She was stern in demeanor and strict with her children. Her household was as neat and organized as a military barracks and Raven unconsciously rubbed her behind as she remembered the stinging whacks her ma doled out with a wooden spoon when she and Buddy got out of line. And yet, Raven missed her terribly. She never realized how much her ma had done for her, and she hated seeing what her death had done to her pa. He was a hollow shell of a man going through the motions of life.

Although it was still daylight, at just after five o'clock in the evening, the New Year's Eve party at Dotson's Emporium had already begun. Everyone wanted to celebrate the New Year. The raucous laughter and noise from inside the bar was muted, until a back door opened, flooding the backyard with light and noise. Raven turned to see Simpson and Buckley Dotson slipping out the door. They didn't notice her in the twilight, but she knew what they were up to. Simpson held a pack of cigarettes, pilfered from the bar, and Buckley carried an oil lamp. They were headed into the closet on the back porch for a smoke.

Seeing those two gave her a shiver that added to her feeling of being cold. They weren't bad as individuals – Buckley could be downright nice at times – but together they were as mean as a pair of junk yard dogs. Their family didn't seem to have much money anymore. They got by on their good looks and the Dotson family name.

Calvin puffed on his just lit cigar and looked around the smoke-filled room. The New Year's party had drawn quite a crowd. Cyril Dotson's bar seldom attracted this many people. It was simply too remote – fourteen miles from town and set back from the road. The noise was beginning to get on Calvin's nerves. When he finished his beer and cigar, he would walk back to the cottage.

"Hello, Cal," Cyril Dotson said with a jovial slap on the back. "Happy New Year."

"Nice party," Calvin replied without a hand-shake or a smile.

"Thanks," Cyril said. He looked around the room, wobbling slightly. "People are ready for a new year. What about you, Cal? You don't look too happy."

Calvin looked around the room. He wasn't sure why he had come inside. He was sad to see what this house had become. The ballroom now had a bar running its length with a mirror and shelves of bottles behind it. Small round tables filled the room and men played poker here on most nights. Calvin remembered the fancy dinner parties the Dotson family once held in this room. He remembered the laughter and recalled peeking through a crack in the door at the people in their fancy clothes. He had imagined that he would someday be allowed to join them.

"I'm happy," Calvin said dryly. "I just choose not to show it."

Cyril laughed uncertainly. "Come on, Cal. Lighten up. It's a new year."

Calvin looked at Cyril, but did not reply. He wondered what had happened to make things turn out this way. For a few summers, when they were boys, they'd been like brothers – hunting, fishing and running all over the property together. They had drifted apart as teenagers, when the realities of class distinction had set in. Then about twelve years ago, Cyril's older brother Cecil had decided to run off to California to seek his fortune and, much to everyone's surprise, Cyril had joined him.

Calvin was left to run the estate under the guidance of their father, and the place had flourished. Calvin felt like a son and secretly hoped to inherit the estate. But Cyril returned after a few years and, like the prodigal son, he was welcomed with open arms. Calvin was once again relegated to the role of manager.

People assumed that Cyril Dotson would continue operating the estate after his mother and father died in quick succession, but he showed little interest. Something in his California experience had changed him.

"Cyril," said a woman who had moved up behind him, "we need a case of whiskey brought down."

Cyril's wife, Dora, looked like a bar-maid in her heavy make-up. It was her idea to turn the house into a bar. It was she who liked the high-sounding name 'emporium' and it was she who had transformed Cyril Dotson from one of the most important men in the county into a saloon keeper.

"I've already sent Koch," he said.

"That clumsy oaf had better not break anything."

A crash from somewhere upstairs punctuated her remark, followed by the thumping of a case of whiskey bouncing down the stairs.

"You need to get rid of him," she said with disgust. "He's worthless."

Cyril moved away and Dora turned her attention to Calvin. Her blouse was open at the top revealing her breasts and as she used her hands to push them up from below they almost spilled out of her top.

"How about these, big man," she said seductively. "Want to ring in the New Year later?"

Calvin swallowed the last of his beer and left without a word.

As Calvin walked out the door, Dora's eyes fell on a young man sitting alone at a table in the front corner of the saloon. He had three shot glasses in front of him and a blank look on his face.

"Got everything you need here?" she asked as she drew near.

"I'm fine," he said without looking up.

"Are you sure?" she asked bending over the table. Her blouse was loose and as his face rose to meet her eyes, his gaze fell on her pendulous breasts. His mouth opened slightly and she knew she had him. He was a little young for her, but that had never stopped her before. He was very good looking in a boyish sort of way. He wore a dark suit, a white shirt, and a red tie that was pulled loose at the collar. He said his name was Jim.

"I wonder if I could get you to help me with something in the back room, Jimmy."

She had not changed her position and his eyes had only left her breasts long enough to glance at her face. She moved her shoulders slightly causing them to jiggle.

"What do you say?" she said softly.

He rose, downed his last shot, and said, "Sure, why not?"

Dora smiled. He followed her to the back of the room, but before she opened the door she looked up the stairs on the far wall. Her husband was still upstairs cleaning up the mess. He would be busy for a while. As she reached for the doorknob with her left hand she reached back with her right. He was ready, she could tell. This would not take long.

Three miles up-river from Dotson Park, Andrew Flanagan thrust another piece of firewood into the glowing pot-bellied stove. He had lived in this house by the river for most of his sixty years. It was the perfect spot for him – remote from any other homes and in a swampy area that discouraged casual visitors. He liked his privacy. The only company he needed was his pet alligator, Florida.

Andrew had acquired Florida from a traveling peddler over twenty years ago, and the beast had grown from the size of Andrew's arm to over six feet in length – big enough to bite off that arm. For some reason, Andrew had the knack for rearing an alligator in a climate in which an alligator would not naturally survive. Florida loved his diet of whole chickens and swamp rats, and he thrived in the pond that Andrew had dug out and fenced in behind the house. The only tough time was now, during the winter, but Andrew had figured that out as well. He built a special den under the center of the house beneath the pot-bellied stove, where Florida could comfortably sleep away the winter in hibernation.

The stove sat atop a massive steel plate that radiated enough heat under the floor to keep the gator from freezing. The only problem was that the house was stifling inside. Alligators down in the south, he knew, just burrowed down in the mud during winter cold spells. He was creating a natural environment for Florida, it just lasted a little longer in these parts.

There's no better feeling than being buried under a pile of quilts and blankets on a cold night. The cottage was warm and comfortable around the stove, but in the bedroom it was cold enough to see your breath. Raven wasn't sure how long she'd been asleep, but it was long enough that she didn't wish to be pulled back to life. Her pa's shouts were urgent, but took a moment to register. When he ripped off her covers, she sat up, instantly alert and aware that something was terribly wrong.

"Get up and get some warm clothes on!" he shouted. "And get your brother."

"What…" she began feebly, as Buddy appeared in her doorway.

"The big house is on fire. You two get dressed and get down by the river."

Raven and Buddy looked at each other, then toward the window. They saw the shadows of light dancing across the walls and smelled smoke drifting in through the open doors. Their pa had disappeared and they scrambled to get dressed, as much to follow his orders as to see for themselves what was going on outside.

The fire was the most impressive sight they'd seen in their young lives. Flames licked the night sky, as sparks and embers floated to the heavens. They could feel the intense heat, even far from the blaze. The roar of the fire sent shivers through them. People were shouting and running around with buckets of water, even though it was clear that this fire was not going to be put out with a bucket brigade.

Buddy pulled Raven away from the fire and toward the river. As she turned, she caught sight of Zeke, tied to his tree. He was at the end of his rope and trying to get away from the heat and flames. Raven ran back inside, grabbed a knife, and headed toward the blazing inferno.

"What are you doing?" shouted Buddy, as he followed. "Pa's going to whip you!"

"Zeke's burning up," she said over her shoulder. "I'm going to cut him loose."

"Are you crazy?" he stopped. "That bear's a killer."

She didn't reply. She walked up to the tree and began sawing at the knot.

"Hey, you get away from there," Henry Koch said gruffly, as he appeared out of the smoke. "Get away from my bear."

"He's too close to the fire," Raven replied defiantly, holding the knife higher than she had intended.

Koch looked at the knife and back at her, as if questioning her intentions. Raven quickly lowered the knife. The heat from the fire was beginning to burn her face and she wanted to get away from that spot. She stepped to the side, away from where she knew the bear was still tugging at his rope, and turned to run back to her brother. As she glanced back, she could see Koch untying the bear from the tree and leading it away from the heat and flames.

When Raven and Buddy reached their mother's grave, they knew they could stop. Not only had the heat and noise faded, but they felt safe in her presence. They turned, just in time to see the roof of the burning house collapse in a crash of smoke and sparks. As they gazed on the devastation, they knew that their lives would be changed forever. That mansion had always been there, watching over their existence. Their father drew his living from it. They had played in and around it all their lives. Even as a bar, it provided a connection to their past. What would happen now? What would happen to the estate with the house gone?

"You guys OK?" asked a familiar voice, as a figure emerged from the darkness. Their friend, Al Doyle had made his way up the creek in the dark and found his friends where he had expected, at their mother's grave.

"Yeah," they said in unison.

"What happened?"

"We don't know," Buddy said. "Pa just woke us up and told us to get out."

"Someone out front said that people are still inside," Al said. "They must be burned up by now."

The frigid night air sent a shiver through her body as Raven pulled the collar of her coat up around her face. It smelled of smoke.

   "I wonder if Simpson and Buckley got out." She said quietly.

   Henry Koch had tied Zeke to another tree and stood behind it, watching Raven intently. The firelight played off his face as he spat a dark stream of tobacco juice. He wondered what she was telling those boys. He'd seen the look she had given him, when she confronted him with the knife. Had she seen him set the fire? Did she know? Who else would she tell? This was a threat he would have to deal with.

8

"You can't kick me off my own land," Cyril Dotson protested. "I'm going to rebuild!"

"No, you're not," countered Mayor Crofton. "The deed is clear. Your father left this land to the City. Now that the house is gone, you have no claim here."

Dotson was silent, as he stared at the Mayor. He couldn't think of anything to say. The Mayor was right, but it wasn't fair. He looked over the ruins of his family's house, now reduced to a pile of charred lumber. Three brick chimneys stood as silent memorials to a once proud home. The family was staying in town with his wife's parents. Since the bar had been their livelihood, they had no means to rebuild and the mayor had little interest in allowing them to do so. He now had his park.

Cyril and his brother, Cecil, had grown up on this land. Their father had bought it when he came home from the War. He'd built the house with profits from his dry-goods store. After his wife died, he threw himself deeper into his work. His business thrived and he became wealthy.

His sons had grown up with everything they needed. After Cecil moved to California, Cyril figured the house and property would be his. He had no idea what was in the old man's will, until it was too late.

Now he had to face the shame of living with his wife's family and figuring out a way to support his kids. He had never in his life had to work at anything and didn't look forward to starting now.

"According to your father's will," the Mayor continued, "we're to turn this land into a public park and that's what it is – Dotson Park – in honor of Cyrus."

The final words were said to Cyril's back as he stomped angrily toward his wagon. Clouds hung low in the fading afternoon light and the smell of burned wood clung to the area. The Mayor turned to go, but paused to watch Calvin Griffith's daughter walk out of her house and cross the yard behind the rubble of the old house. She cradled a large wooden bowl in her hands. It took him a moment to realize where she was headed. He hadn't seen the bear, until she dumped the contents of the bowl and retreated. The bear moved to the food and began to eat. The girl sat on the ground to watch.

As the scene unfolded, the Mayor chomped on his cigar and stared intently. The City owned this property and the City owned that bear. What he had here was more than just a park. He had the makings of a zoological park. He'd seen them in Cincinnati and Pittsburgh, and he knew some big cities like New York and Philadelphia had them, as well. Excitement welled up inside him, as he realized the possibilities. He rushed back to his wagon to begin planning the Dotson Park Zoo.

Raven placed the bowl in the sink and walked back out of the house toward the barn. She met Lizzie Harner coming her way.

"Hey, Liz," she said brightly.

"Hey, Raven."

"Want to help me feed the animals?" Raven asked.

"Sure," Lizzie replied.

Lizzie was Raven's best friend. They had met years ago when Lizzie's pa began delivering hay for the Dotson's animals and Lizzie rode along. She was a good bit shorter than Raven with skin the color of chocolate milk, large expressive eyes, and a smile that never seemed to leave her face.

As they stepped into the barn they were met with the familiar sound of a ball hitting the wooden wall of the barn. Buddy was practicing baseball inside to escape the cold. He had created a clever way of outlining the strike-zone of a batter. He stood a bale of hay on a bench against the wall at the far end of the barn and stepped off the distance from home plate to the pitcher's mound. The hay-bale was about the size of a strike-zone. If he hit the hay, it was a strike.

"Is he up there?" Raven asked Buddy.

"No," Buddy replied without looking at her. "He went out somewhere."

Raven did not like to be in the barn when Koch was in his room upstairs.

"He gives me the creeps," she said to Lizzie. "I've seen him watching me."

"My pa says he's pure evil," Lizzie said. "Ain't nothing but trouble going to come from him."

"He's not so bad," said Buddy, just to be contrary.

"He is too," Raven said from the hay stall. She emerged with a pitchfork full of hay and stopped to watch Buddy wind-up and throw another baseball. It thudded into the wall. He was supposed to be helping her, but she didn't mind. She liked feeding the horses.

"What's going to happen now that the big house is gone?" Lizzie asked.

"I don't know," Raven replied, "but pa's plenty worried. He won't talk about it, but he's sure worried."

"I'm not worried," Buddy said. "The Dotsons will probably build a new bar and pa'll keep looking after the property. Who else is going to do it?" He threw another baseball which caught the edge of the hay bale and careened into the adjacent stall.

"What if they don't," Raven said as she pitched hay into the horse stall. "We'll have to find a new home."

"We're not moving," Buddy said as he heaved a ball. "I wish we would, but pa will find a way to stay here." The ball hit the center of the hay with a swish. "You'll see."

Calvin couldn't remember the last time he'd been this nervous. He threw his cigar away and wiped his sweaty palms on his shirt as he walked up the steps. The small wooden shack served as an office for Walker Brothers Construction Company. Rollo Wilson had told him they were looking for a foreman on the site of a massive new state prison that was under construction in the nearby town of Claxton. Calvin figured Rollo was just trying to push him out of the way, but that was all right.

"I'm here to see about the foreman's job," Calvin announced to the man behind the desk.

The man looked Calvin up and down and pointed to the construction site behind the building.

"See Gruber," he said. "He's on the yard."

Cal turned and walked back into the cool morning air, unsure of how he would recognize this Gruber, or even what was meant by 'the yard'. The area behind the office was quiet, with one solitary figure looking down into a deep hole that had been cut into the landscape. The man, it turned out, was Richard Gruber and the hole was larger than any excavation Calvin had ever seen.

"This is the basement," Gruber explained after their introduction. "Ever have any experience with something like this?"

"No." Calvin said simply.

"Refreshing to find an honest man," Gruber replied with a sidelong glance. "Where you from?"

"Over in Thomasville," Calvin said. He told the man about his work on the estate, which included everything from farming to game management, and even some construction.

"Well," Gruber said when Cal had finished, "I need a yard foreman. You don't need to know much about construction. You just need to be organized. You'd receive materials, keep track of supplies and order stuff before we run out. Think you can handle that sort of thing?"

"Yeah," Cal replied. "I can handle that."

"I have another fellow coming in this afternoon. I'll let you know in a couple of days."

Rollo Wilson strode out of the mayor's office with coffee cup in hand and a frown on his face. He said nothing as he passed the desk of James Purtle, the mayor's assistant. Purtle was a nice looking young man with quick, shifty eyes. He always wore a dark suit, white shirt and red tie. He had an air of friendly, quiet efficiency – but he was none of those. He was a con man.

"What's the matter?" asked Purtle as he stood at the door to Rollo's office.

"A zoo is the problem," said Rollo staring angrily out the window. His office was small and cluttered so Purtle had no place to sit. "The mayor has decided to build a zoo out at the old Dotson place."

They both knew that when R.C. Crofton made up his mind, he was not likely to change.

"You going to run it?" asked Purtle.

"It'll be in my department," Rollo replied. "But he wants that caretaker to run it."

"Griffith, what does he know about zoos?"

"What does anyone around here know about zoos?" Rollo replied. "He's obviously good at managing the property and he knows about livestock."

They stood in silence. The quiet in the room was punctuated by the clip-clop of someone walking down the hall outside door.

"I could run it," said Purtle quietly.

"You don't know anything about zoos either," said Rollo as he continued to stare out the window. "I really don't want a zoo way out there. A park is bad enough, but not a zoo."

"How about making me assistant director of parks," asked Purtle. "I'm sure the mayor can see you need help."

Rollo Wilson did not respond.

9

"I don't want to be a zookeeper," Buddy muttered, "I'm going to play baseball."

"What?" asked Calvin sharply, looking across the table.

Silence hung in the air as Buddy stared into his boiled potatoes and ham, and Calvin continued to glare at him.

"Why did the mayor ask you to run the zoo?" asked Raven to break the tension.

"He knows I can't say no. I'm tied to this property."

"I think he knows you're good with animals," Raven said brightly, trying to lighten the mood.

Calvin did not reply. He wasn't ready to tell them about the job application.

"What kind of animals will we have?" she asked.

Still no reply.

"Does this mean you'll work for the mayor?"

Calvin chewed his dinner and avoided looking at his daughter. "I'll work for Rollo Wilson."

Buddy looked up, ready to pounce on the negative, "He's mean. I hope he doesn't come around here."

"He'll be here plenty," Calvin shot back. "He's director of parks and this is a park. You'd better be nice to him."

"I've never been to a zoo," Raven said, changing the subject.

"A zoo is nothing but a big, smelly barn yard," Buddy said knowingly, even though he had never seen one either.

Raven liked the idea of having more animals around. She was the one who fed Zeke most of the time. It would be fun to live in a zoo.

"Will Zeke have to live in a cage?" asked Raven.

"Yep," Calvin replied as he rose, put his plate in the sink and poured a cup of coffee. "Get this place cleaned up and both of you do your lessons," he said as he left the room.

The big mountain lion was on her in two bounds. His front paws hit her in the back, knocking her to the ground. His canine teeth severed her spine at the base of her neck, killing her instantly. He had been stalking her for nearly an hour as the plump woman in the dark skirt, white blouse, and floppy hat stalked around the pond looking at the ground. Her stumbling walk and slow moving way signaled easy prey. When she faced his hiding place he remained motionless but when she turned her back, he seized the opportunity.

Now with the kill complete, he would drag his prey to safety and take his time eating. But the clip-clop of a passing horse pulled his attention toward the road and he bolted for the woods. Dinner would need to wait.

Raven didn't like washing dishes, but it was one of those simple chores that allowed her mind to wander. That's why the loud knock at the back door startled her. She jumped and looked sharply at Buddy who was at the table behind her with an open book in front of him, but with the look of one whose mind was also somewhere else.

The kitchen had been quiet since the argument at dinner. Calvin was in the front room in his chair, probably asleep. The faint smell of smoke permeated the room as the fire in the wood stove warmed the room. Buddy scraped his chair noisily back from the table as a second knock jarred the room.

"Coming!" he hollered.

Alvin Doyle bounded into the room looking like he had just received good news.

"Well?" he asked expectantly.

Buddy and Raven looked at each other and then back at Al, who just stood there grinning.

"We're going to build a zoo," Al said finally.

"Oh," Buddy said and sat down.

"Yes." Said Raven with a little more enthusiasm.

"That's great," Al beamed his red hair and freckles seeming to glow. "We can help build it. We can work there after school and in the summer. Buddy can become a zoo keeper when he graduates this spring."

"Not interested," Buddy shot back.

Al turned to Raven, who had resumed washing dishes. "What about you, Raven?"

"I'll work there, if Pa'll let me," she said.

"Sure he will. Why wouldn't he?"

"Because I'm a girl," she replied. She dumped the dishwater down the sink and began to dry her hands.

Al sat at the table, leaned back and clasped his hands behind his head. Al lived across the road in a modest, wood-frame house. He was the youngest of the twelve Doyle children, and they were quite a sight when they were all together. Every person, including the parents, was short and muscular with hair the color of fresh carrots. Mr. Doyle was a traveling salesman who was seldom home and Mrs. Doyle worked hard to keep her brood fed and clothed. Al had his chores, but he also had plenty of freedom. His sisters were usually charged with looking after him, which meant he was mostly on his own.

Calvin strode back into the room and placed his coffee cup on the counter for Raven to wash. She glanced at him as if to complain about more dirty dishes, but thought better of it.

"Hey Uncle Cal," said Al brightly. Calvin wasn't his uncle but addressing familiar adults as aunt and uncle was common in these parts. "I hear you're going to be in charge of building a zoo."

"Looks that way," said Calvin as he made for the door.

"I know where you can get animals," Al said.

Cal had moved out of sight but stuck his head back into the room.

"My Aunt Bea takes care of animals," Al continued when he saw the interest.

Cal had forgotten about Bea Taylor. Al was named after Bea's late husband. Alvin Taylor had been a veterinarian who had joined the army after the bombing of the battleship Maine down in Cuba. He had been in charge of Teddy Roosevelt's horses until he died of yellow fever a few years ago. After Alvin died, Bea took to supporting herself by doctoring animals, even though she wasn't a real veterinarian.

"My Aunt Bea sees lots of animals. She helps Miss Janey with her birds. She even told me about an old man up the river who keeps an alligator under his house. Can I work at the zoo, Uncle Cal? Boy, this is going to be great."

Calvin left the room without replying.

Raven smiled as she took a seat at the table. Al was like a breath of fresh air in the stuffy household. She hoped her pa would let Al work at the zoo. She hoped he would let her, too.

"How do you keep an alligator under your house?" she asked.

10

"Mornin, R.C.," Calvin said.

"Mornin, Cal," said the mayor with his customary vigorous pumping handshake.

Calvin and the mayor showed a familiarity that might have surprised the casual observer. In fact, they had a friendship that went back twenty years to the time R.C Crofton was a school teacher who tutored young Calvin. As James Purtle led the horses and wagon to the barn, Calvin and R.C. turned to face the property. They stood in the old driveway facing the river. A cold wind whipped across the landscape tossing leaves and bits of paper. The leafless trees waved at the low flying clouds. Calvin tugged at the collar of his shirt pulling it up around his neck. The mayor hardly seemed to notice the cold.

"What do you have in mind for this, R. C.?" Calvin asked.

"You can start by pulling down those chimneys," he replied, pointing at the three tall, brick chimneys that remained from the old Dotson mansion. "Maybe we can reuse the bricks. I figure we've got about five or six acres to work with, from the barn," he pointed to his left, "down to the creek," he gestured casually to the right. "I'd go maybe half way to the river. Any more than that will be too far for people to walk. I don't imagine you'll find enough animals to cover more than that anyway. Have you found any animals yet?"

"A few," Calvin replied. "I'll put some goats and donkeys around the barn. I hear tell of some buffalo and maybe an alligator in the area. And I may want to talk with Miss Janey about some of her birds. I'll need your help with that one." They walked slowly toward the river. "And the bear, of course."

They glanced toward the barn where Zeke the black bear was tied to a tree and Raven poured water into a metal bucket that was tied to a stake that had been driven into the ground.

"Your girl going to work for you?" asked the mayor absently, thinking back to the scene of her feeding the bear.

"No," Calvin replied without explanation.

"What about the layout and the construction of the cages?" asked the mayor.

"I won't know about cages until we get some animals," replied Calvin. "We'll need to buy supplies – wire, wood, nails, concrete, and such."

"You'll get all that," said the mayor with a touch of impatience.

"I'd like to bring the entrance off the drive way where the old house stood. We can use the bricks from the chimneys for the walls and walkways there," Calvin said.

"I've seen zoos in Cincinnati and Pittsburgh," said the mayor. "They're pretty impressive. They also have zoos in Washington, New York and Chicago. Maybe you could talk to those folks."

"Any pictures?" Calvin asked.

"I can get some. I want the cages large enough for the animals but not so big that people can't see them. Maybe you can build around these trees," continued the mayor, pointing to the large chestnut and elm trees that dotted the property. "That would give the animals some shade."

"How much are you going to pay me?" Calvin asked.

"Sixty dollars a month plus the house," the mayor replied, "But you'll work for Rollo. It's his park."

Calvin didn't respond for a moment. He knew he had no choice. "I can't manage a bunch of animals seven days a week by myself. I'll need a couple of zookeepers. I'll also need help from your city work crews and I'll need to pay Koch to help with the bear."

Henry Koch's name hung in the air for a moment.

"That's a lion track, sheriff," Allison Janey exclaimed, "and a big one, too."

"I can see that," he replied.

There was no mistaking the print in the mud. It was nearly the size of a person's fist. It lacked the tell-tale points at the end of each toe that would have identified it as a large dog.

"Well, I want to know what you're going to do about it," she challenged. "He's after my birds."

There was not much doubt about that either. Allison Janey had an impressive collection of birds in cages and pens strewn all around her house and barn.

"I've never known you to worry about varmints," he said as he leveled his gaze on the elderly woman. She glanced at him and looked away. He was right. There was a time that she would have stayed up all night with a shotgun across her knees to protect her birds. But, they both knew that she was too old to do that, now.

"You're the sheriff," she said quietly. "It's your job to protect people. If that cat kills someone's child it'll be on your head."

He watched her walk away and knew she was right. The tracks led nowhere and the cat could be anywhere. He looked around at the collection of pens and cages that dotted the property. He was one of the few people allowed on the property. He had seen the pheasants, pigeons, parrots and other assorted birds. She had spent the better part of forty years building this collection and he wondered what would become of it. Her man, Albert, had recently left her to care for his ailing wife, and she was simply too old to handle these birds on her own. Maybe it would be better to let the cat take care of them after all.

He knew his search was a waste of time. That cat was long-gone, but he walked the grounds anyway. He figured he had better make a good show of it.

The house was a big, two-story on the edge of town. It backed-up to the woods and her neighbors were far enough away that they were not bothered by the squawks and cries of the birds.

It did make him nervous to be walking around the back of these cages looking for a mountain lion. What if it was watching him, getting ready to pounce? That's why he jumped when the large, blue and yellow parrot pierced the air with a deafening squawk a few feet behind him.

"Son of a bitch," he said as he instinctively reached for his pistol.

James Purtle stood at the door of the barn, looking at the mayor and Calvin Griffith stroll the property. Henry Koch sat on a bale of hay behind him in the shadows.

Purtle had drifted into town a few years earlier, found a job as an accounting clerk at city hall and worked his way up to the mayor's office. Those few people who were close to him knew that behind that pleasant, boyish exterior lurked a dark, ruthless person who would stop at nothing to get what he wanted.

"I'll need more money this time," Koch growled.

"You'll get what we agreed to," Purtle replied. "I'm not asking you to do anything yet. Just keep your eyes open. Let me know what's going on out here."

"Why don't you just run em out of here?"

"We can't run em off. Griffith is friends with the mayor," Purtle said. "Just do what I'm paying you for and I'll keep you dirty little secret," Purtle stiffened and backed into the shadows as Raven emerged from her house.

"It's that girl, isn't it?" asked Koch as he studied Purtle's reaction.

Purtle didn't reply.

"She's trouble, that one," Koch said menacingly.

"She's a kid," Purtle replied.

"That whole bunch needs to be run off from here," Koch said.

"You want this place for yourself?" Purtle asked, mockingly.

Koch did not reply.

"Well, you do your job and you might just get your wish."

The mayor appeared to be finished with Calvin and they were walking toward the barn.

As he moved outside to meet his boss Purtle said, "You just remember our deal."

Olivia was frightened. Her sister, Bessie, had never been missing this long and Olivia had never seen her ma this worried.

"You'd better get back to the house," said her pa without looking at her. "It'll be dark soon."

"But, Pa."

"Don't argue with me," he said sharply.

Olivia knew he meant business. He was small, thin, and looked too old to be her pa. She'd come late in the marriage of

Myron and Bertha Kettle. They already had two grown daughters – Alice, who was married, and Bessie, who never would be. Bessie was twenty years old and had the mind of a ten year old. She and Olivia were best friends. That's why Olivia hated to give up the search. Bessie had wandered off before, but this time was different. It was getting dark and there had been talk of a mountain lion in the area.

Olivia walked across the barnyard past the chicken coop and pig pens. Where could she be? They often played in the woods, walking into the hills to pick black berries and down to the creek to hunt for arrowheads. They didn't get out as much in the winter so Olivia couldn't imagine where she'd gone, especially with a lion on the loose. They'd talked about it this morning, about the tracks down by Adams Pond.

One of their favorite activities was to look for deer, otters, and beavers. They occasionally saw foxes and once glimpsed a bobcat before it disappeared into a thicket. About the only animals they hadn't seen were bears and mountain lions.

"Lion," Olivia said to herself as she stopped in mid-stride. "Adams Pond."

Suddenly she knew Bessie had gone to the pond to see a lion. She'd told no one because she knew they would all say no.

"Pa," she shouted. "Pa, I know where she is!"

11

"How'd you get that rope up there?" Raven asked as she craned her neck to look up at the top of the chimney.

"Ladder," Buddy replied, "and a long pole"

"Pa know you're doing this?"

"Course he does," Buddy lied. "He's busy with that man from Claxton."

Raven was pretty sure that was not true. Their pa would never have sent Buddy to pull down these chimneys alone.

"You'd better get back," he warned as he pulled on the rope to take up the slack.

Raven backed up a few steps. She wondered where her pa was and what he would say when he found out what Buddy was up to. Koch, she knew, was in town picking up supplies to build cages.

Buddy had chosen the largest of the three chimneys, the one that had once served the kitchen and the parlor. It had two fireplaces back to back. The other two chimneys were smaller and looked like they would blow over in a heavy wind. It was just like her brother to choose the hardest one.

"Here goes," he said as he leaned into the rope that was wrapped around his body.

As the rope tightened, she looked at the top of the chimney. Puffy white clouds moved across the blue morning sky making it difficult to judge whether the brick tower was moving. It did not appear to be. Buddy grunted with effort. The rope was taut but nothing happened. After a few moments of grunting, straining and slipping he dropped the rope to bend over and catch his breath.

Raven took a step toward him but a loud crack stopped her. She looked back at the chimney. It still wasn't moving – or was it?

She stared hard and finally, slowly she caught sight of a tree in the distance and she could see movement. The chimney was falling directly where Buddy was standing.

"Buddy!" she shouted. "Look out!"

He looked at her then back at the chimney. He couldn't see movement because it was coming straight at him.

"Look out!" she said again, taking a step toward him.

This time he moved quickly in Raven's direction just as the massive pile of bricks crashed to the ground with an earth shaking thud and a cloud of dust. Raven and Buddy stood grinning at each other like a couple of fools who had just cheated fate, when Calvin came charging out of the house with Richard Gruber behind him. Gruber had just offered him the job in Claxton when the crash of falling bricks had halted their conversation. As soon as they saw the fury on his face, their smiles faded. Raven knew in that instant that their pa had not known what Buddy was doing.

"What are you doing?" he bellowed. "I told you to get it ready, not pull it down."

He eyed the scene and looked back at Raven and Buddy who now stood together.

Turning to Gruber he said, "I'll need to get back to you."

"Don't take too long," Gruber said.

"I just need to sort some things out here," Cal said. He was excited about the prospects of change and had every intention of accepting the position, especially at the generous salary of twenty five dollars a week. But something about the situation with Buddy and Raven was making him hesitate.

Gruber paused, then turned and left.

"Get over to the barn," he said, "and get on your chores."

"But Pa," said Raven, prepared to defend herself.

"Git – both of you!"

"You said he knew what you were doing," said Raven as they walked away.

"I figured he'd be pleased if I went ahead and finished the job," said Buddy.

"Well, if he was pleased he sure didn't show it," she replied.

Calvin was furious with Buddy and Raven. They could have been killed, he thought as he stood looking at the jumbled pile of bricks. Now he wasn't sure if he felt anger or fear. How would he feel if anything had happened to Raven or Buddy? He was still bitter over the loss of his wife and maybe he somehow blamed them for living when she had died. Now he felt something different. Like losing them might be like losing her all over again.

As he stood rooted to that spot sorting out his emotions, his gaze wandered from what had once been the top of the chimney down to the fireplace – which had remained upright. The falling of the chimney had broken the fireplaces at an angle and he saw something unusual where it had broken. As he moved closer he discovered a cavity between the two fireboxes. He pulled a few bricks out and peered inside. Something had been bricked-up in a cavity between the fireplaces. It was a large metal box which he carefully pulled out and brushed off. Why would anyone hide something behind a fireplace? He carried the box to the house, careful that no one would see.

"You two get this wagon unloaded," Koch growled as he tied off the reigns and climbed down.

"You're not our boss," said Buddy defiantly.

He and Raven stood in the door of the barn. Koch had just returned from town with a pile of lumber, rolls of wire fencing, and boxes of nails. They didn't move as he walked away, looking intently at the pile of rubble in the distance. Their pa had pulled down the other chimneys, so the whole area was a jumble of bricks and mortar. They watched as Koch picked carefully through the rubble, struggling over bricks with his wooden leg, peering here and there. He seemed to be looking for something. His attention was captured by something at the big brick fireplace that Buddy had pulled down.

"What's he doing?" Raven asked.

"I don't know," Buddy replied, "but it looks like he found something.

Koch was on his hands and knees reaching into the rubble. He came up empty, looked carefully back into the bricks and suddenly turned in their direction. His hard stare lock onto them as they stared curiously back at him.

"What is he up to?" asked Raven quietly.

12

"Strike 'em out," yelled one man.

"Come on, Buddy," shouted another.

Hundreds of people had crowded around the baseball field at Dotson Park to see if their Thomasville Giants could finally beat the Claxton Knights. It was the largest crowd this part of town had ever seen. Rollo Wilson, as director of parks, had made it happen and he had made it known that he wanted it to expand. If he had his way, the whole park would become ball fields and recreation areas. It was obvious that this was the type of activity people wanted to see.

As he hovered around the edges of the crowd, he could see all the people standing shoulder to shoulder around the field craning their necks for a look at the action. A few lucky folks sat high in the seats of their unhitched wagons while others stood in the backs of those wagons. One person was even perched in the branches of a tree on the edge of the outfield.

Calvin stood at the front of the crowd, along the first-base line. He had seen Richard Gruber from the prison job in Claxton standing with the opposing players. They had nodded to each other from across the field, but now he was gone.

"Quite a game, isn't it?"

Calvin was startled and turned to see Gruber standing behind him.

"Sure is," Calvin said as they shook hands.

"Any of these boys belong to you?"

"That's my son," Calvin said, pointing to Buddy.

Gruber was silent for a moment. "Have you thought any more about my offer?"

Calvin looked around, worried that someone might hear. "I thought you hired someone," he said, trying not to sound rude.

"He didn't work out," Gruber replied. "I'll keep it open for a few more days if you're interested," he said before retreating into the crowd.

It was the third year of their rivalry, and the Knights always won handily. This year Thomasville had a 5 – 3 lead going into the ninth inning. Their star player was Davis Wagner, whose Uncle Honus played professional baseball for the Pittsburgh Pirates. Wagner had hit two home runs and pitched a nearly flawless game, until he wore down in the seventh inning. After Claxton had scored three runs, the Thomasville coach replaced Wagner with Buddy Griffith. The fate of the team, a group of young men in their late teens and early twenties, rested on the arm of a seventeen-year-old.

Buddy stood on the mound with his back straight and his hands folded into his glove. He gave his best glare toward the batter, and then glanced at the man he had just walked to first base. The batter was a wiry little guy, whom Buddy knew was well able to hit a home run to tie the game.

Buddy could offer him one of two pitches – a blazing fast-ball that would make the catcher's mitt pop like a gunshot, or a curve-ball that sometimes fooled batters into swinging at a ball that moved away at the last minute. The only problem was that he didn't always know where the ball would end up. On a bad day, he was as likely to hit the batter as strike him out.

"Your boy's turned into quite a pitcher," said Cyril Dotson as he moved next to Calvin.

"Thanks," replied Calvin, without taking his eyes off the action.

The two men could hardly have looked more different. Calvin wore the rough clothes of a workman – overalls, flannel shirt, and heavy boots, with a floppy, wide-brimmed hat on his head. Cyril, on the other hand, sported a flat-topped, white straw hat and the high-collared, dapper clothes of a businessman.

"There are professional baseball scouts here," Cyril continued. "I could introduce them to Buddy, if you like."

"He's only seventeen," Calvin said, chomping his cigar and looking at Cyril out of the corner of his eye.

"He could play summer ball on the Junior Circuit," said Cyril. "I'd be glad to represent him – maybe get him some money."

Calvin was silent for a moment, as though thinking it over. In reality, he had no intention of letting Buddy spend his summers playing baseball. He needed him to help around the park.

"I don't know," he replied, taking off his hat and mopping his forehead with a handkerchief. "I'll need to think it over."

Both men's attention shifted back to the field.

Raven didn't care for baseball. Grown men running around playing games seemed silly to her. But she knew plenty about the game from listening to talk around the house, and she cared enough for her brother to hope he did well at it.

Calvin had told her to help mind the zoo, so she watched the action from the outfield, halfway between the game and the zoo. The Dotson Park baseball field was located at the front of the park along the Road. Raven stood facing the field, close enough to see the action but well able to look over shoulder and watch the zoo construction site behind her.

Raven had never seen so many people in the park. This whole neighborhood had a bustle to it that was exciting. She could see a house across the street that was under construction, one of several in the area, with workmen standing on the unfinished roof watching the action. All of these people gathered here would have been unimaginable just last year. She leaned against one of the trees that lined the driveway and wondered what her Pa and Mr. Dotson were talking about. Next to them stood a couple of girls that Buddy and Al were seeing frequently these days. Mary Hampton and Rebecca Malone wore wide-brimmed hats with flowers stuck in the bands and clapped their gloved hands politely.

Buddy completed his wind-up and let his pitch fly. The batter swung and missed. The pop of the ball hitting the catcher's mitt arrived at Raven's ear a couple of seconds after the event. The umpire's right arm stabbed the air, indicating strike three. The crowd erupted in cheers and ran out on top the field. The Giants had won and her brother was the hero. Raven smiled and turned back to the zoo.

"What'll we feed em?" asked Rondell Boyd as he peered into the large box that sat on the work table outside the barn. He had been hired as Calvin's first zoo keeper just two weeks ago on Bea Taylor's recommendation. He was a cousin of Nat Harner's and an experienced farm hand.

"Meat," Al replied. "Aunt Bea said to feed 'em rats, mice, chicken, even meat-scraps from the table"

Red foxes were pretty common in these parts. They were often seen on the property – their crimson fur glowing in the sunlight as they hunted for mice in the fields. These little guys peering back at her weren't much larger than house cats. They had prominent ears, pointed muzzles and slanting clever eyes. Their tails were long and bushy and the tips looked as if they had been dipped in white paint.

"How old are they?" asked Raven.

"Probably born last summer," Al replied, proud of his status as an authority.

In truth, the foxes had been orphans that were raised by his aunt Bea and had spent the winter in a pen behind her house. They were quite tame, though they would nip if they were teased or hungry – a fact which caused Al to rub the scar on his left index finger. It had mostly healed, but it still itched a bit.

Though Al was a little younger that Raven, their mutual interest in the natural world brought them close. He was impulsive and bold while she was shy and reserved. He was smart but did poorly in school while she did well at nearly everything she put her mind to, but they seemed to speak a common language when it came to animals. They had what people called 'the gift'. It was almost as if they could talk to the animals.

"Where's your pa going to build their pen," he asked.

"Over by Zeke," she replied. "He wants to group the animals by type – carnivores, birds, hoofed stock."

"They're diggers," Al said. "We'll need to put rocks around the edges to keep 'em from digging out."

"Mr. Calvin's going to try something else, said Rondell. "He's going to lay a row of fence on the ground around the edge of the pen and cover it with dirt."

"Hmmm," Al said thoughtfully, "that's pretty smart."

These little animals looked harmless enough, but Al knew that if they decided to dig out they would be difficult to stop. And, as every chicken coop owner knew, it didn't take much of a hole for them to squeeze through.

"Did they come from this area?" Raven asked.

"No, they were brought in by Mrs. Hardaway from up near Weaverville. Her husband killed their mother. The babies were in a den under the front porch."

Raven was relieved. Her pa regularly shot foxes on this property. He said he was protecting their chickens but she thought he really enjoyed shooting. He hunted all sorts of animals that were no threat to the livestock – deer, pigs, birds. It seemed odd for someone who liked animals and even looked after them in a zoo, to want to kill them. She'd never understood that.

"Pa," said Raven quietly. "Lunch is ready."

She hated to disturb him as he sat in the sun near the small copper beech tree and looked over the creek, lost in thought. The tree hadn't grown much in the few months since it was planted, but Calvin loved this spot next to his wife's grave. It was where he came to think. He didn't speak to her anymore, but he did feel her presence. The most difficult part of taking the job in Claxton would be leaving this spot to someone else's care. He'd come to tell her he had decided to take the job.

"I'll be right there."

Raven turned and walked back toward the zoo to tell Buddy. The gravel path crunched beneath her feet and the scent of honeysuckle washed over her.

Mr. Harner's hay wagon was backed up to the end of the barn, and Mr. Harner was tossing bales of hay up to the open loft door. Raven could see Rondell and her brother snatching the bales as they rolled in and stacking them to the side. Buddy had been working hard in the days following his big baseball game. With the final game coming next week, he hoped his Pa might soften his stance on letting him spend next summer playing in a traveling league.

"Buddy, Ron," said Raven to the open door. "Lunch."

"You're welcome to join us, Mr. Harner," she continued.

"Thank you, Miss Raven, but I've got four more deliveries to get out before sundown. I'll toss the rest of these up and Rondell can stack 'em later."

Raven smiled up at the enormous, black man who stood on the back of the wagon mopping his head with a handkerchief.

"I'll pick up Lizzie before supper time," he continued, nodding toward the house.

Lizzie and Raven had been inseparable all winter, working at the zoo, playing down at the creek, and, today, fixing a hot lunch of cornbread and black-eyed peas. As Raven returned to the house, Lizzie was setting the plates on the table.

"Your pa says you can stay 'till suppertime," said Raven.

"Good," said Lizzie. "Maybe we can take Able out for a walk." The girls enjoyed hitching a rope to the nose ring of the gentle, old bull that had recently been donated and parading him around the park.

A knock came at the door before Raven could reply.

"Is Calvin here?" asked Cyril Dotson.

"You're just in time for lunch," replied Calvin from somewhere outside the house.

Raven pushed open the screen door and in walked Cyril, his son Buckley, and a man Raven did not recognize, followed by Buddy and Rondell.

Raven looked at the five men in frustration. She and Lizzie had not fixed enough for all these people.

"This is Isaiah Roberson," said Cyril waving his hand at the stranger. "He's a scout for the Pittsburgh Pirates baseball club. Rollo said you might be interested in talking to him"

Raven observed her pa stiffening slightly as she set the food on the table. A baseball scout, she knew, was someone who looked for new talent to sign to a team. She glanced at Lizzie, then at Buckley and nodded her head toward the door. The three of them hastily dished up their food and retreated outside. They found a bench outside the barn and sat side by side with their plates resting on their laps. The odor of pigs wafted over them.

"My p-pa thinks B-B-Buddy is good enough to p-p-play p-professional b-b-baseball," stammered Buckley.

"Well, my pa will never go for that," said Raven.

"Why not," asked Lizzie through a mouth full of cornbread?

"He wants Buddy to stay here and run the zoo."

"You should be the one to take over the zoo," said Lizzie.

"Yea," said Buckley. "You know way more than B-Buddy."

"I know, but pa says I'm to find a man and get married. Zoo keeping is man's work."

"He lets you do it now," said Lizzie defiantly.

"He doesn't have much choice right now," said Raven. "Maybe I can prove him wrong someday."

"Buckley," said Cyril Dotson as he and the stranger emerged from the house. "Let's go."

"I wish you'd reconsider," he said to Calvin as they left without waiting for a reply.

13

Rondell leaned on the handle of his shovel and propped one foot on its head. He was working with young Raven, and they had been shoveling goat, sheep, and donkey droppings into buckets and hauling it to the dump pit for half-an-hour. A dozen animals lived in the pen outside the barn, and the pit Calvin had dug for manure and old hay was way down by the river. They hadn't made much progress. Two loud booms shook the air and they both glanced across the creek to where Calvin was shooting at something. Raven was dressed like a boy, in work pants, a flannel shirt and heavy boots. With her hair in a long braid that hung to her waist like a thick rope, she almost looked like one. It was her actions that gave her away. When she wiped her nose as it dripped in the cool afternoon air, she did not drag her sleeve across it like a boy. She gently pushed up at the tip of her nose with the cuff of her shirt and gave a quiet sniff as she stared up the lane toward the road and watched Buddy stroll toward the zoo.

"Where have you been?" she asked her brother with a touch of irritation.

"I had to stay after school."

"Did you get in trouble?" she mocked.

"No," he replied. It was his turn to be irritated. "Mrs. Carson asked me and Jason Kinder to help move her desk so she could clean under it."

"That wouldn't take half an hour."

"Well, I guess it did," he said as he picked up a shovel and began to make deposits into the bucket.

The Dotson Park Zoo was taking shape. A few animals had been added to the sheep and goat pen, Henry Koch looked after

Zeke the bear and most of the remains of the old Dotson house had been cleared away. The tree-lined driveway that had led to the old house now made an impressive entry to an unimpressive zoo. Though not officially open to the public, people regularly wandered in to check the progress.

Most visitors walked up the driveway from the street. At the circle that once marked the front of the house, they turned a little to the right and encountered the black bear. Zeke had worn a rutted path around the edge of his pen near the fence. Koch apparently had little interest cleaning. Mounds of poop littered the dirt floor of the pen. The smell was intense on a calm day.

Beyond the bear pen lived the foxes, with their new wire cage already showing the first signs of rust. The foxes loved to dig and their pen was littered with holes of all sizes. The one bright spot was the area around the barn. Though the building was unpainted, the fencing was rough-cut split-rail, and the doors hung at odd angles, the animal pens were clean and neat. Raven frequently heard the complements.

The animals with which people should have been impressed, like the bear and the foxes, brought complaints. The common barnyard animals brought squeals of delight. Raven even provided a bucket of oats for people to feed the animals on busy days. She took pleasure in seeing city kids touch a goat or a pig for the first time. And it made her feel good to overhear people say that this was going to be the best part of the whole zoo.

Buddy, on the other hand, cared little for that. If he had to work here, he wanted to work with Zeke. He wanted to go inside the cage with the big, killer bear – at least that's what he told anyone who would listen.

Buddy reached down and grabbed one of the sheep by its hind leg and laughed as it tried to kick free.

"Let her be," exclaimed Raven. "She doesn't like that."

"How do you know?"

"You can see she wants loose."

"I'd like to see you catch one of 'em," challenged Buddy.

"I can catch 'em better than you."

"Prove it," He said.

"You go first," said Raven. "Let's catch big Jake."

Big Jake was the adult billy goat. His massive horns and rugged disposition made him king of the pen. Nobody messed with big Jake.

"You two help Rondell get this place cleaned up," said Calvin as he strolled by their pen headed to the barn. He cradled his shotgun in his left arm as a dead fox dangled lifelessly from his right hand. "Miss Janey will be here soon."

Buddy did not look at Raven. He simply resumed his shoveling, relieved to be rescued from having to wrestle the big goat and risk being shown up by a girl. Raven watched the lifeless fox swing from side to side as her pa walked away. She was struck by the conflicting position her father was in. He occasionally needed to kill wild animals in order to prevent them from harming the animals he cared for at the zoo.

Allison Janey stepped primly from the smoking motor car clutching her handbag in one hand and accepting the assistance of her driver with the other. She wore a long dress with a pink flower pattern and black high-button shoes. Her silver hair glowed in the afternoon sun. Though she appeared thin and frail, she held her head high as she addressed Calvin and Rollo Wilson, shaking their hands in turn. The long plumes on her hat swayed in the breeze and the folds of loose skin under her chin shook like turkey wattles as she moved. The driver remained with the car as the three walked into the area that might now be called a zoo.

Allison Janey was well known around town. She never married, had lots of money, and was crazy about birds. She had a long row of wire cages behind her house, but since she was something of a recluse, nobody but her servants had ever seen what was in them. Now she had taken ill and wanted to donate them to the zoo.

As Calvin and Rollo escorted her toward the row of cages that Calvin had built near the zoo's entrance across from the bear pen, Buddy and Raven watched intently from their vantage point near the barn while Rondell continued to work. They knew this was a big deal for the zoo, and they knew she was a particular and peculiar old lady. Would she approve of Calvin's handiwork?

Calvin had visited Miss Janey's house several times. Raven had accompanied him one time to help him measure and draw and he had been astonished at the number and variety of birds he had seen. Pheasants of all shapes and sizes pecked along the ground like great, colorful chickens while pigeons and doves sat calmly overhead. Some cages held familiar birds like crows and robins. They had been injured and had drooping wings or missing eyes. In one large wire cage colorful parrots squawked loudly. These parrots would need a warm place to spend the winter.

The cages Calvin built at the zoo were exactly like the ones at Miss Janey's, and most of them were prominently located at the front of the zoo. They were the first thing people would see after they looked at the famous bear that had killed a man. There were a dozen cages in two groups of six. Each cage was long and narrow, but tall enough for a man to stand up in. Calvin had used twenty rolls of chicken wire to cover the wooden framework of the two runs, and another twenty rolls for the tent-like structure he had built for the parrots up near the barn.

"These cages are well done," she said turning to Calvin. "You did a nice job on them."

"What is this square opening in the door?" she continued.

"Those are feed and water ports," Calvin replied. "They will allow us to feed and water the birds without going inside the cages." He demonstrated by dropping a bowl into a wooden frame, lifting the flap over the opening, and sliding the bowl into the cage. She was clearly impressed.

Raven and Buddy were leaning on the fence watching the tour when the three adults suddenly turned in their direction. Looking away, they quickly returned to their cleaning chores.

"Who is that man?" they heard her ask after they had passed the bear pen.

"Henry Koch," replied Calvin. "He takes care of the black bear."

Miss Janey stopped and looked back. Koch seemed not to notice, though he did turn his back to his observers in an effort to hide his face. Miss Janey had a puzzled look. When she resumed walking, Koch stopped working, looked up, and stared back at her.

They walked past the goat pen and, as they approached the parrot pen, a thought occurred to her. She looked at the cage, then at the kids, and finally at Henry Koch.

"Who will care for my birds?"

"Mr. Rondell Boyd is my new zoo keeper," said Calvin gesturing to where Rondell was working.

"A Negro?"

"Calvin will care for them personally," said Rollo with authority as he looked directly at Calvin.

"Hmm," she mumbled as she gazed again at the now busy bear handler. "I feel as though I've seen that man before."

As she drove away Raven and Buddy looked at Henry Koch. He was glaring at the departing car with the intensity of someone who knew he had been discovered. As Raven looked in his direction, Koch's head suddenly turned toward her. Raven looked away, but too late. Koch looked at her for a long time before returning to his work.

14

The barn was one of the few dry places in the zoo and Rondell was glad to be inside. The rain had eased just after noon, but he could still hear taps on the roof which indicated that it had not stopped altogether. He could smell the dampness drifting in through the large open door at the end of the barn.

Ron liked doing the evening feed in the barn. The sweet smell of fresh hay drifted about like dust in a sunbeam as he broke off a flake and shook it into the feed manger for the goats. The animals would munch on it, play with it, and sleep in it overnight. After he finished feeding and watering Able the bull, he would go home and eat his own dinner as darkness closed down the zoo for the evening.

As he came out of the goat stall into the hallway, a movement caught his eye. A horse filled the opening of the barn door – a large horse. It was the type of horse that pulled heavy loads, not the kind that people usually rode. But people rode this horse, a gangling, weather-beaten man with a floppy hat and in front of him a young, barefoot girl in a dress that looked like an old feed sack. They looked at Rondell with the shifty eyes of people who are unaccustomed to meeting strangers. They must have come from way out in the country, Ron surmised, and he couldn't imagine why they sat in the door to his barn.

"You the manager here?" asked the man in the raspy voice of one who smoked cigarettes.

The question caught Rondell off guard. Was this man seriously suggesting that he, a Negro, was in charge? Calvin was in Claxton on business. Raven was in the house and Buddy was across the street helping the Doyles repair a broken barn door. He was alone and felt uneasy about admitting that to this stranger who blocked his exit.

"What do you need?" he said, evading the question.

"My name is Myron Kettle. This here is my daughter Olivia. She has something she wants to give to the Zoo," he replied. Rondell had seen the Kettles on the roads and around town but had never actually spoken to them. They were dirt-poor country folks who kept to themselves.

Rondell looked at the girl with her smudged face and muddy legs. She wasn't holding anything, but he watched as the girl reached down the front of her dress and produced a cotton bag that was moving.

Ron's fears melted as he stepped forward to take the bag from the girl's outstretched hands. Inside, three baby cats squirmed and mewed in the dim light.

"These bobcats washed out of a hollow log in the woods behind our house. They were wet and nearly drowned, but the girl warmed them up and brought 'em back to life. There were four, but one died. We can't keep 'em," he said with authority as he glanced at the girl.

Rondell looked into the bag, then at the girl, and finally at the man. He was trying to decide what to say. Calvin wasn't here, and these people appeared ready to turn and leave. The bobcats would not survive without some expert care, but he wasn't the one to give it. What to do?

"We'll take 'em," he said with more confidence than he felt. "We'll take good care," he said directly to the girl.

After a brief pause instead of a reply, the man wheeled the horse and they rode silently into the gloom. Rondell unbuttoned his shirt and stuffed the bag against his warm body, in imitation if the farm girl's instinctive good sense. His chores were done so he headed to the house, where he met Calvin returning from Claxton. Raven was greeting him at the door as Rondell produced the bag from his shirt.

"Mr. Cal," he began. "I know I'm not supposed to take in animals. But these were dropped off and the people left."

"What are they," Calvin said as he peered into the sack.

"Bobcats."

"Pa," said Raven, taking the sack and looking inside. "We can raise them for the zoo. Can we keep them?"

"Sorry Mr. Cal," said Rondell. "I didn't have any choice."

"That's all right," Cal replied. "We'll see if we can keep em alive. You go on home. I'll see you in the morning."

"What's for dinner?" asked Buddy as he kicked off his muddy boots outside the door.

"I've got a pot of beans going on the stove," replied Raven, "and I'll whip up some cornbread."

Calvin emerged from his room in his undershirt. He had been in a good mood since his return from Claxton and Raven and Buddy had wondered what was going on.

"We've got some baby bobcats," she announced proudly.

"You're not supposed to take in animals," said Buddy to Raven.

"I didn't," she said. "Rondell did. They were brought in by country folk who weren't going to raise them. We couldn't just let 'em die."

They were all silent for a moment as the tiny squeals leaked out of the bag. Calvin looked annoyed but Raven was relieved to hear him say, "I guess you'd better mix up some milk."

For all of his expertise with animals, Calvin had no experience with raising babies. He was confident however, that with mammals, it would involve milk. He was a little irritated with Rondell, but he had done the right thing. Besides, these tiny critters would probably die anyway.

"Tomorrow, if they're still alive," he said, "we'll get a bottle from Bea Taylor. She'll know how to raise babies."

Raven finished preparing the cornbread for the oven and turned her attention to the kittens. She carefully scooped one of the kittens into her hand. It was so young that its eyes were not yet opened. She had no bottle, so she dipped her pinkie finger in the milk and shoved it into the tiny mouth. To her relief, the kitten sucked eagerly. She repeated the process for a few minutes before feeding the other cats. Then she placed them in a wooden milk crate near the stove that her pa had lined with an old blanket. They weren't getting much milk so Raven would be up most of the night. She was greatly relieved at her pa's reaction and couldn't wait till morning to find out what Aunt Bea could teach her about raising babies.

Sunshine can cheer up even the bleakest of landscapes, especially after what seemed like weeks of rain. Raven stood at the door and looked out over the zoo. Sunlight glinted off the many puddles like diamonds on a sandy beach, but she barely noticed. She was awaiting the arrival of Aunt Bea. Her pa had sent Buddy over to ask for help and she had promised to come over after church. The cats had survived the night, but they were not as active as they were last night, so Raven was anxious.

"Hello Raven," said a lady's voice.

"Oh, hello," said Raven.

Aunt Bea seemed to appear from nowhere because she had come from around back. Her fancy dress indicated she had just arrived from church.

"Fetch me an apron, dear," she said kindly as she carefully removed her straw hat with its band of flowers.

Raven handed her a faded, red apron with small white teapots all over it. It didn't go with the shiny green dress she was wearing, but she didn't seem to care as she slipped it over her head and walked briskly to the box near the stove. Her motion was silky smooth, her touch soft and gentle, and her voice quiet and soothing as she picked up one of the kittens.

"OOOO," she cooed to them as she held one close to her face. "You're a cutie."

"I like to hold babies close to my face so they can get my smell in their little minds," she explained to Raven. "They look to be in good shape. I don't see any runny noses or patchy fur. What have you been feeding them?"

"Milk," replied Raven.

"Did you warm it?"

"No."

"That won't do," Aunt Bea said kindly as she put the kittens back in the box and produced a bottle of milk and two tiny baby bottles from her bag. "They'll need the milk warmed to body temperature. We'll use these two baby bottles. They'll need to be fed every four hours all through the night." Aunt Bea warned. "Are you up to that?"

"Oh, yes," said Raven eagerly.

"Have you stimulated them to go, yet?" continued Aunt Bea.

She could tell by Raven's blank look that she had not. "When they are this young, their mother licks their bottoms to stimulate them to relieve themselves. You'll need to do that for them. They won't be able to do it on their own for a few weeks."

"I have to lick their bottoms?" asked Raven in disgust. "I can't do that!"

"No, no, no, dear," laughed Aunt Bea. "Just use a rag that is dampened in warm water to gently rub their bottoms after you feed them."

"Did the cats make it through the night?" asked Rondell.

"Yep," Cal replied. "I sent for Bea Taylor to help my girl figure out how to keep them alive."

"If anyone can do it, she can," Rondell said between sips of coffee.

He and his boss had developed a comfortable relationship over the past few weeks. He had held many jobs in the past, but never one where he was treated with such respect. It was almost as if he were an equal. Calvin had fashioned a kind of office in a corner of the barn hallway. It consisted of planks on sawhorses for a desk and some rickety old chairs. They met there early each morning to plan their day, but the conversations were wide ranging. They talked about baseball and current events, such as Scott and Amundsen's race to the South Pole.

"Hello, Bea," said Calvin as he walked through the door. "Thanks for coming over."

"Glad to do it," she replied. She rose and walked over to shake his hand.

Calvin had known Bea Taylor for years, ever since Alvin had moved back to town after the Spanish-American War. She had been a real beauty and Alvin was justifiably proud to show her around. She was from Cuba, but spoke perfect English and her black hair and dark eyes were captivating. She had a tiny waist, a large bosom, and fine features, but when Alvin died, she let herself go. She seemed to care little for how she looked, though that meant little to Calvin, as he wallowed in grief of his own.

So it was a remarkable moment when they touched hands that day. It was as if a veil had lifted when they locked eyes – the dark-haired beauty and the strong, determined man recognizing needs that neither had felt for quite some time.

Calvin was surprised to see Raven up so early the next morning. He was always first to wake. It was his time for coffee and a quiet moment to begin the day. He didn't like having his routine disrupted. He was also surprised at the mess in the kitchen. The sink was piled with dishes, towels littered the floor and the room smelled something awful. The box on the table emitted the squeals of a hungry bobcat kitten and a second animal was perched on Raven's lap. She held the squirming animal like Aunt Bea had taught her – upright and facing away. Raven's hand cradled the bottle and the baby's head at the same time.

As it dawned on Calvin what was going on here, his surprise turned to annoyance. She had school today and she had stayed up all night nursing these animals.

"You been up all night?" he asked sharply as he pulled the coffee pot from under the sink.

She didn't respond but when their eyes met he could see that she'd been crying.

"What's the matter?" he asked with more anger than he intended. He half expected her to say something silly about how much she loved the cats, but his mind swirled around the other possibilities, such as the fact that she was missing a cat. "Where's the other cat?"

"It died," she said.

"What happened?" he said quietly.

"I don't know," she began to sob. "I fell asleep. I wasn't asleep long but when I woke up, he was dead. The others were hungry and squealing and crawling all over it."

She placed the cat she was feeding in the box, leaned on the table and cried. Calvin hadn't seen her cry like this since her mother's funeral and it began to touch him deeply. He moved up behind her and wrapped his arms around her.

"I haven't been much of a father to you," he said softly, "But I'm going to make that up to you. I've accepted a job in Claxton. We're getting away from this place"

"What?" she said sharply, pulling away from him.

"I'm going to be the yard foreman at the new prison."

"What about the zoo?" she asked.

"I'm just doing that for Buddy," he said.

Raven felt a stab of jealousy as she walked around the kitchen thinking.

"But, pa, this is perfect for you. No one else can do this job. Besides, Buddy doesn't even want to work here. All he wants to do is play baseball."

"Baseball's no life for him."

"Yeah, but he doesn't see that and you're not going to change his mind. What about me? What if I want to work here?"

"No," he said more sharply than he intended. "No daughter of mine is going to have to grub for a living. There are plenty of men who'll jump at the chance to take care of you."

She could see there would be no changing his mind on this

"I love this zoo," she said finally, "And I want to see it completed by you and Buddy and me. You're the only one who can do it. Please stay at least until its open. I'll stop asking to work here. It'll be for you and Buddy," she paused, "Besides, we can't leave ma behind. What would she think?"

Calvin put his head down. He knew she was right. She pulled him into her arms and hugged him fiercely. It was frightening how much she was like her mother.

"I think that's exactly what your ma would have said," he pause, "she also would have told you that losing the kitten is not your fault," he said softly into her hair. "You did well to keep these two alive."

He held her tightly, "Where is it?"

"I wrapped him in a towel and put him on the front porch."

"Let's go bury him," he said as he loosened his arms and moved away. "We'll put him down by the copper beech tree with your ma. I think she'd like that."

"What about Claxton?" asked Raven.

Calvin thought for a moment and said, "I guess we'd better stay here and see if this zoo thing works out."

Raven moved quickly and grabbed her pa in another embrace. She loved the feeling of safety and of being loved once again. "Thanks, Pa."

15

"Unsinkable, they said. Can you imagine that?" said Rondell. "Unsinkable and fifteen hundred people drowned in the ice cold Atlantic ocean."

"I read that there were only seven hundred survivors," Cal said. "They sailed into New York harbor yesterday on the ship that found them floating in the water."

"That must have been one big ship to hold over a two thousand people," said Rondell. "I guess that's why they named it Titanic."

Calvin stood looking out the door of the barn and lit his first cigar of the day. It was raining again and the zoo pathways were ankle deep in muddy water. It would be a miserable day for working but he and Rondell would at least get everything fed. Cleaning would have to wait.

"I have to go downtown to meet with Rollo," he continued.

Rondell was sitting in one of the chairs staring out into the gloom of a soggy morning. The constant rain was depressing enough, but thinking about all those people freezing to death in the ocean made him feel even sadder. Now, on top of all that, Cal had to meet with Rollo Wilson. They hated each other for some reason.

"Koch'll feed Zeke and the fox area, you feed the barn and the birds," said Calvin without changing his gaze from the outside.

The rain grew more intense and the pounding on the metal roof momentarily drowned out any conversation. When it slacked off Rondell asked Calvin, "Why are you meeting with Mr. Wilson?"

"I don't know. He probably wants to chew me out."

"He still doesn't like the zoo much, does he?"

"No," said Calvin. "He still thinks it's a waste of money feeding all these animals and paying me to run it."

Calvin was now content with his job at Dotson Park. He worked out of his home, every day brought some new challenge, and even his children were able to participate. But Rollo Wilson had other ideas.

"Do I need any supplies while I'm in town?" Calvin asked.

"We're down to our last sack of oats," replied Rondell. "The hay is damp and getting moldy in spots. While you're at the feed store, you'd better see if Mr. Jenkins can find us some dry hay."

"How about hitchin up the wagon for me," said Calvin as he stepped out into the rain. "I'll go see if the kids are ready for school."

Three miles upriver from Dotson Park, Andrew Flanagan stood in the rain clutching his chest. The pain was paralyzing and he bent over slightly to catch his breath. He had been digging a ditch to channel the rising floodwaters away from his house and he had to get the work done. He had to do something to stop the river, even though he knew his little ditch wouldn't stand a chance against the massive amount of water that appeared to be headed his way. Spring floods often presented some problems because they came before Florida was ready to emerge, but Andrew used sandbags and ditches to keep the water at bay. This year's floodwaters, however, were the worst he'd seen and the water was going to flood under the house if he didn't work fast. He had to push himself to keep digging in spite of the pain. Florida would not survive long if this cold water reached his den.

He straightened himself and the pain eased somewhat. His oilskin coat bulged in front as his big stomach pressed at the buttons. Rain dripped from his wide-brimmed hat. He turned his pudgy face to the sky hoping for some relief from the rain and the pain, but he received neither. Rain pelted his face and the pain returned. His left arm went numb and, as he sank to his knees, the pain in his chest seemed to be crushing the life out of him. He was dead before his face hit the mud.

"Is Rollo in there?" Calvin asked with a touch of impatience. He had been to Rollo's office and found it empty. Mayor Crofton was in Cincinnati looking at their zoo and Calvin knew the park director liked to play mayor when R.C. was out of town.

"Yes," James Purtle replied stiffly. "I'll tell him you're here."

"I'll tell him myself," said Calvin as he brushed by the self-important little man.

The mayor's office was surprisingly small – not much larger than the outer office.

"Is the park going to flood?" Rollo asked without looking up.

"The swamp on the south side of the creek is under water. The rest of the park'll be OK."

Rollo weighed his next question, not wishing to appear concerned. "What about the zoo?"

"The zoo's fine."

"Do you have any new animals?" Rollo asked.

"A couple of bobcat kittens."

"And construction?"

"We're on schedule," Calvin replied. "We'll be ready for the mayor's opening in June."

"Don't take in anymore animals without my permission," Rollo said ominously.

"The mayor wants more."

"You work for me," Rollo said. "The mayor can't protect you forever."

"That boy of yours is quite a ballplayer," he continued after a short pause. "I hear the pro scouts are interested in him."

Calvin was silent.

"I know some baseball people. I could have a word with them."

"Mind your own business," Calvin said angrily. "Are we finished here?"

Rollo stood. "Yes, we're finished. But remember, no more animals."

"Right," said Calvin as he turned on his heel and walked out.

Florida the alligator awoke to find himself floating in cold water. His small brain told him it was not yet time to wake, but something was terribly wrong. He needed air to breathe, but he was under water. He needed warmth for his body to operate, but cold was draining the life out of him. He needed desperately to get away from this place. It was difficult enough to get moving after five months of sleep without having to do it in freezing cold water. His back was pressed against the underside of the house but he could feel the tug of the water's current pulling him. Since reptiles are unable to control their body temperature, the cold water would continue to sap his strength until he froze to death. He still had a little life left and he had a deep-seated instinct to survive, so with a twist of his body and a swish of his powerful tail he pushed out from under the house and into the churning current. From there all he could do was drift, unaware of where he might be headed.

16

Raven, Buddy, and Calvin stood on the bluff overlooking the river, in awe of the ominous, steady roar of the floodwaters below. They had just finished lunch on this gray, warm Saturday and had come to check on the status of the rising water. Calvin's meeting with Rollo Wilson had left him with a bitter feeling about his job and he almost wished the flood would wash away the whole place. That wasn't likely to happen, though. The zoo was built on the highest part of the park. It was the area across the creek, which was in danger. The waters were creeping into the swamp and would soon be halfway to the Road.

Out in the river, the normally smooth-flowing, placid waters were choppy like an ocean in a storm. The strong current drove uprooted trees and massive logs along in the torrent. Houses on the far side of the valley were surrounded by water as the muddy river swallowed up the banks and engulfed anything in its path. The power of the flood was humbling to Raven and even a little frightening. There was nothing to be done but wait and hope.

Raven wondered what it would be like to jump into that water. She imagined rolling and tumbling along, pushed under water, and struggling to the surface to catch a breath. She felt her whole life was like that, tumbling out of control.

She was helping her pa build a zoo, she was raising her bobcats, but she was uneasy about – even frightened of – Henry Koch. She leaned slightly toward her pa and touched him with her shoulder. At least she had him. Maybe he would pull her back to shore.

Florida the alligator was slowly becoming aware of his surroundings in the darkness. His sluggish body was warming, his senses were returning, and he was hungry. He had drifted out from under the house and floated in the tumbling, cold water for quite some time, eventually coming to rest in some type of warm-water pond. He swished his tail, moved forward, and discovered that everything was working again. His hunting instincts were buried deep within but seemed unconnected to the relief of his hunger. He had always relied on humans to provide his food. He would need to wait until morning when humans were around, and then he would eat.

Mason Benson lived across the road from the steam plant. He was a chubby, eight-year-old who had long dreamed of daring acts but had never mustered the courage to act, until his friend Corbin talked him into sneaking a swim in the pond. Getting caught meant his folks might be forced to pay the two-dollar fine for trespassing, and a whipping was sure to follow. When Mason had acted cool to the idea, Corbin called him a chicken. Now, as Mason pushed his way through the weeds around the pond, Corbin was nowhere to be found. Mason was tired of being called names just because he was overweight and timid. He would show Corbin.

"You should be proud of those bird cages," said Bea as she placed the steaming mug of coffee on the table in front of Calvin. They were at her kitchen table and spread before them were pieces of paper with drawings on them.

"I had her cages to copy," Calvin replied. "All I did was make some improvements."

"I'm not so sure about these," he said pointing at the drawings. "I don't know much about bobcats and foxes but I do know that chicken wire is not going to hold them."

"Sure it will," she said. "Just stretch it over some of that farm fence. All you need to do is make a big box. You already know how to keep the foxes from digging out."

"Here," she said, as she shuffled through the papers on the table. "Use this plan."

"Where will I get the meat," he said pushing back from the table. "We can't afford to buy it."

"Good question," she replied. "Maybe the slaughter house would give you scraps. You'll figure it out."

She got up, walked around the table and sat on his lap. He placed one hand on her back and rubbed her thigh with the other. She bent her face to his and their lips came together, gently at first then with more force as she grabbed him in a fierce embrace.

"Hello," said a loud voice from the door of the barn. "Is the zoo manager here?"

The voice belonged to a young man who had apparently run a long way. He was bent over with both hands on his knees to catch his breath.

"He's not here," said Rondell. "What do you need?"

"My boss, Mr. Pendergrast, sent me to fetch the zoo manager to the steam plant to see about the crocodile in our warming pond," said the man breathlessly.

"What?" Rondell laughed. "There's no crocodiles around these parts."

"There's one in our pond," said the man. "He's a big one. I saw him with my own eyes."

Rondell paused to think. He was in the process of training a new zoo keeper and Cal had gone to survey the flood damage across the creek. William Radditz, or Will as he preferred to be called, was the son of Mayor Crofton's sister. He claimed to be a farm hand, but Rondell could see no evidence of any expertise. The man was razor thin, had a flat face and short hair, and was as dull as a butter knife. He figured the family was desperate to find this guy a job so they pushed him off on the zoo.

"The zoo manager is out," said Rondell. "He'll be back in a little while."

Rondell was curious to see what was going on but he had work to do. The steam plant was a few miles down the road towards town. It stood on the banks of the river, producing steam from three giant boilers and sending it through square, wooden underground tunnels into nearby homes and businesses. The water it discharged went into a large pond for cooling before it overflowed back into the river. Most people knew about the warming pond even though it was not visible from the road. It was a great place to sneak a swim, especially on a cold day.

"Maybe we'd better go have a look," said Will hopefully.

Rondell did not reply right away. He wanted to go, too but he didn't want Calvin to get mad at them for leaving the zoo unattended.

Henry Koch was watching the commotion from a crack in the wall of the barn loft. He had seen Calvin leave and now watched the keepers saddle up their horses. James Purtle had hired him to burn down the house, but he had refused to pay. He kept wanting more, kept asking him to keep an eye on things. He wouldn't tell him the real purpose, but when he found the empty cavity in the broken fireplace, he figured Purtle was after some kind of treasure. The old man had probably brought back some loot from the war – lots of men did. Purtle wanted it all for himself.

His family back in Pittsburgh had been out to get him as well. His ma, pa and older brother had been plotting to put him in that asylum. They said he was crazy but he had showed them. They were the ones who were crazy and he had given them what they deserved. He had burned the house down while they slept.

Now he had new threats to deal with. He'd fix this girl, but first he had to find the treasure. Then he would take his bear and move on. The house was empty and he figured that was where Cal had stashed the treasure. He needed to move fast.

"Aren't you going to bring something to catch him with?" asked the young man as Rondell and Will climbed on their horses.

It had not occurred to Rondell that there would be anything to catch, but he rode over to the corral and picked up a rope that was hanging on a post. "We'll tie him up with this."

The man looked at Rondell for a long moment to see if he was kidding, then with a shrug, he started a smooth, loping run in the direction of the plant.

The three of them covered the distance fairly quickly and found two men standing beside the road awaiting their arrival. One man Rondell recognized as Mr. Sullivan, a reporter for the newspaper. The other must be Mr. Pendergrast. He did not look pleased to see two workmen accompanying his messenger.

"The zoo manager was not home," said the young man, anticipating the displeasure of his boss.

As Mr. Pendergrast opened his mouth to reply, a shrill scream rolled up the road from the area of the pond. After a brief hesitation, as if not sure of what they had heard, the three men on foot began to run toward the pond. Rondell and Will quickly overtook them on horseback. They arrived at the edge of the pond and, as they dismounted, another scream erupted from the pond. A splash at the water's edge a few yards to their right caused the horses to rear up and shy away. A large reptile held a young boy by the arm.

"I'll get the rope," said Rondell as Will ran toward the commotion.

The animal thrashed back and forth shaking the boy like a ragdoll and blood began to fill the water. Will ran hard but he was unsure of what to do when he got there. As he started down the embankment, the rain-softened mud gave away. He pitched forward and fell face down – right on the back of the reptile. As his hands flew forward to break his fall, his arms encircled the great beast's neck while his legs straddled its back. The enraged creature opened its mouth as it swung around to face this new threat and the young boy flew up onto the bank.

"Hold on, Will," yelled Rondell as he slid down the bank with the rope in his hand. "Hold on while I get this rope on his head!"

"Hurry," said Will through gritted teeth. He could feel the power beneath his body and smell the foul breath just inches from his nose. Scaly knobs pressed into his chest making it difficult to breathe. Suddenly the creature stopped twisting, rose on its four legs, and started walking out toward deep water.

"Hurry up," said Will desperately. "I can't let go."

"I'm coming. I'll try to get his tail."

Rondell slipped a noose around the animal's tail and tossed it to the three men who had joined him on the bank.

"We've got the tail, Will," said Rondell. "Jump off."

"I can't," said Will. "He'll bite me." Will was holding on so hard, his arms were cramped and he couldn't let go if he wanted to.

Slowly the men pulled the human and the thrashing reptile up onto the bank of the pond. Rondell took the other end of the rope, tied a noose, and fastened it around the animal's snout. With the mouth tied shut, Rondell grabbed Will by the back of his shirt and said, "Let go!"

As Rondell pulled his new partner free, the animal began to spin and the men let go of the rope. Soon it was wrapped tightly in the rope and it seemed to give up, lying helplessly on its back.

With the danger past, the men turned their attention to the little boy, who was lying in the mud groaning. Blood oozed from a large gash on his right arm and the men worked quickly with their handkerchiefs to stop the flow. As people began to appear from the road and from inside the steam plant, a woman claiming to be a nurse took over care of the boy and someone went for the doctor.

"Are you all right, Mister?" Mr. Pendergrast asked Will.

"That's the bravest thing I ever saw," said the newspaperman. "What made you think to jump on that thing's back like that?"

"Well, I…"

"Rondell!" shouted an angry Calvin Griffith as he rode up on his wagon. "You should have waited for me!"

"Don't get too upset, mister," said Mr. Pendergrast pointing to Will. "This young fellow saved that little boy's life. He's a hero."

"Hmp," said Calvin. "You still should have waited. You OK?"

"Yes," said Rondell as they turned their attention back to the still immobile beast.

"That's the biggest alligator I've ever seen," said Calvin.

"Alligator," said Rondell. "I thought it was a crocodile."

"No," said Calvin. "A crocodile has a long skinny nose. This is an alligator. If a crocodile got a hold of that little boy, he'd be dead. Will would probably be dead, too. Let's get him on the wagon."

"What's going to happen to the gator?" asked the newspaperman.

"We'll make a place for him at the zoo," said Calvin as he clicked at the horses and said, "Get up".

17

"How long has he been in there?" asked Will as he and Rondell peered through the slats of the chicken coop.

"Since day before yesterday," said the old man who owned the coop.

"Looks like he's killed all your chickens," said Rondell. "Why didn't you just shoot him?"

"That's not our way," he said, with a nod toward his eight year old daughter. "The Lord says 'Thou shalt not kill'. We don't hold with killin' unless it's for the table."

Myron Kettle was a thin, wiry man with thick gray hair and a full, bushy beard. He looked much older than his sixty years. He had been a drummer-boy in the War Between the States and some said it had aged him. It was his daughter Olivia who had insisted that they ride all the way in to the new zoo to deliver the bobcats and it was she who has asked him to send for help with this lion. They scratched out an existence on their small farm, growing their own food, sewing their own clothes and making their own way in the world. He couldn't even bring himself to kill the animal that had probably killed his daughter, Bessie. That too, he figured, had been God's will.

Rondell peered through the slats for a long while and then stood back to think. The coop wasn't much bigger than a large outhouse. Fortunately it was sturdily built and able to hold a full-grown mountain lion. Where the big cat had come from, Ron had no idea, but why he was here was obvious. The inside of the coop was covered in chicken feathers and the cat's face was smeared with blood. When he showed his teeth and hissed at his tormentors, he had an evil appearance.

"What are we going to do?" asked Will.

Calvin had instructed Will to let Rondell handle things. Cal had doubted the report of a lion in a chicken coop, but he had sent Rondell and Will anyway.

"I'm thinking," said Rondell impatiently.

"Maybe we should just shoot him and be done with it," said Will.

"I could have done that myself," said old man Kettle.

"Maybe we can rope him out of there," said Rondell as he looked in.

"Yeah, right," replied Will sarcastically. "I'll hold the door open for you while you go in with a lasso."

"Nobody needs to go in," said Rondell, ignoring the insult. "If we put the crate up against the door to the coop and pass a rope through the back of the crate, maybe we can get the rope on him and pull him out."

"And how do we get the rope on him?"

"With this," said Rondell, picking up a long stick off the ground.

Will looked at the stick and then glanced around at the small assembly of people that had gathered.

"Fine," Will said finally, clearly wishing to be done with this. "Let's get the crate off."

When the crate was in place and the doors to the coop and the crate opened, Rondell carefully opened the back door of the crate and threw the noose end of the rope as far into the coop as he could. Will worked through one of the slats with the long stick, picking up one end of the rope and draping it over the cat's head. The cat snarled, showing its teeth, but seemed not to notice the rope over his head. He pushed the rope further back on the cat's body until it encircled its neck like a necklace, then pushed the knot tighter.

"Take up the slack on the rope," he ordered.

Rondell and the old man looked at each other and began to reel in the rope. As the noose tightened, the cat swatted at the rope, which had the effect of tightening it more.

"We got him," shouted Rondell as he jumped on the crate, ready to slide down the door. "Pull him in."

Will and the old man pulled the screeching cat toward the crate. They were surprised at the strength of the animal as it fought and thrashed. When it became wedged in the doorway they thought they were beaten but, with one final pull, the cat flopped into the crate and Rondell dropped the door. The cat was caught, but as they stepped back to savor the moment they heard an awful gagging sound coming from the crate.

"He's strangling," said the old man.

"We've got to get that rope off his neck," said Rondell as he carefully pried open the back door of the crate. The cat's eyes bulged and his tongue hung limp. The rope was so deeply embedded in its neck that he could barely feel it.

"Give me some slack," he said urgently. Lying flat on his stomach and working with both hands, he dug his fingers under the rope and pulled it free. When the cat failed to respond, Rondell shook it by the neck and banged its head on the floor of the crate. The angry cat swung a paw and caught Rondell's hand with one of its claws, but the skin tore loose as he pulled back and the door slammed shut.

Rondell lay on the ground panting as the cat hissed in the crate a few inches from his head.

"That was close," said the old man as he wrapped Rondell's hand in a handkerchief.

"Yeah," said Will a bit impatiently. "Let's get going," he continued as he coiled the rope. "We need to get unloaded before dark."

"Looks like you're almost finished here," R.C. Crofton said. He lit Calvin's cigar then his own.

"It's looking real nice," agreed Bea Taylor.

"Thank you," replied Calvin, knowing that it was neither almost finished nor looking real nice.

In fact, he had much work to do if he was to meet the mayor's opening date of Saturday, June eighth – just two weeks from today.

The zoo's most impressive feature was its entrance. The brick path was framed by two low brick walls that led visitors from the driveway into what was once the Dotson's garden. Straight ahead, the rows of bird cages pulled visitors in. A right turn led to the bear and fox pens and to the left was the barnyard with the gator pit beyond. The buffalo pen was still under construction while the three animals waited in a small make-shift corral. Lumber and bits of wire mesh were strewn around the pathways. If Rondell came back from the Kettles with a mountain lion, which he doubted, he would be forced to build yet another cage.

"Let's have a look," R.C. said. The big, jovial mayor with the cigar clamped between his teeth wasn't looking so good. Cal thought he looked pale and tired. "I'm anxious to hear what Bea has to say."

Bea Taylor knew more about animals than anyone else in town and the mayor wanted to make sure their zoo was built correctly. He didn't know that Cal and Bea had already spent a lot of time reviewing the plans. They walked the brick path and stopped at the bird cages.

"These are exactly like Allison Janey's cages," Bea told the mayor. "Cal and Raven took measurements over at her house and built copies of them here at the zoo."

The simple, wood-frame structures were covered with chicken wire. They were nothing special, but the careful workmanship made them seem better than they were. The wood was square and the wire was tight, making the cages blend in and the colorful, active birds all the more attractive.

They moved to their right and stood in front of the bear pen.

"He's worn this place out," the mayor commented. The bear pen had been in place for months and already looked its age. Zeke had worn deep ruts where he paced. He had dug numerous potholes looking for worms and grubs. Any grass that had once grown in this area had long-since been worn or eaten away.

"Zeke's doing well," Bea said, "but you're going to have a hard time keeping this area looking nice. You might want to spread some straw or leaves to cover the ground. He might even like rooting in it for something to do. Same for the foxes," she continued as they turned to view a similar scene in the fox pen.

"Where will you put the bobcats?" the mayor asked Cal.

"Over there," Cal replied, pointing to a spot next to the fox pen. "But we'll do that later, when they're old enough to be on their own."

"Raven is doing a nice job with them," Bea offered.

Calvin did not reply. They walked a little further and stood before an expanse of grass with a pile of wood posts and several large rolls of wire lying in a jumble.

"This'll be the buffalo yard," Calvin explained.

"Will you have it done in time?" asked R.C., clearly concerned.

"Yes," Calvin replied with more confidence than he felt.

"Let's see the alligator," R.C. said.

Bea and Calvin walked across the zoo talking, but when they stopped at the gator pit the mayor was not with them. He had lagged behind. He slowly caught up, but he was wheezing and looking like he needed to sit down.

"This alligator is the hardest thing they'll be keeping at the zoo," Bea said to R.C. as he walked up.

"Why is that?"

"They're cold blooded," Cal said. "Which means they can't warm themselves when it gets cold. We'll have to make a place for him in the barn next winter."

"How in the world will you get him inside?" R.C. exclaimed.

"If we can get his mouth tied shut with a noose, two or three of us will jump on his back and hold on. Then we'll tie him up and carry him inside."

"You've done a magnificent job here, Cal," he said after a few moments. "Someday, people will thank you for this."

"That old man loves that place," Henry Koch said about the mayor as he looked around Rollo Wilson's office. This was the first time they had met here. Rollo and Purtle stood together near the window as though they did not want to get near the scruffy man with the wooden leg and the awful odor.

"It's time for you to move on," Purtle said.

"I'm not finished yet," Koch replied.

"Yes you are," Purtle said. "We hired you to do a job. Now, we're telling you to back off."

"Hired me, or black-mailed me?" Koch replied.

"We didn't blackmail you," Rollo said. "We just kept your dirty little secret. If people find out what you did back in Pittsburgh, they'd probably lynch you."

"What about the treasure?" Koch asked.

"What treasure?" Rollo replied.

"You know what I'm talking about."

"You're crazy," Purtle said.

"No, I'm not. You two are hiding something." Koch stood up menacingly, forcing Purtle to back up a step.

"I've had enough of this," Purtle said in exasperation. "Let's call Sheriff Taylor."

"They've got it and you want it all for yourselves," Koch said, "But I'm going to get it. I know where it is." Koch looked back in defiance. He was clearly getting tired of this little game, but he eventually rose and left without a word. They heard his peg-leg clomping down the hall.

18

Raven always looked forward to her Saturday trips to town and this week even her Pa seemed excited. It was their last trip before the zoo opened and, to Raven's dismay, he talked about seeing Bea Taylor. Raven loved Aunt Bea, but her pa was paying entirely too much attention to her these days. The leisurely wagon ride covered the fourteen miles in just less than two hours, with a few stops along the way. Thomasville's main street was paved with bricks and lined with gas street lamps. The clip-clop of horses' hooves and the familiar smell of horse manure were giving way to the putter and smoke of motor cars.

Raven had their stops in town memorized and she found the routine comforting. Their first stop was at Thompson's General Store for food and clothes. Then they went to the far end of town for animal feed and supplies at Jackson's Feed and Livery. On the way back through town Pa called in at the bank, the Post Office and City Hall. It was at this last stop that he had learned that Mayor Crofton was critically ill – a fact that ruined the mood of their day. If anything happened to R.C. Crofton, Rollo Wilson would be in charge and the Dotson Park zoo would be in jeopardy.

The last stop was Mr. Fister's barbershop where her Pa got his haircut and they both caught up on the latest town gossip. It was there that she ran into Buckley Dotson as she sat on the bench outside the shop, bottle-feeding her bobcats.

"Hey," he said shyly. Now that he lived in town, they hardly saw each other. His family now lived with his grandparents and his father had started selling real estate. People now called him Buck.

"Hey", she replied looking up to meet his eye.

Buck was a handsome boy and seemed to have grown up over the winter. He was tall, fair-haired, and smooth-skinned – and he had a stutter in his speech. Raven and Buck had known each other all their lives, since they were both raised on the estate, but they had always lived in different worlds. Now however, the Dotsons seemed less like royalty and more like common folks.

Her reply seemed to catch him by surprise and he hesitated. She had changed over the winter, too. She was much more self-assured, more confident. She even looked different. Even though her skin was broken out, she was prettier, somehow. She had cut her hair. The long braid was gone and her black hair framed a strong, square face and those pale, gray eyes. When she continued to look at him, he stopped to chat.

"Are these w-wildcats?" he asked.

"They're bobcats," she replied, holding up the one that squirmed on her lap. The other one was squealing in the box on the ground next to her chair.

The cats had changed in the last few weeks. Their eyes were open and they wobbled on their feet rather than crawling on their bellies. Their feedings were down to three times per day with no mid-night feedings, and in another month they would be weaned altogether. Raven had never been a proud or boastful person, but she was pleased with her success. The kittens depended on her and she was pleased with the attention they brought her and the zoo her pa was building.

"We're m-moving b-b-back out to the farm," Buck said.

"You are?" Her eyes grew large with surprise.

"Well, not exactly to the farm. Pa b-bought the old Torgerson Farm and he's dividing it into lots for p-people to b-b-build homes on. We're going to b-build on one of the lots."

"So we'll be neighbors again," Raven said brightly.

"Yep."

They sat in silence for a moment. She recalled seeing Buck and his brother on the back porch of their house on New Year's Eve. It didn't seem possible that this nice young man could have done something as terrible as burning down a house and not owning up to it. She had to know the truth.

"I saw you on your back porch the night your house burned down. It looked like you and your brother had an oil lamp." Her implication was clear.

"It wasn't us," he said. "Our p-pa thinks it was Koch. They had an argument that evening and p-pa threw him out."

"Why didn't your pa have him thrown in jail after the fire?"

"We couldn't prove it," Buck replied. "And I think p-pa was a little afraid of him. Anyway, I hear Miss Janey recognized him as a criminal from somewhere b-back east and identified him to the sheriff."

"What?" she replied in alarm.

As she stared at Buckley with her mouth open waiting for the rest of the story, the barber shop door opened and her pa burst out. Sheriff Taylor strode out behind him and stood with his thumbs in his suspenders. He was a skinny man with a big belly and a long, gray beard. You'd never know it to look at him, but folks considered him to be a first-rate sheriff. He was polite to town folks, good enough with his fists to beat an unruly prisoner senseless, and uncommonly smart. Many a criminal had come to justice by underestimating Sheriff Taylor.

"I'll be out Monday morning," said the Sheriff, "as soon as I get my Warrant."

"Let's go, Raven," Calvin hissed, without responding to the sheriff.

She knew by the look on her pa's face that he meant business. In a moment, they were on the wagon and rushing home.

Buddy didn't like the way Henry Koch was looking at him, but he didn't dare disobey.

"I said, get in here and help me clean up this bear crap," the man growled.

Calvin had given Rondell the day off and had told Buddy to feed the animals, clean the pens, and pick up all the trash on the walkways. He still had work to do, but figured he'd better not disobey. Besides, he had always wondered what it would be like to enter the bear pen. No one was allowed in there but Koch and, with his Pa gone for the day, this was his chance.

The gate to Zeke's pen was held shut by a short length of chain and a large padlock. As Buddy rattled the chain and opened the gate, the bear looked up and watched the boy enter. Buddy knew how to loop the chain back through the gate and hook the lock without snapping it shut. As he turned to face Koch he checked on the status of the bear. It was a creepy feeling to be in the same space as an animal that was large enough to kill you – an animal that had already killed someone. Buddy's heart was racing.

"What do you want me to do?" He asked.

"Start picking up here," he said as he pointed, "and work your way around the pen."

Buddy followed the sweep of Koch's arm. The path he suggested would lead right to the bear.

"I'm not doing this," said Buddy as he headed for the gate.

"Get to work," growled Koch as he moved to block Buddy's exit.

Buddy was surprised at how afraid he was. He was afraid of the bear. He was afraid of Koch. And he was afraid to make a run for it. His stomach was knotted up and he suddenly felt like he was going to throw up.

As Buddy turned to start working, Koch asked, "Where's the box you found in the fireplace?"

Buddy looked at him, unsure of what he was talking about. "Where is it?"

"I don't know what you're talking about," Buddy replied.

Koch just looked at him as if he expected more. "I saw the hole it came out of."

Koch continued to stare at Buddy.

"I never saw any box, I swear," Buddy said. "I didn't know there was a hole."

"Then your pa must have found it. What did he do with it? Did he take it to that lady vet's?"

Buddy just kept working. His mind was racing. This guy was crazy.

Koch grunted, apparently satisfied that the boy knew nothing, and moved back to his cleaning as he continued to eye Buddy.

Buddy worked his way around the pen, putting sticks, rocks, and bits of paper in his bucket. He was so intent on watching the bear that he forgot about Koch until he heard the padlock to the cage snap shut. As he turned toward the sound his heart froze.

Somehow, Koch had slipped quietly out of the cage, locked the gate, and was walking away.

"Hey," Buddy shouted. "What are you doin'?"

Buddy's shouts got the bear's attention and the sight of his master walking away brought him to his feet. As Buddy turned his back to the bear and ran to the gate, the bear was on him with amazing quickness. In fact, Buddy couldn't imagine what was knocking him to the ground. The last time he looked, the bear was across the pen. A lady screamed and he knew what it was before his head hit the ground. He heard a deep, quiet growl in his ear and felt the hot breath on the back of his neck just before everything went black.

Calvin had urged the horses as best he could all the way from town. Now, as he turned onto the service road toward the barn, he saw a crowd gathered around the bear pen in the distance. A scream pierced the air as a grim looking Henry Koch came charging around the barn in his undertaker's wagon. He galloped up the lane toward the road to town. Fighting the urge to give chase, Calvin jumped to the ground and ran toward the commotion with Raven close behind. A small crowd had gathered around Zeke's pen. Some were pointing, most had surprised expressions, and none had any idea what to do. Was this normal procedure? The bear had a young boy pinned to the ground with both paws squarely on the boy's back. The bear looked around as if unsure what to do next.

Raven stopped in surprise when she saw Buddy's position, but her Pa kept running and started to holler.

"Out of the way!" he shouted. "Get back."

Raven wasn't sure if he was hollering at the people or the bear, but his shouts jarred her into action. She wheeled and ran back to the barn. Grabbing two shovels and a bucket of oats and carrots that had been prepared for the goats, she made it back to the bear pen just as Calvin was closing the gate from inside.

"Here, Pa," she said handing him a shovel.

"You stay here," he said as he took the weapon and barred her way.

"But Pa," she exclaimed.

"No," he said. "You stay here and mind the gate."

Calvin advanced slowly toward the bear holding the shovel like a club. One swipe from a massive paw or a bite to the neck and Buddy would be dead. Calvin hesitated, not sure how far to push. The crowd grew silent and a low rumbling growl emanated from the bear. Buddy did not move.

"Pa, let me put some food in for Zeke," said Raven quietly.

"OK, but do it from outside."

"I can't get around."

Calvin scanned the perimeter of the pen and saw she was right. The crowd had pressed around all sides of the pen. Calvin didn't want to endanger his daughter, but he didn't know what else to do.

"He's used to me, Pa," she pleaded. "He's used to me feeding him."

"OK," he said. "But stay by the fence and don't let him get between you and the gate."

Raven entered the pen, carefully hooking the lock through the chain but not snapping it shut, and moved to her left along the fence-line. She had to get to the far side of the pen in order to lure the bear far enough away to give her pa a chance to drag Buddy out. She had never felt this way before. She was scared, but not of the bear and not for herself. She was scared for Buddy. Until this moment, she had never cared much for him. He had always been ma's favorite and he was so cocky and sure of himself. She just couldn't stand that. Now, seeing him on the ground under the jaws of a bear, she just wanted to grab him out of there and make everything all right.

Zeke watched her as Calvin watched Zeke. Raven moved slowly but with confidence, watching the bear closely but showing no fear. As she reached the far side, the bear shifted his weight, placing one foot on the ground but leaving one on Buddy's back.

"That's far enough," said Calvin, but Raven had already stopped.

In one smooth motion she tipped the contents of the bucket onto the ground and was moving quickly backwards toward the exit. As she continued toward the gate, she could see that the bear was no longer looking at her. He was eyeing the food. She was feeling good about her mission, feeling it was going to work, when

Buddy moved and groaned, shifting the bear's attention back to him.

Raven stopped as the bear looked down. Buddy's legs moved as he began to regain consciousness and as the bear moved his nose toward the back of Buddy's head. Raven threw the bucket and hollered, "No!".

Zeke was startled to see the clanging metal bucket rolling in his direction and moved off the boy. Calvin continued the commotion by banging his shovel on the ground and hollering. The bear pursed his upper lip and put his head down as if to charge, but apparently decided not to take on the challenge. He suddenly turned and shuffled toward the food.

Calvin grabbed Buddy by the collar of his shirt and dragged him to the gate. Raven was ready with the gate open and the three of them tumbled to safety as the crowd cheered.

As Raven and Calvin helped Buddy walk toward the house, Calvin asked, "You OK?"

"Yeah," mumbled Buddy. "What happened?"

"You tell me," said Calvin a bit crossly. "What were you doing in with that bear?"

"Koch told me to come in and help him, then he sneaked out and locked me in."

"Any idea where he went?" asked Calvin.

"No. He seemed mad about something. He wanted to know about a box. He seemed to think you found it and hid it at Aunt Bea's."

Calvin and Raven looked at each other. "That man is nuts." She said.

"Raven, you get Buddy to bed," said Calvin as he ran to the phone in the barn. "I'll call the sheriff."

Raven filled Buddy in on what they had learned about Koch, and then joined her pa at the barn.

Calvin rushed out of the barn and headed for the still-hitched wagon.

"Come on," he said. "We've got to see about Bea."

"What did the sheriff say?" asked Raven.

"He wasn't there."

Bea's house sat on a large piece of land about half way between the park and the town. It was a small, unimposing structure that kind of spread out in several directions. A visitor facing the front door would see a small addition of rooms to the left and, to the right, a larger barn-like addition. It was in there that some of her more delicate animals spent the winter, and it was from there that flames flickered through the windows and a cloud of thick, black smoke billowed into the clear mid-day sky.

Calvin raced his wagon up the winding driveway, passing Henry Koch's wagon parked near the main road and several horses tied to some shrubs near the house. Sheriff Taylor was already there. Calvin pulled the wagon up near the horses and jumped to the ground.

"Stay here," he said as he ran toward the house.

Raven watched him leave and threw a leg over the side of the wagon to climb down. She climbed to the ground using the spokes of the wagon wheel like a ladder. She took the final step with a hop down, turned to run, and plowed into something solid. It was Henry Koch.

"You're just the one I wanted to see," he growled.

He dragged her to his wagon, shoved her in the back, and locked the door. It smelled of stale bear urine and rotting hay. The thick wooden walls muffled her shouts and kicking at the door did no good. She could tell by the bounce of the wagon that they were moving quickly and, after what seemed a long time, they stopped. She was surprised when the back door opened onto her own barn. They were back at the zoo.

"Get over here," the man snarled.

She hesitated, but when he started in after her she scrambled to the door. He grabbed her by the arm, pulled her roughly out of the wagon, and dragged her toward the barn. She twisted and struggled, but he squeezed her arm so tightly she thought it would break. As they entered the barn, he threw her forward and she used the momentum to break free. She ran to the end of the hall toward the far door. She could hear the peculiar sound of someone running behind her with a wooden leg and, quicker than she expected, he was on her and dragging her to the ground. He smelled awful as he wheezed from exertion and dripped sweat onto her face. She screamed, but there was nobody to hear.

"Be still you little bitch," he growled. "Get up," he commanded, "or I'll break your arm."

He dragged her into an empty stall and tied her to a post with baling string.

"What are you doing?" she asked through her tears, when he returned carrying a can of lamp oil.

"I'm going to burn this barn down with you in it," he said.

"Why are you doing this?" she sobbed. "I haven't done anything to you."

"Shut up. I have my reasons." He said.

He lit a match and watched her with twisted amusement. He loved fire – the way it danced with color, the way it changed smell depending on its fuel and the way it consumed everything that it contacted. It had a way of making his problems go away. He didn't even mind a little burn once in a while. Fire was such a wondrous thing and it made him feel so powerful.

Raven had always been frightened of him. He had a glint in his eye that was pure evil. She was terrified and he was getting a thrill out of her fear. He was going to murder her and enjoy every minute of it. Her pa had gone to Aunt Bea's house with such purpose, she was certain he had not seen her being taken. No one would know where she is. No one could save her. Koch spit some tobacco juice into the straw and as the match burned out, he threw it down and bent over to pick up the can.

"Why are you doing this?" she pleaded. She was scared and began to struggle against her ropes. She could see he was crazy and didn't need a reason. He poured oil into the straw, splashed it onto the walls, and moved to the door of the stall. With his back to the door, he lit another match but before he could toss it, he grunted, his mouth fell open, and his eyes became wide with surprise. It all happened in slow motion. He appeared to be moving back into the stall but his feet were still. He was actually falling forward with a pitchfork stuck in his back. At the other end of the pitchfork was a grim-looking Rondell Boyd.

As Koch hit the floor the match fell into the straw and caught fire at once. Rondell pulled out his folding knife and cut Raven free. She appeared to want to stop and help Koch, but Rondell pulled her from the smoky stall.

"We have to get the animals outside," she screamed.

Together, they opened stall doors to let animals outside to safety before they both came choking into the fresh air. The barn was fully engulfed in flames by the time Calvin came rushing back with Sheriff Taylor.

"What happened," Calvin asked as he grabbed his daughter in a fierce embrace.

She told most of her story as the Sheriff walked around the building.

"Where's Koch?" asked the Sheriff.

"He ran off," Raven lied.

Sheriff Taylor stared at the still burning structure as if lost in thought. "You need me for anything?" he finally said to Calvin.

"Not much you can do here, Sheriff."

"I'd better go see if I can find the son of a bitch before he hurts somebody else," said the Sheriff. He glanced at Rondell, who sat on an overturned bucket apart from everyone, mounted his horse and left.

With the sheriff safely out of sight, Raven told her pa the whole story.

"Why did you lie?" Calvin asked.

"When we came out here to wait for help, Rondell told me he once killed a man in a fight," she began. "They were going to hang him for murder when it was really self defense. He escaped and has been on the run ever since. If they find out he killed someone else, he'll hang for sure."

"He saved your life. They can't hang him for that," Cal was looking at Rondell as he stared sadly at the ground out of earshot.

"The man he killed before was the son of the local sheriff," she explained. "If they find him, he won't get away again."

The roof of the barn collapsed in a shower of sparks and smoke. They knew that inside that mess lie the remains of an evil man who could ruin one more life, even in death.

"Tonight, when this is burned out," said Cal. "We'll pull Koch out and bury him. No one will ever know what happened here."

Buddy wandered out from the house rubbing the bump on his head, as Raven and Cal drifted into quiet thoughts. Calvin's heart ached for his wife, but he now appreciated what a precious gift he had in his children and the opportunity for a new life with Bea.

"There is no treasure," Cal said in response to Buddy's question. "But I did find something."

He disappeared into the house and emerged carrying a battered metal box. He sat it on the ground and opened it. Raven and Buddy crowded around to see inside. The box held a carefully folded white baby dress and a tiny pair of white shoes. Calvin reached into the box and produced an official-looking document.

"It appears that Mr. Dotson was married before," he said somberly. "The mother died of cholera and the baby must have died soon after. The fireplace was some kind of shrine to his first family."

He was interrupted by a horseman riding up fast.

"Do you know where the sheriff is?" the man asked, pausing to catch his breath. "Mayor Crofton is dead."

19

Saturday, June 8th, 1912

Rollo Wilson lifted his flat-topped straw hat and mopped the sweat from his head. It was a scorching hot Saturday morning, hot enough to burn up a wet mule – as the saying goes. While most people were gathered in spots of shade, he was forced to stand in the sun on a small wooden platform. This day, after months of hard work, was the day he would open R.C. Crofton's new zoo.

It wasn't much of a zoo, not compared to the ones in Washington, New York, and Cincinnati, but it was a start. From his platform with the zoo entrance to his back, he looked up the avenue of trees that had once been the driveway to the Dotson home. James Purtle was not there. He disappeared when the business with Henry Koch had unfolded. Bea Taylor was there with Allison Janey. He also saw the unmistakable red heads of the Doyle family. Even the Kettles were there. The crowd was small, but as he watched the workers laying tracks in the street for the new streetcar line, he had an idea. He called one of his assistants to his side, whispered some instructions, and soon the crowd had swelled by twenty or so ragged men.

The location of the zoo, set back from the street near the river, was the one battle that Rollo had won. He hadn't really wanted a zoo in the first place. When he realized he couldn't stop it, he decided to place it as far from the public view as possible. He persuaded the Mayor that what the people wanted near the road was open space for picnics, baseball, and the like. The zoo, he reasoned, would be much better overlooking the river along with some beautiful gardens.

The entrance to the zoo was blocked by a red ribbon across the grass pathway. People facing Rollo looked south toward the zoo and the river beyond. The bear, lion and foxes all paced nervously while the bison munched hay. Birds chirped, Able the bull mooed and the parrots squawked. Calvin had just completed cages for the newest arrivals, including the tame raccoons and the injured eagle that had all been donated by the Doyles. He also built a wood and wire hutch for the six rabbits donated by Jackson "Bunny" Raymond. They were culled from his feeder operation. Beyond the little zoo, the pathway continued down to the bluff overlooking the river. This served as Rollo Wilson's garden area. Calvin had taken special care with this section, planting new trees, shrubs, and plenty of colorful flowers. It stood in stark contrast to the hard edges and barren conditions in the animal areas.

"Come on," Raven urged, "we'll be late."

"I'm not going," Buddy announced.

Raven, Lizzie and Al looked at him and then at each other. Buddy had emerged from his bedroom carrying a small suitcase and a baseball bat. They knew he had secretly been talking to baseball scouts, but they never figured he'd run off like this – without even a goodbye to pa. Buddy had never really fit into the world of animals and, lately, he had quit trying. He didn't respect the animals and many seemed to know it. Zeke perked up whenever Buddy came around, which wasn't often anymore, and the mountain lion paced and snarled at him. Buddy wasn't much good with people either, and the zoo was as much a people business as it was an animal business. Baseball was his passion. He was good at it, he didn't really need to talk to people and there were no animals involved.

"You sure you want to do this?" Raven asked.

He picked up his baseball glove, slipped it over the handle of the bat and looked at her in reply. She gave him a fierce hug, which he did not return.

"Want to stay and see us let the foxes out?" Al asked hopefully. "Rollo's going to have a fit."

"No," Buddy said. "They're waiting for me at the street. Tell pa goodbye for me." And he was gone.

Calvin couldn't believe his eyes. The three foxes were out of their cage and trotting up the path in the direction of the speaker's platform. In what must have been a moment of premonition, when a person senses he is being watched and he is, Rollo turned and saw the creatures scampering in his direction. He jumped off the stage in a panic and fell down in an undignified heap.

The small crowd laughed and scrambled out of the way. Calvin rushed toward the barn for a net but he only traveled a few steps when he stopped in his tracks. There standing in his path stood Raven, Lizzie and Al with nets already in hand and grins on their faces. In that instant, he knew what had happened and he couldn't help but smile as he approached them. The zoo was now open, and it was as much their zoo as his. They had made sure this would be a day to remember.

"Where's Buddy?" he asked, looking around.

Part 3

20

Tuesday, October 11th, 2011

John Stokes wondered why, in this age of computers and internet search engines, he found himself sitting on a hard, wooden chair at the public library scrolling through microfilm to search the newspaper archive. There was no easy way to do this. After the librarian helped him load the film into the machine, he had to turn the knob to advance the film. The more he turned the knob the faster the film advanced – and he was advancing pretty fast at the moment. He wasn't even sure what he was looking for. He was scanning for the words 'zoo, 'missing', and 'murder' and he was looking in the 1930's. he was up to 1933 when his phone vibrated. He had a text message. He fished out his phone out of his pocket, looked at the message, and smiled. The message read 'miss u. can't wait till tonite!'. It was from Chelsea.

The dining room at Ivanhoe Country Club commanded one of the most beautiful views in town. The eighteenth green outside the floor to ceiling picture windows was no different from other fine golf courses. The view, however, was made spectacular by the Tecumseh River which flowed down the right side of eighteen. In fact, there was no rough on that side of the fairway. If a golfer, who was playing back to the eighteenth green, hit a hook to the left, the ball was not in the rough, it was in the river. Willow trees lined the shore and the ducks and geese were a nuisance to the golfers but a delight to the diners. Joanne Dotson Newman was not a golfer, but she loved coming here. It was a beautiful, sunny, fall day. The leaves were changing and the golfers were out in force. Her lunch partner had not arrived yet so she was content to enjoy the scene before her.

"Sorry I'm late," said Susan Wagner breathlessly. "My tennis match lasted longer than I expected."

Joanne sized her up and quickly realized that the flush on her cheeks was not from tennis. Susan had a reputation for sleeping around. Joanne wondered who her latest conquest was.

Joanne smiled broadly and offered her hand, "I was just enjoying the marvelous view, and I'm still on my first martini, so I don't consider you late."

The two women were obviously comfortable with their surroundings. Susan Wagner was married to a very successful attorney who served on several boards, including the zoological society. Joanne married the owner of the region's largest chain of grocery stores, and her family on the Dotson side had money, as well. Dotson Park was named after her great grandfather, Cyrus Dotson.

"Did your husband make it to the zoo board meeting?" asked Joanne.

"No, he hates going to those things. He says they're mostly small minded people trying to make themselves feel important"

"I don't like those meetings either," said Joanne. "I love the zoo and want to help it grow, but until the zoological society gets stronger, there is not much anyone can do."

Joanne was a strong woman who was used to getting what she wanted. As she looked out the wall of glass at the fabulous scene of river and golf course, Susan wondered what motivated her. Joanne came from a wealthy, privileged background. The Dotson family was well known in this city. Cyrus became fabulously wealthy as owner of a regional group of dry goods stores. His son, Cyril, built his own real estate empire and the family's net worth grew. Joanne had little to do but throw herself into doing good works for the community. Her elegant good looks, her regal bearing, and her money made her much sought after as a board member by all the community's non-profit organizations. She was active on the symphony board, the children's home, and the art museum, but her favorite, for sentimental reasons, was the zoo.

"Milt says it will; be a disaster if the City stops funding the zoo," said Susan. "He says they will disband the Society and give it back to the City if they do."

"I can't imagine them being short-sighted enough to do that."

"According to Milt, the City is in such bad shape financially they might be desperate enough to do it."

"I'm starved," said Joanne. "Let's order lunch."

"Everyone in the monkey house gets the same thing, only in different proportions," explained Billy Scales.

Chelsea Johns looked around the monkey house kitchen. Eggs boiled in a large pot on the stove, fruit and vegetables covered the counter by the sink, and five stainless steel buckets stood in a row on the wooden chopping-block table that filled the center of the room. Billy was cutting oranges on a small cutting board next to the sink while Chelsea cut apples on the table. She had finally earned a transfer out of the Children's Zoo. She was not in large mammals yet, but primates were the next best thing.

"Some of them like their fruit cut a little different, too," he continued. "The chimps are pretty much like us. They peel the whole bananas and they seem to like the fruit and vegetables cut into large pieces. The lion-tailed macaques, the spider monkeys, and the gibbons like everything cut smaller. I peel the bananas for the gibbons, since their thumbs are practically useless."

Chelsea looked up from her apples with a puzzled expression.

"The gibbon's hand is adapted for swinging in the trees," said Billy holding his hand up and curling his fingers into four little hooks. "The thumb would just get in the way, so it's way down here," he said pointing to the inside of his wrist.

They worked in silence for a few moments while Billy seemed to gather his thoughts. Chelsea liked working with Billy Scales and she was sure she would enjoy being relief keeper in his area. Billy, who was lead keeper in the area, was enthusiastic but professional and he loved his animals without being anthropomorphic.

"The black and white colobus monkeys are very picky eaters. They eat almost no fruit and very few vegetables. They seem to live mostly on lettuce."

"What do they eat in the wild?" asked Chelsea.

"I'm not sure," admitted Billy. "Judging by what they eat here, it must be mostly leaves, though."

They worked for another spell in silence, chopping bananas, carrots, celery, eggplant, and escarole. They peeled hard-boiled eggs, and then Billy pulled the diet cards from the cupboard and placed one on the table in front of each bucket. He did not need the cards, and soon Chelsea would not need them, either. Each bucket had a species name scrawled on it in Billy's hand writing with a black marking pen.

"I like to put the monkey chow in the bucket first," he said. "That way it picks up some of the juice from the fruit. The monkeys seen to eat it better that way."

Monkey chow, Chelsea knew, was a nutritious biscuit about the size of a person's thumb. It was hard and rather tasteless, as Billy had demonstrated in his standard demonstration for new keepers. She opened the lid on the thirty gallon garbage can that sat next to the table and began to scoop chow into the buckets as prescribed on the cards.

The cages in the monkey house were starting to dry from their morning cleaning as Chelsea and Billy carried the buckets down the hall and placed them in front of the cage doors. Small puddles remained on the floor in a few areas and the faint smell of chlorine bleach hung in the air. Billy stood in front of the empty chimp shift cage, removed the bananas from the top of the bucket, and slung the remaining contents of the bucket into the cage with enough force to evenly scatter chow, fruits, and vegetables over the entire floor. He locked the door and shifted the chimps into the cage, handing each animal one banana as it passed through the shift gate. He and Chelsea watched as the chimps gathered as much fruit as they could carry and went to their favorite spots to eat.

"Where did you learn to cook like that?" asked John Stokes.

"When I was in Africa," Chelsea replied.

"Africa!" he said. "What were you doing in Africa?"

It was their second date and he clearly had much to learn about this red-headed beauty, beyond the fact that she was gorgeous and she worked with monkeys at the zoo.

"I was working on my Doctorate in Biology studying chimpanzee communication in the Congo. Political unrest forced us out of the country so my thesis is on hold. I needed a job and this seemed like a good opportunity to get some hands-on experience."

"Hosing monkey shit at the zoo doesn't seem like much of a career," John said. "Pardon my French."

"I didn't think so either, when I first started," she replied as she cleared the dishes from the table. "But it's starting to grow on me. This zoo is more progressive than most, with their emphasis on animal welfare. And this new exhibit they're planning is really exciting."

"Why is that good for animal welfare?" he asked, stacking dishes to carry into the kitchen. "Won't the elephants and chimps fight?"

She paused in thought as she picked up his stack. "They might, but they are two of the most intelligent species in the animal kingdom. It will be a fascinating study in animal behavior to see how they learn to get along."

They cleared the table, loaded the dishwasher, and moved to the living room. He sat at the end of the couch, leaving plenty of room for her to join him – and she did. She brought her refilled wine glass and a fresh bottle of Sam Adams for him.

"How is your zoo murder-mystery coming along?" she asked as she sat down closer to him than was strictly necessary.

"I don't know for sure that it is a murder," he replied, "but it sure is a mystery. I can't find any record of anyone connected with the zoo dying or disappearing, and I've got a hundred years of history to look through."

"Have you Googled it?"

"Yes," he replied, "but I'm not sure what to Google – 'dead bodies at the zoo'?"

"Why did you get stuck doing this alone," asked Chelsea. "Don't you guys usually work in pairs?"

"My partner is on maternity leave. She just had a baby. She's the senior partner since I've only been out of uniform for eight months, so this is a nice safe place for Division to put me."

He took a swig of his beer and casually put his arm along the back of the couch, testing the waters. She inched closer and sipped her wine.

"Do you want to go back to Africa?" he asked.

"No," she said. "I like it here just fine." She looked up at him to make sure he caught her meaning.

He did.

21

Sonny began his pant-hoots as soon as Asa Wright walked in the door to the Monkey House. Chelsea was down the hall, already cleaning the colobus monkeys when Asa arrived, late as usual. Chelsea had seen these displays several times a day for the past few weeks. They were directed at her when she worked the chimp side, but her instincts told her to ignore them. With Asa, they were different. The displays were much more aggressive, and they ended with Sonny spitting at Asa. That was, Chelsea knew, because Asa not only didn't ignore the displays, he actually displayed back. When Sonny banged his food pan, Asa banged a bucket against the bars. When Sonny screamed, Asa screamed. Chelsea had even seen Asa spit back at the angry ape. And when the displays were over, Asa turned the hose on Sonny. Chimps hate water. Chelsea shuddered to think what would happen if Sonny ever got his hands on Asa Wright.

Amos loved the musty smell of the basement archive at the newspaper. It was a place he had spent many happy hours researching a book or a historical project, and he associated the satisfaction of discovery with it.

"I'm finished with 1936," he announced. "I'm putting this box away and starting on 1937."

He and Mildred Jones, the archivist, had known each other for years and he was the only person she trusted to be down here. But he still had protocol to follow. She had to know exactly what boxes he had out.

Amos had made a lot of progress in the past month and a half. He had established the facts around the founding of the zoo and he had dug up everything there was on the pre-1030's era – which wasn't much. He expected to find much more documentation on the WPA period of the 1930's up until World War Two. He was more than half way through the newspaper archives and he had more than enough material for this section. He scanned quickly, searching for specific dates that he already knew, like the date the old elephant house had opened on October 9th, 1937. He already had a good copy of the photograph of the Mayor riding the elephant, but he wanted to see more details from the news account of the day.

The newspapers were stacked vertically in the boxes so he could just make out the headlines without pulling out the entire copy. The white gloves that Mildred made him wear made it difficult, but he had learned to cope. His natural curiosity and his fascination with history forced him to look at headlines from every day, even though he already knew the date he was looking for. That is why his eyes fell on the headline of Sunday, September 5th where a name he had already seen connected with the zoo caught his eye. He pulled the paper from the box and began to read.

"Hey Mildred," he called. "Do you know anything about this?"

"Sure," she said with barely a glance. "That happened in the 1930's."

Amos stared at the headline. There was no mention of the zoo in this story, but he pulled it for copying anyway. He had a feeling he may have stumbled onto something useful.

"We'll keep 'em inside today," Tommy had said of the elephants that morning. Tommy liked to be in charge when Sam Kest was off, even though Sal had been with the elephants longer. Tommy was a take-charge kind of guy and Sal was not. It was not too cold for them to be outside, but on a chilly Friday during the school year, nobody would be there to see them anyway. "Sam said to work them on their routines and to check that spot on Elke's foot," Tommy had said.

The zoo owned three female African elephants. Elke was the oldest at about thirty three. She had been with the circus for many years. The other two, Sally and Bebe, were in their late teens and had been imported from South Africa as youngsters from culled herds. Elke was calm and obedient while Sally and Bebe were high-strung and needed to be watched. They would push their keepers around if they were given the opportunity.

"Elke, move up," said Tommy. With the stalls cleaned and the animals finished with their training session, it was time to look at Elke's foot. Elephants are prone to foot problems in captivity. The theory is that since they don't walk for miles in search of food like they do in the wild, thick calluses form on the bottoms of their feet. Little bits if dirt get in the cracks and cause infections, and an infection in the bottom of an elephant's foot is a big deal. It has even been known to be fatal, if not treated in time.

The big elephant moved toward the two keepers who stood at the bars of her cage. The two elephant stalls had poured concrete walls on two sides and vertical, six-inch steel pipes on the others. The pipes were set about a foot apart, wide enough for a man to squeeze through but not an elephant. There were no cross bars that might hinder a quick escape.

"Elke, turn around," Tommy commanded. The animal turned her backside to the bars.

"Elke, foot," he said, tapping the right rear leg.

Elke stuck her foot backwards through the bars and Sal guided it to a short, metal stand that had been fabricated in the zoo's maintenance shop for this purpose. He straddled the foot and, with it sticking out from between his legs, he went to work with his hoof knife.

"Elke, steady," said Tommy, maintaining control with his elephant hook from outside the cage.

"Foot looks pretty good," Sal said as he shaved off bits of the heavy, leather-like callus that formed the bottom of the elephant's foot. Sal's knife was about eight inches long with a wooden handle and a tip that was bent into a U. It was razor sharp. He worked quickly, making firm strokes and brushing at the pad of the foot as he went. There didn't seem to be any hot spots or infection, so he just opened up the narrow fissures and smoothed the pad. When he was finished, he straightened up and turned to tell Tommy he could release the elephant. He was shocked when he turned to see Tommy in the cage with Elke rubbing her head.

"Detective Stokes," said Don Laskey. "Thanks for coming."

"You said it was important," said Stokes. "So here I am."

"Have you met Amos Morris?" asked Laskey. The two men shook hands and everyone sat down. They were in Laskey's office. "Amos is a historian who is writing the book about our one hundred year history. His research has turned up something that might be of interest to you."

Amos opened his folder and handed the detective a paper. It was a photocopy of an old newspaper headline, and it was most definitely of interest. He would, of course, need DNA confirmation, but his gut told him that this was his victim. This was the man he had laying in the morgue. Now all he had to do was find out how he came to be there.

The routine in the monkey house was that, after the morning coffee break, the keepers would let the animals into their outside cages for the day and begin the cleaning of the indoor areas the animals had spent the night in. That's why Chelsea found herself in the outdoor colobus cage with a hose in her hand when John Stokes came walking by.

"Deep in thought?" she asked as he walked by.

He looked up, startled. "Actually, I just received some good news," he replied breaking into a smile. "I have just discovered who my victim is."

He explained the discovery of the disappearance more than seventy years ago. He had some work to do in order to prove it, but he was sure this was it.

"How do you suppose he came to be here?" she asked. "They don't generally bury people at a zoo and keep it a secret."

"Definitely a suspicious death," he replied thoughtfully. "He could have fallen into a hole and somehow got overlooked, but I doubt it. I think we've got a murder."

How do you solve a seventy year old murder?"

"I'm not sure, yet. I don't even know how he died, let alone have a clue who killed him. I need to get down to the Medical Examiner's office and get them to run some DNA."

"See you tonight," she said.

He waved a hand as he walked away.

She was thinking about those broad shoulders and how they would feel after dinner when she heard strange sounds from inside the building. Asa was still cleaning inside because he had been late and slow that morning. It sounded like he was struggling with something. There were no loud noises, only muffled grunts, groans, and bangs. She stepped out of the cage she was cleaning and walked around the building to peer in the door to the hallway. She was horrified by what she saw.

Asa was lying on his back in the middle of the hallway and Sonny was out of his cage standing over him. Sonny's fur was bristled and his teeth were bared. Chelsea was frozen for a moment. Asa kicked at the chimp. Sonny grabbed Asa's leg with both hands and bit into his calf like it was a drumstick, tearing muscle and sinew as he pulled back. Blood splattered over man and chimp and, for the first time, Asa let out a terrifying scream.

Chelsea was shocked into action as she yelled into her two-way radio, "Code Red at the monkey house. Code Red at the monkey house. Keeper is down. Sonny is out!"

Code Red was the signal for an animal escape and would bring staff running from all over the zoo. Mentioning the big male chimp would mean vets with tranquilizer guns and the shooting team with rifles. She knew that they would not hesitate to shoot Sonny to save the keeper's life. That would be standard operating procedure in an emergency.

Asa became still. He had apparently passed out, and Sonny lost interest. He looked around and caught sight of Chelsea through the glass door. She wondered briefly if she should run away, but Sonny turned and scampered back into his cage. He moved to the back of the cage and climbed to his sleeping bench to lick the blood off his fur.

"What happened?" asked Janice who was first to arrive.

"Sonny got out. He bit Asa and ran back into his cage."

More keepers arrived followed by the vets in their golf cart. The rifle team consisted of Tommy Ross with the 30.06 rifle and Sal Martinez with a twelve gauge shotgun. Don Laskey was last to arrive and he quickly took charge.

"What do we have?" he asked.

Chelsea stepped forward and explained what had happened. Lasky had not had any contact with Chelsea and wasn't sure what to make of her. He was a bit wary of good looking women because they often got where they are by their looks.

"Sonny's back in his cage," she said. "Let me go in and close the door."

"No," said Tommy. "He'll tear her apart. Let me go in and shoot him."

The director thought for a moment before asking Chelsea, "What makes you think he won't charge you the minute you open this door?"

"He trusts me," was all she said.

Laskey weighed his options. Finally he said, "OK, but the gun team goes in with you."

"No," she said. "The guns will freak him out." Before anyone could protest, she pulled the door open and walked calmly inside.

She stopped in the hall when the door closed behind her. The only sound was the whir of the fan motor in the heating system. She looked briefly at the big chimp and then looked away, careful not to make eye contact. She didn't want to appear at all threatening. She could see his shape out of the corner of her eye as she slowly made her way to the door. He wasn't moving, but he was definitely watching her. The door opened into the cage, so she would need to reach in and grab it to pull it shut. That is when she would be most vulnerable. That is when he might fly off his bench and tear her face off like the chimp in Connecticut had done to that woman a few years ago. Chelsea was totally focused on her own movements and those of the chimp. She was not aware of Asa lying on the floor a few feet away or the eyes of her colleagues and boss watching from outside the door. She needed calm, slow, sure movements. She could show no fear and relay no threat. She walked to the door of the cage, reached in, and pulled it shut. The bolt slid into place and she snapped the lock. It was over.

Eric and Joanne Newman had invited nearly three hundred people to Eric's seventy-eighth birthday party. In spite of the cold November weather, the lavish affair spilled out of their home on the Dotson estate, into tents, and across the expansive lawn down to the river. Red-jacketed valets parked cars and tuxedo-clad musicians soothed the crowds in various ensembles that were spread around the estate. Guests wore dinner jackets or suits and dresses that ranged from the lavish to the revealing. The Newmans had invited friends, relatives, government officials, and the fellow members of the various boards on which they both served. Even the governor was arriving later in his helicopter.

A small group of people, all members of the Dotson Park Zoo board, had gathered in the second floor library of the Newman home. The room was comfortable but devoid of that rich feeling found in most book-filled rooms. The bleached oak bookshelves and the off-white walls lacked warmth. The sofa and two wing-backed chairs had a tiny, dark red floral pattern that complemented the burgundy carpet. The Dotson mansion was visible out the window, a reminder of true elegance and character.

"We ought to get Betty up here now and start working on her," said Milton Wagner.

"I can go find her, if you like," said Evelyn Woodson, looking around the room. Evelyn was the director of the local humane society and was very much out of her element in these surroundings. She was eager to please.

Rodrick Olsen nodded his agreement and they all turned to their hostess, Joanne Dotson Newman. They were puzzled by her hesitation. She had been one of the most outspoken proponents of change on the zoological society's board and Betty Bexley, the wife of cardiologist Byron Bexley, was the vote they needed to swing things their way. They had all grown tired of the politics and incompetence that characterized the city's administration of the Dotson Park Zoo.

"Before we get Betty," she said at last, "we need to decide what we expect to accomplish."

"We're going to give the zoo back to those crooks at City Hall and let them run it," blurted Milt.

"I guess I'm having second thoughts," said Joanne. "Look at what we're giving back. Look at what we have built."

"Do you have another idea?" asked Rod Olsen, "because if you're asking us to do nothing, I don't think I can stand any more of those good-old-boys and their politics."

"I'm just saying that we should take it in small steps," said Joanne. "We need them to pay their fair share, but they will run it into the ground. Maybe we need to work the political angle a little longer. Maybe we can convince them to continue their funding support."

"We've been trying to do that for months," Milt said in frustration. "We need the City to fund at least thirty per cent of our operation. That comes to four and a half million a year. They say they don't have it. The State's not going to help us. The County's not going to help us. I can't imagine where we are going to pull that kind of money."

His last sentence hung in the air. Everyone in the room knew the only people with 'that kind of money' were the various families in the Dotson Clan.

"Joanne," said Milt. "We have to do this. It's the only way. I hope we are just bluffing, but we must be ready to carry out our threat."

No one spoke for a moment.

"I think we should elect Joanne president of the board," said Evelyn suddenly. All eyes turned to her and no one spoke as the obvious wisdom of this washed over them. Then, slowly, all eyes turned to Joanne.

"The election is in two weeks," Joanne protested. "The nominating committee has already decided on another term for Ralph."

They all knew that Ralph was part of the problem.

"According to the by-laws, Ralph has to open the floor for nominations," said Milt. "I'll place Joanne's name in nomination."

"I'll second the nomination," said Evelyn.

Rod nodded his approval. In the silence that followed, everyone paused to consider the implications. For fifty-four years, the Dotson Park Zoological Society and the city's administration had operated the zoo as a team. Shortly after being incorporated in 1922, the zoological society was forced to lead the zoo through the dark days of the depression and through the renaissance of the Franklin Roosevelt's New Deal. The City funded the zoo's operation and the Society raised money to fund improvements. In 1988, the roles reversed when the Society took over operations and the City funded infrastructure improvements and subsidized any shortfall in the operation. Now, with the recent world-wide financial crisis, the City claimed it did not have the funds to support the zoo. They threatened to cut all funding at the end of the fiscal year in June. The solution the Society Board had arrived at was a drastic one. They were volunteers. They would simply resign from the board, dissolve the organization, and go back to their regular lives. The City would be forced to operate the zoo.

"We had better go find Betty," said Joanne with obvious acceptance. "And let's get Evelyn back in here."

"I'll look for Byron," said Milt. "Betty won't do anything without his support."

They all stood when Joanne opened the door. Noise from the party flooded into the room as Milt marched out and they pondered the possibility of changing the face of the Dotson Park zoo forever.

22

If any area of the zoo could handle the frigid, December weather it would be the polar bears. The animals seemed to thrive in this kind of weather. It was probably just good luck that kept the problems of the rest of the zookeepers from occurring in this area – no frozen water pipes, no frozen locks, no balky heaters. But it was really the animals that made things seem better. The polar bears, and the seals next door, were oblivious to the cold.

John Bullard unlocked the door to polar bear holding and stepped into the wire safety cage. He flipped on the lights, closed the door behind him, and looked down the row of cages to see if it was safe to enter. Polar bears were considered by many to be the most dangerous animals in the zoo. They were meat eaters with teeth that were meant to tear flesh. They were big and strong. The male, Gustav, weighed over a thousand pounds and the females, Freda and Zaleska, weighed in at about eight hundred each. What really made them dangerous, however, was that they were ruthless and clever at catching prey. John had seen one of the females stick her paw out the space under the mesh cage-front and wiggle it as though it was extended as far as she could reach, when John knew she could actually grab things much further out. She was trying to lure him into a trap. Their beady little eyes never revealed any intentions, but John was pretty sure their intentions were never good.

The polar bear and seal exhibits opened in 2002 and were still in good shape. The bear holding pens had concrete sides and backs with stainless steel, wire mesh fronts. The mesh was a heavy duty weave with openings about two inches square. It provided good visibility and was plenty strong enough to hold a bear. From his vantage point in the safety cage, John could see that each cage door was locked and no bears were roaming the hallway. He retrieved his stainless steel buckets of feed from the cart outside, brought them inside, and placed them on the stainless steel kitchen counter next to the stainless steel sink. The zoo was going to make sure nothing turned to rust in this corrosive, salt-water environment.

John went down the line of cages, talking to the bears and checking to make sure nothing was amiss. Gus was his usual amiable self, lying at the back of his cage. He barely raised his head when Sam walked by. Freda was much the same. Both she and Gus had come to the zoo as youngsters in 1996. Zaleska was another story. She was born at Dotson Park four years ago to Gus and Freda. She was nervous, high strung, and hard to deal with. She had bitten at the wire mesh cage-front so badly, she had broken one of her bottom canine teeth. She gave John her usual greeting. She pursed her lips, blew out sharply with a repeated 'chuffing' sound, and charged forward with her head down. It was when she backed away that he noticed the problem. The lower left side of her jaw was so swollen it looked as though she had a golf ball stuffed into her cheek. Something was very wrong. He would need to call the curator, Clarence Watts.

"What are we going to do in the winter?" asked Sal, "when everybody is locked inside."

"We are building an indoor arena," said Don Laskey. "It will be a large dirt-floor space, like a horse show arena and it will be designed to house both chimps and elephants."

This was the first time the keepers had been allowed an opportunity to sit down with the zoo director and hear his vision for this new area. Neither the elephant keepers nor the chimp keepers had been particularly optimistic about this working out, but they had little choice in the matter. The space was very nice and both chimp staff and elephant staff liked the idea of occupying it – just not with the other department involved.

"If something bad happens," said Tommy, "are we going to be allowed to go in with the elephants?"

"Absolutely not," said the director. "The animals will have to sort it out. Besides, if chimps are there, you can't go in."

They paused as that thought sunk in. They all knew what had happened a few weeks ago to someone who found himself in with the chimps.

"Maybe we need to start cross-training," Chelsea broke the spell.

"With who?" said Tommy sarcastically, "animals or people."

"Both, maybe," she laughed. "Actually I was thinking of us. Billy and I could train on elephants and you guys need to learn chimps."

"I know all I want to know about chimps," said Sam, "which is nothing." He laughingly looked at Sal and Tommy, but they appeared to be buying in to this nonsense.

"Great idea," said Laskey back to Chelsea. "I'll have the curators set up a schedule to get you keepers into each others' areas. I wish we really could train the animals to get along, too."

"There may be a way," said Chelsea.

They all looked at her, Laskey with curiosity and the elephant keepers with contempt. This new zoo keeper with her fancy college degrees sure thought a lot of herself. What did she know about any of this? She had never even worked with elephants. It was Sam who challenged her. "Are you going to bring the chimps over to see us, or shall we bring the girls over to the monkey house?"

"Neither," she said unphased. "We can start the minute they are moved to the new building as long as we have a common space where they can have some kind of protected contact with us and with each other."

"The chimps will figure things out pretty quickly," said Billy, speaking for the first time. "I imagine they'll be freaked out at first, but they'll work out how to deal with elephants. They might even enjoy messing with them once in a while."

"They had better not mess with Bebe," said Tommy. "Bebe'll stomp them into the dust."

"She'll have to catch em first," said Billy, rising to the challenge.

"Aw," said Sam, who knew more about elephants than anyone in the room. "The girls might like having some little, furry human companions. They used to like having us go in with them. If that keeper in Tennessee hadn't been killed by an elephant, we'd still be going in with them ourselves."

"Good," said Laskey. "Let's get through the Christmas holidays and we'll start the cross training after the first of the year. Good work, everyone." This last phrase was delivered as he and Chelsea made eye contact.

Clarence had taken his sweet time getting to polar bear holding, but then everything seemed to move slower when it was this cold. He had agreed there was a problem and had called the vets. That is why Clarence and John were now joined in the hallway by associate veterinarian Dr. Salinda Donaldson and veterinary technician, Eve Stewart. The head veterinarian, Dr. Herb Schroeder, had stayed in the clinic on this frigid morning. Dr. Donaldson, or Dr. D as everyone called her, was young but she had done her veterinary residency at the San Diego Zoo, so she knew her stuff. The female keepers liked dealing with her because she was knowledgeable and decisive without being rude or condescending. The male keepers liked her for the same reasons, not to mention the fact that she was tall, blond, and nice looking.

"When did you first notice this?" she asked.

"Just this morning," said John. "Must have swelled up overnight."

"Is she eating?"

"She ate some yesterday," he replied. "But she did leave some, which is unusual for her."

"Are you thinking abscess?" Eve asked the doctor.

"Yes," Dr. D replied. "And I don't like the prospects of what we need to do to treat it."

They were all quiet as the bear eyed them suspiciously from the back of the cage.

"OK," said Dr. D finally. "We'll need to knock her down, but we won't be able to do it until this evening when Doctor Hardin is available." Doc Hardin, they all knew was the local dentist who did consulting work for the zoo from time to time. "No food today and no water after noon. Eve, you can call Hardin and make sure he can come in. then get our stuff ready for a knock down. We'll meet back here at seven."

An uneasy calm filled the room as Ralph Polaski called the Dotson Park Zoological Society board meeting to order. He was aware of the financial challenges they faced. He had also been experiencing increasing opposition at these meetings from certain members of the board. They had started as innocent questions or challenges but lately, they had become more direct. He had grown to dread these meetings and was sorry he had already agreed to one more term.

"The first order of business," he began, "Is to welcome our newest board member, Rhonda Bailey." He pointed his gavel unnecessarily toward the only black face in the room.

With that formality out of the way, Ralph steered the meeting efficiently through the approval of minutes, the treasurer's report, and the staff reports.

"The final order of business is the nominating committee's report. Ivan, do you have a slate of officers to present?"

"I do," said Ivan Robson as he stood and read his list of names.

"Are there any nominations from the floor?" asked Ralph.

He was stunned to see Milt Wagner's hand raised. "Milt?" he said in a questioning tone.

"I nominate Joanne Newman for president."

The following thirty seconds seemed like an eternity as Ivan tried to decide what his next move should be.

"We'll split the slate," he said finally, "And we'll vote by show of hands. Is there a second for Joanne?"

"I will second," said Evelyn Woodson.

"All those in favor of Joanne Newman as president of the board for the three year term, please raise your hands."

Milt's hand went up immediately, followed by Rodrick Olsen and Evelyn. Joanne raised her hand, obviously accepting the nomination. As the four people with hands raised looked to Betty Bexley to help carry the vote, they were surprised to see another hand go up. It was Rhonda Bailey who cast the fifth, and deciding vote before Betty could raise her hand. Ivan, Ralph, and Sam Wilson looked at each other and then looked at Don Laskey. They were clearly stunned. The old guard had lost control and Don knew that he was in for a rough time with Joanne Newman at the helm.

With the election over and the business of the Board taken care of, Ralph asked, "Is there any new business before we begin our annual Christmas party?"

Milt's hand went up again and he began to speak before being recognized by the Chair. "I have a resolution to offer under new business." Ralph appeared confused, so Milt continued.

"Whereas the City does not have the funds to support the operation of the Dotson Park Zoo," he began, "and whereas the Zoological Society cannot operate the Zoo without those funds, The Dotson Park Zoological Society hereby dissolves its organization and returns the operation of the Zoo back to the City."

Ralph was dumbfounded. He looked around the table for some clue as to what to do next, but people were evidently either already onboard with this, or they were as shocked as he was.

Sam Wilson was the first to speak. "This is crazy. The City won't take it back. It would cost them millions."

"That's the point," said Joanne.

"That's blackmail," said Sam.

"I'm not sure this is legal," said Ralph.

"Oh, it's legal alright," said Milt, the only attorney in the room. "And all we need is two readings and a two thirds vote at the final reading, which will be at our February meeting."

"Why don't you call for a show of hands to see who is already in favor of this," Rhonda said to Ralph.

Before he could respond, five hands went up. They would only need one additional vote in February to change the face of the zoo forever.

"Doc," John Bullard called down the hall. "I think she's down."

Doctor Schroeder, or Doc as everyone called him, broke away from the quiet conversation he had been having with Doctor Donaldson and their consulting dentist, Doctor Ira Hardin. Doc Schroeder was one of the few people who had been at the zoo longer than John. He was a stocky man who had the look of someone who had been powerfully built in his youth. Now his shock of white hair and his soft physique gave him the look of a big teddy bear. He peered in at the sleeping bear. "Let's have a look," he said, pointing at the lock on the cage door.

John knew that meant Doc wanted to go in with the tranquilized bear, poke it with a broom handle, and grab it by the scruff of the neck for a good shake. Whenever he tranquilized an animal, Doc was always the first in. He wanted to make sure the animal was completely out – and this one was.

"Ira," he called. "Let's get started."

The team had been waiting quietly and patiently for the tranquilizer drugs to take effect and for the bear to go to sleep. If they could avoid noise, excitement, and stimulation while the bear was awake, they knew she would go down quicker and stay down longer. Now that she was down, they could go to work. Each person there had a job and most of the jobs had not even been discussed. John and Clarence, for example, were to handle the bear. They would try to keep the animal still and try to control the head during the delicate procedure. Doctor Donaldson and Eve Watts would perform any veterinary procedures which included monitoring the level of anesthesia that would ensure that the bear stayed down. And Doctor Hardin would work on the tooth that they knew must be abscessed. The dentist was a small man with thinning dark hair, close set eyes, and a hooked nose. He did not talk much, but he was quick, efficient, and the team liked working with him.

Doc kneeled down next to John and pried the mouth open. He peered inside and felt the lump under the chin. "Abscessed lower left canine," was all he said as he straightened up.

Salinda and Eve moved in to the space he vacated. Eve held a glass beaker under the chin as Salinda slit open the abscess with a scalpel. The odor of pus and rotting flesh filled the room as Eve squeezed the bloody mucous into the beaker with a gloved hand. The next few minutes were spent flushing out the wound with an iodine solution and packing it with a powerful, antibiotic ointment.

When they were finished, Doctor Hardin moved in with his portable drill. He used equipment that he had specially modified for the animals at the zoo. He had been doing this long enough that he was no longer surprised at the size of the teeth he worked on. He received no pay and only charged the zoo for materials. He must enjoy this, John thought, to be out at the zoo, kneeling on the wet concrete floor of a polar bear den, with his hands in the mouth of an animal that would surely kill him if it was awake.

Eve had carefully place a towel on the floor next to him and unwrapped a sterile cloth that held the small, hair-like files that he would run down into the root canal. When he was finished drilling he carefully and thoroughly cleaned out every bit of root to ensure there would be no need to do this again. As he was jamming the file into the rot for what would be the last time, the bear lifted his head.

"Better hurry up, Doc," John said as he pushed down on the top of the bear's head.

Doctor Hardin did not panic, but he did cast a worried glance at the two vets who stood by the door.

"I don't want to give him any more drugs," said Doc Schroeder. "Just keep going."

Doctor Hardin mixed the filling material and filled the tooth as the rest of the staff cleared everything out of the stall. The bear was moving around more and would soon be awake. The dentist was finished and picking up his instruments when the bear roared and lifted John off the floor by raising her head. It was time to go.

She was getting up off the floor as Clarence scrambled to the door. He held the door as John gave the bear a push and jumped out the door. Clarence pulled it shut as she hit it with a crash.

"Whew," said John as he sagged against the wall. "That was close."

23

Mayor Wilson Parker breezed through the zoo offices with his entourage and past Wilma Watson's desk like a predatory bird in silent flight. Wilma had seen him coming, but he still made it past her and into Don Laskey's office before she could stand and say good morning. His driver took a seat opposite Wilma's desk and picked up a magazine from the coffee table. Joanne Newman and Milt Wagner were already inside and had been talking near the desk. Don Laskey was standing and looking out the window. Laskey appeared nervous. The Mayor introduced city attorney Raymond Delbridge and acknowledged his other companion, Sam Wilson, with a wave of his hand as everyone found a seat.

Wilson Parker was finishing his first term as mayor and would probably have little opposition in the fall election. He had been an enormously popular and effective mayor whose background as the owner of a successful chain of dry-cleaning shops would have given little indication of suitability for the office of mayor. He had simply taken charge and blossomed. He was of medium height and average build, and he used his dark eyes and deep, booming voice to their fullest advantage. He had ridden into office as the city's first black mayor, but no one mentioned that anymore. He was simply the best, most charismatic leader the city had seen in recent history.

"I have considered the Society's proposal to return the zoo to the City," began the Mayor, "and I can't support that when you present it to City Council. I'm going to counter with a five year support package with decreasing amounts each year, so you will be on your own by year six." No one in the room was surprised. The Mayor couldn't afford the bad publicity associated with a destabilized zoo. If he could reach an agreement with the Society, it should help assure his re-election.

"I do have a few conditions, though," he continued. "As long as we are subsidizing your operation, I want some type of free admission benefit for city residents and school children."

Mayor Parker stood to gaze out the window. The sun was burning away the last of the morning fog and, though the sky was still hazy, this day would surely live up to the forecast of sunny and cold. Everyone in the room remained silent as the Mayor watched the first zoo visitors of the day, an elderly couple, stroll around the fountain and toward the lion house. An odd sight, thought the Mayor. He had expected to see children.

"What is the timing of the announcement?" asked Joanne.

"As soon as possible." replied the Mayor without turning. "Mr. Delbridge is drawing up the papers now. When is your next board meeting?"

"Tuesday the seventh," Milt replied.

The Mayor looked at his City Attorney, who shook his head slightly. "Can't do it by then. We'll have the papers ready to sign by the following board meeting. You can work out the details with Mr. Delbridge. I want this wrapped up by Memorial Day."

"How long is this likely to take?" asked Susan Daniels.

"Hard to say," Dr. Donaldson replied. "It dep..."

"Oh, I've seen these things last for six or eight hours," she was cut off by the man standing between them. He was Parks Jones, the new deputy director who had started at the zoo on Monday.

Susan had been given the task of showing him around the zoo and introducing him to staff. They had worked their way around the zoo this week and had arrived at the giraffe house this cold, Thursday morning to find vet staff and zoo keepers watching this female giraffe. She had a pronounced bulge under her tail and was pacing nervously. She was, it appeared, preparing to give birth.

"You've seen these before," asked Susan.

"Sure," he replied, "Lots of them."

Dr. Donaldson looked down at the man. He was, she guessed, about five foot three, probably in his early forties, with dark hair and plenty of bravado. He had been the Curator of Herpetology for the New York Zoological Society and he had done his PhD thesis on the Tortoises of Madagascar. She doubted that he had seen 'lots' of giraffes give birth.

"Should I call the media?" Susan asked Dr. Donaldson.

"No," the vet said, a little more sharply than she meant to. "No press until it's over. Too many things could go wrong."

"What could go wrong?" asked Parks condescendingly. He gestured toward the giraffe. "This is the most natural thing in the world. It'll make great news footage when that baby hits the floor."

"Hits the floor?" said Susan.

"She'll give birth standing up," Dr. D. explained with a disapproving glance at Parks. "And plenty could go wrong. This is my procedure and I say no press." She walked away.

They stood in silence for a moment as Susan took in the scene. The giraffe house consisted of three large indoor stalls that were visible to the public and several off-exhibit stalls behind the doors in the back wall. The pregnant female had been separated from the male and the other females. Her stall had been bedded down with fresh straw and sweet-smelling pine shavings. The doors to the building were locked, although the zoo had no visitors on this frigid, weekday in January.

"I need to get to Don's office," he said finally. "I'm supposed to meet the Society President."

"Why did you find it necessary to hire someone from New York?" asked Joanne. "With all of these people running around this place, we couldn't find anyone qualified to be your Deputy?"

"Nobody with the right combination of education and experience," Don replied. "I need someone who can step in and run things in my absence. This chemotherapy is going to take its toll."

Joanne had to fight back the urge to argue. Don was not her favorite person and would not have been her first choice to run the zoo. But with his recent revelation that he has cancer, she did not wish to press the issue.

"So, what is his education and experience?"

"Forty two years old. A native New Yorker, so this will be a big change for him. His Doctorate is in Herpetology."

"What's that?"

"The study of reptiles and amphibians."

"Oh, God," she said. "A snake man."

"He has fifteen years' experience at the New York City zoo," Don continued. "He worked his way up the ranks from zoo keeper."

"Is he married?" she asked. "Does he have a family?"

"No. He's still trying to convince his fiancé to move out here with him."

"What does a reptile guy know about polar bears, chimps, and elephants?"

"He doesn't need to know everything," Don replied. "He just has to trust his curators and vets."

"Mr. Jones is here," said Wilma from the door. Parks Jones brushed past her before Don could reply.

"You must be Joanne," he said with extended hand. "I've heard so much about you."

Amos Morris and Detective John Stokes were an unlikely pair as they stepped out of the elevator into the basement of the newspaper offices. The tall, good looking man in the trench coat and the small rumpled historian made their way down the hallway lined with boxes toward a counter where an unsmiling, middle aged woman in a grey suit waited.

"Morning Mildred," said Amos.

"Hello Amos," she replied.

"This is Detective Stokes," said Amos with a gesture. "I've brought him to have a look at the box you showed me."

"I'm afraid that won't be possible," she said without making eye contact.

"What?" Amos said. "Why not?"

"Mr. Appleton said so." She said. "He said no one was to look inside this box until he had a chance to go through it himself. He said I was to hold it here until he came down later to pick it up." She looked down at the cardboard box sitting against the wall behind her desk and then back up at the men. Making eye contact for the first time she said, "I am going to lunch. I trust you can see yourselves out." Without another word, she picked up her purse, gathered her coat and walked to the elevator.

"Appleton is the Publisher," said Amos. "He'll fire her if he finds out."

"Appleton will go to jail for obstruction of justice and tampering with evidence," said Stokes. "Let's have a look."

Amos was well aware of the search for the identity of the body found at the zoo and when Mildred had told him of the discovery, he knew the detective would be interested. She had been moving boxes and organizing them for a move to a new, climate controlled storage building when she had come across a box marked 'Bertram Wallace'. It appeared to be the contents of his desk.

Amos snatched up the box with surprising agility for a small man and quickly moved to the back of the room. He found an empty table behind a stack of shelves, removed the lid and slid on a pair of white gloves that he had in his pocket.

"You need to find a pair of gloves up by Mildred's desk," he ordered.

While Stokes was getting gloved-up, he began laying out the contents of the box. A handful of file folders, a stack of newspaper clippings, two framed pictures, a coffee cup filled with pencils, three ledger books, and a name plate that said *'Bertram Wallace, Publisher'*.

"Who are the people?" asked Stokes picking up one of the photos.

"This is Bertram," said Amos pointing to the unsmiling man in the business suit. "I've seen his picture before. I don't know the others."

Stokes scanned the files then picked up one of the ledgers, while Amos unframed the pictures to see if anything was written on the back.

"Jesus," said Stokes. "This guy was a piece of work."

"Why?"

"He was blackmailing everyone," said Stokes stabbing a page in the ledger, "and keeping a record of it!"

He read further and asked "Have you come across someone named Bobby Crofton?"

"He was the first architect of the zoo in the 1930's. He drew up the master plan that will be in my book."

"How about Buddy Griffith?"

"Son of the zoo's first director, Calvin Griffith. He disappeared for years but showed up in the 30's to handle the elephant."

"And Gunther Liebherr?"

"Nope. Haven't come across that one."

"These are all people at the zoo he was blackmailing or paying to do his bidding," said Stokes closing the book and setting it back on the stack. "I'm taking these ledgers."

"Don't you need a warrant or something?" asked Amos.

"Probably," said Stokes. "But this'll never go to trial. Everyone involved is long dead. Besides, if I do turn up anything useful, I'll get the newspaper to release these under the Freedom of Information Act."

"We'll need to work fast," said Amos. "Mildred will be back soon. Let's get through these files and clippings. I'll photograph them as we go."

Amos pulled a small, digital camera out of his pocket and Stokes began laying out the materials.

Any change?" Chelsea asked, knowing as soon as she said it that there had been a noticeable change. She stood beside Dr. Donaldson and Eve Watts. Susan Daniels and Parks Jones were there, as well, but standing a little apart.

"Legs are out," said Eve, stating the obvious.

The giraffe paced. She appeared nervous, but not frantic. She walked with purpose in a figure eight in the stall, stopping every few minutes to contract. Two legs protruded from the opening under her tail.

"Is everything normal?" Chelsea asked, not really knowing what she was seeing.

"Yes," said Dr. D. "These are the front legs. We should see the nose next and then the head. Once the head comes out, gravity will help take over and it will go fast."

A crowd of zoo staff had gathered and a murmur of voices filled the room. The giraffe appeared not to notice as she kept up her routine – walk, stop, squeeze, walk, stop, squeeze. Soon Chelsea could see a third bulge under the tail. The nose was out. Then she could see the head and, miraculously, the baby moved its ears.

"That's a good sign," said Eve. "It's alive."

It had not occurred to Chelsea that being stillborn was even a possibility, but she didn't have long to ponder the thought. The female gave a push and the baby slid much further out and was now dangling four feet above the floor. The female stopped, spread her back legs and gave another push. The baby slid all the way out and flopped onto the straw covered floor. The murmur grew to a muted cheer as the baby lifted its head and took its first look at the world. Another giraffe called the Dotson Park Zoo home.

"Damn it's cold!" Fred Williamson closed the door to the construction trailer and sat down to take off his slush-covered boots. He hated the cold weather and complained about it constantly. Lyman wondered if he was going to hear the usual threat to move to Florida this summer. "I swear, Lyman. I'm going to be living in Tampa by next winter."

Lyman was seated at his desk with lunchbox on it, but unopened. He always waited till Fred came in so they could eat together. Their 'office' was a trailer that had been moved onto the construction site when they began work last summer. It had a bathroom at one end, a storage room at the other, and it was piled with boxes, rolled up architectural drawings, and samples of everything from carpet to glass. To the occasional visitor, it was a jumbled mess. To Lyman and Fred, it was home. Fred picked his way across the dirty floor carefully in his socks, retrieved his lunchbox and joined Lyman at the table.

"Got a call from Gardeau Steel this morning," said Lyman as he unwrapped his sandwich. "The cables are ready to ship but the posts for the outdoor exhibit are running behind. It may be two to four weeks before they have them ready for the trucks."

"Hard as the ground is," said Fred with his mouth full, "a few weeks won't make no difference."

"We've got a lot of work to do in four months," said Lyman shaking his head.

"Yeah," agreed Fred. "Good thing we got the buildings under roof. We can keep working inside till the weather breaks. What about the chimp caging? When will that get here?"

"On its way," said Lyman. "Be here Monday."

"Good."

They ate in silence and cleaned up their trash, before Fred spoke again. "I think I may have spotted a problem in the outdoor exhibit."

Lyman had been over the plans a thousand times and couldn't imagine what his foreman was talking about, but Fred's instincts were very good. Lyman knew from past experience that if Fred thought there was a problem, there usually was.

Fred moved to the tall, slanted table and began flipping the large sheets of architectural drawings. He stabbed a finger at a spot as Lyman joined him.

"See where the post and cable, elephant fence comes near the wire mesh, chimp fence?" he said. "Here and here."

"Yes," said Lyman peering in.

"The architects specified a minimum distance of twelve feet between each fence," said Fred. "That's to keep the chimps from climbing the elephant post and jumping out, right?"

"Right," said Lyman. "But they have given us a twenty foot distance just to be on the safe side."

"Right," agreed Fred, "except here and here. These two spots are down to twelve."

"So?" Lyman wasn't sure where this was heading. "That's still within the safe distance."

"But what about the overhang," asked Fred. "Have they accounted for the fact that the chimp fence has a four foot overhang? In these two spots, a chimp can stand on the elephant post and look across eight feet of open space to the top of the overhang. Don't you suppose those monkeys could jump eight feet? Hell, I could jump eight feet."

Lyman looked at the big man's belly.

"Well," Fred grinned, "I used to could."

Lyman thought for a moment. He could easily make a field-change in these spots and simply move the fences farther apart. But if something happened down the road, he would be responsible.

"I'll get with the zoo people this afternoon," he said finally. "See if they want to do a change-order. Good catch, Fred."

Lyman knew that Fred Williamson was not the stereo type – this large, slow moving, uneducated black man. He had just caught a flaw in the design of a twelve million dollar project, a design that had been approved by architects, engineers, zoo animal experts, and even himself. He wondered what he would have been like if Fred wore the suit and had the college degree. Lyman figured he would be working for Fred.

"You look like the cat that swallowed the canary," said Chelsea as John slid in the booth opposite her.

"I just had a huge break in my case," he smiled.

He reached out discretely and covered her hand with his. She turned her hand to grasp his fingers. He longed to sit beside her and put his arm around her, but he knew Mario's was not the place for that. Their relationship was no secret, but dinner across the street from the zoo was too much like being on duty for her.

"I ordered a pizza and two Cokes," she said.

"I'd rather have a beer."

"You're on duty," she admonished. "Forget it."

"You look pretty happy," he said.

"We had a giraffe born today," she said. "I watched the whole thing."

The waitress placed cokes and two straws on the table, "pizza is on the way," she said.

"Have you ever seen a giraffe give birth?" he asked after he took a sip of Coke.

"No," she replied. "So, tell me about your big break."

He explained about the discovery of Bertram Wallace's belongings – first the ledgers and the names inside then the newspaper clippings. Amos had filled in the details from his research. The story of those days in the 1930's still had his heart pumping.

Part 4

24

Saturday, March 27, 1937 (Easter Weekend)

The rock was the size of his fist and its smooth surface and rounded edges would make it easy to throw. He tossed it lightly into the air a couple of times to measure its heft, and then let it fly. It was a glancing blow and it fell harmlessly to the ground. The beast just stood there in the afternoon sun swaying from side to side.

"You missed", laughed Adam Swindler.

"He didn't even move", said Danny Tyler.

Nine-year-old Chucky Thompson just grunted as he looked for another rock. He wasn't sure whether he was more disappointed in the lack of reaction from the beast or the failure to impress his thirteen-year-old friends. They had been at the zoo all day getting into their usual mischief and it would soon be time to go home. Chucky was determined to impress the older boys and he wasted no time with his next toss. It flew hard and straight, striking between the eyes, and bringing a rumble of displeasure from the beast and roars of laughter from Adam and Bobby. It also earned him a whack on the head from the handler, who had just returned from a bathroom break.

"You three get out of here!"

Matthew James raised his stick again but the boys scrambled away – the two older ones laughing and Chucky rubbing his head. It was Matthew's first day with this animal and he didn't need these little hooligans screwing things up. He watched them walk away and turned back to the task at hand. He was glad for this assignment and hoped he was up to the task. The stick he held was a stout one, about four feet long and as big around as the small end of a baseball bat. It was not unlike the ones he seen used in the circus a few months earlier which is where he got the idea to lie about having experience. In truth, he had never been this near an elephant, especially one as large as this African male called Bwana.

Simon Poston had watched the little drama unfold from his scaffold on the wall of the new elephant house. Most of his crew was off for the Easter weekend, but he and his laborer, Willie Larder, were setting forms and tying steel rods in preparation for pouring concrete on Monday. As the boys walked away, jeering over their shoulders, the elephant handler fiddled with his stick and eyed the animal. Simon thought he was not much older than the boys he had just run off.

"He's no more an elephant handler than I am," muttered Simon.

"What?" asked Willie, looking up from his work.

"Nothin. Let's get back to work."

A crowd had gathered around Bwana, but that didn't bother the old bull. He had spent most of his life with the circus. They were kept back by a single rope that was tied to posts that had been pounded into the ground. They were laughing, pointing, and throwing bits of food that he happily sucked-up with his trunk and stuffed into his mouth. Bwana had been walked to the zoo from the rail yard by two elephant men from the circus. They had pounded a large iron stake into the ground, wrapped a long chain around his left front leg and tied the chain to the stake. That would be Bwana's home until the new building was finished.

Matthew looked at the elephant for a moment. The animal seemed calm enough, flapping his big ears and swaying in the mid-morning sun. He threw a trunk-full of sand over his back. Matthew gathered an armload of hay and dropped it near enough that the animal could reach it, but careful to remain out of reach himself. He then placed a pitchfork in his wheeled cart and began picking up the elephant's droppings. The turds were large and firm. They had a peculiar odor that was strong and pungent enough to cling to clothing and hair, but not stinky like dog and cat poop.

He wheeled and scooped in a circle around the stake, not wanting to draw near the elephant, and leaving the piles that were out of his reach. He could get those later. As he turned toward the hoofed stock barn where he would empty his load and begin his other chores, he caught movement out of the corner of his eye. The end of the elephant's trunk punched him in the jaw as the animal ran out of chain and Matthew went to his knees like a punched-out fighter. The elephant had moved with astonishing quickness and silence.

"Did you see that?" asked Willie.

"See what?" replied Simon.

"That elephant just knocked that guy down."

The two workers paused from their task on the scaffolding and watched the elephant keeper stagger toward the barn.

"That boy's gonna get hurt one of these days," said Willie.

"Yep," said Simon. "I believe you're right."

"That son of a bitch knocked me down," said Matthew as he stumbled into the barn.

"Did you hit him back?" asked Gunther Liebherr. "You can't let him get away with that."

"Hell no I didn't hit him back! I'm not getting that close to him."

Gunther was the supervisor of the section that included hoofed stock, monkeys, and the new elephant. He was a handsome, blue-eyed, blond who spoke with a slight German accent. He had worked at the Frankfurt Zoo in Germany and, though he had never actually worked with elephants, he had seen elephant men at work.

The hoofed stock barn was one of the first buildings at the zoo, built shortly after the original barn burned down. About fifteen years earlier it had been gutted, remodeled, and enlarged to house more exotic animals. It currently held two zebras, two eland antelope, three Grant's gazelles, and four dromedary camels. The long hallway in which Matthew and Gunther stood was open at both ends and fed into indoor stalls along one side. Each stall, in turn, led into an outdoor yard. Above them was the hayloft which held hay, sacks of feed, animal shipping crates, and some tools.

"You can start with the zebras," said Gunther, showing little concern for Matthew's health. "I've finished the camels so I'll throw down some hay."

He moved to the stairs at the end of the hallway as Matthew pushed his empty cart to the door of the zebra stall. Up in the hayloft, Gunther jabbed his pitchfork into the pile of hay and dropped it through the opening in the floor. He wished the builders had placed openings over each animal stall but they hadn't. One hatch opened to the hallway, which meant they had to fork the hay a second time into the stalls. The barn he had worked in at Frankfort Zoo was so much better designed. In addition to hatches over the stalls, they had a driveway to the upper level so supplies could be dropped off rather than hoisted up by rope, and the hay arrived in rectangular bales that were tied with wire. Some things he missed about the old country and some he did not. He did feel safe here – safe from his past.

"Hello."

Gunther dropped his pitchfork and jumped back. He turned to the man standing at the stairs with his mouth open.

"Sorry," said the man. "I didn't mean to scare you."

"You're not supposed to be in here," said Gunther briskly as he regained his composure.

"Mr. Griffith sent me over here to find Gunther," said the man. "I'm Robert Crofton – Bobby – and I'm supposed to start work today. Are you Gunther?"

Gunther sized up Bobby Crofton and wondered what kind of zookeeper he would make. He was a scruffy old guy who looked to be in his mid-forties. He had graying hair, a week-old beard, and a stained shirt under his coveralls. He also had the sharp eyes and confident air of someone who was once a person of substance, but who had fallen on hard times like thousands of others who were out of work. Gunther was a little annoyed that he knew nothing of the new man's starting to work in his section, but he was grateful for the help. He had been complaining to his boss, and Alvin Doyle had obviously convinced the superintendent that help was needed in the hoofed stock area – especially with a new elephant to care for.

"Right," said Gunther. "We'll start you in the petting zoo."

They walked downstairs to the hallway and Gunther called Matthew from the stall he was cleaning.

"This is Bobby Crofton," he said to Matthew. "Take him over to the petting zoo and get him started mucking out the sheep and goats."

The walk to the small farmyard that served as a petting area took them past the elephant, the water-moated, monkey area called Monkey Island.

"Our area includes Bwana the elephant," explained Matthew as they walked, "monkey mountain, and all the hoofed stock in the barn and petting zoo."

"How long have you worked here?" Bobby asked.

"Been here since Christmas," he replied, "and started with the elephant today."

"And Gunther, what's his story?"

"I don't know much. He's been here a few years. He's a German. Worked at a zoo in Frankfurt."

"I figured him for a Kraut," replied Bobby sourly. "I saw plenty of his kind in the war."

Matthew looked at Bobby as they walked. "You were in the war?"

Bobby did not reply.

Matthew showed Bobby around the petting zoo, which was essentially a large round corral, about thirty feet across with a shelter along one side and a shed for storing tools and hay. The animal collection consisted of ten goats, three sheep, and a donkey. People were allowed to enter the pen and pet the animals. Most folks brought bread, crackers, and other treats to feed them. After showing Bobby how to rake and shovel the droppings and where to dump them, Matthew walked back to the hoofed stock barn. As he passed Monkey Island, he saw a young lady with a long stick trying to fish something out of the moat.

"Can I help you?" he asked.

"My little brother dropped his rattle into the water," said the lady.

She was the most beautiful woman he had ever seen. Dark curls spilled out from under her hat and her light, hazel colored eyes seemed to look right through him. She was plump in all the right places and her smile seemed to be meant just for him.

"I'll get it," he said, leaning so far over the wall that his feet went straight up in the air and then teetering back to the ground. "You'd better rinse it off before you give it back."

Her hand touched his as he handed the rattle back to her and he felt as if he had touched an electric spark. He walked back to the hoofed stock barn feeling lighter than air. He glided into the barn, fell into a cart that someone had left in the hallway, and rolled out the other side onto the floor.

"What the hell," he said scrambling to his feet. "Who put that there?"

The smell of cat shit was his first clue. The appearance of Thomas Chandler at the top of the stairs to the loft was his second.

"Sorry," said the rotund zookeeper from the cat house. "I need a little hay for the lion cubs."

Big Tom was one of the keepers who worked cats, birds, and reptiles. His team was more specialized, with him handling the cats, William Ross the reptiles, and Jacob Zeigler the birds. Big Tom was way too large to fit into the bird cages or the reptile boxes.

"I was going to throw some down," Tom said. "But Gunther is up there with one of his girlfriends."

Neither Tom nor Matthew was surprised. Gunther was quite the ladies man and he regularly took them to the loft.

"Here," said Matthew. "We'll take some from the antelope stall. They're still locked out and it's clean."

Matthew liked big Tom. He was friendly, funny, and easy to work with.

"You need to finish that elephant," said Gunther from the top of the stairs.

Matthew was not quite finished with his chores in the barn, but he knew Gunther wanted him out of the way so he could bring down his girlfriend. Matthew knew better than to argue, so he placed the pitchfork he was holding into the cart and pushed it out the door.

The crowds around the elephant had thinned as the afternoon wore on, but as he drew near he saw a sight that made his step quicken. The dark haired girl he had seen earlier at Monkey Island was at the rope and it appeared her little brother had thrown his rattle into the elephant area.

"Looks like you could use another hand," he said as he strode up behind her.

"Oh," she said. "I am so embarrassed."

"No problem."

He knew he was never to enter the ring without his stick, but it was not in the cart. He had left it in the barn. Bwana was several yards away, throwing dust over his back. Matthew hesitated, then pushed up the rope and walked quickly over to retrieve the rattle. He picked it up and turned to show her, but the smile left him when he saw the look of horror on her face. He wanted to run, but his feet were frozen to the spot. She opened her mouth to scream but he did not hear the sound. Bwana hit him from behind, wrapping his trunk around Matthew's legs and yanking his feet from under him. He drove the zookeeper into the ground with his forehead crushing the life out of him. It was over in an instant. Blood oozed from Matthew James' mouth as his lifeless eyes stared at the sky and the elephant ambled back to the other side of the pen to resume throwing dust.

25

"Is this true?" asked Mayor Jasper Beneman. He was waving the morning edition of the newspaper. "Did Griffith really send this kid into a pen with a killer elephant?"

"He did," said Bertram Wallace without looking up from his own copy. "It says so right here in my newspaper."

"Why would he do that?"

"Because he is incompetent," replied Wallace as he folded his paper into his lap. "Look, Jasper. Calvin Griffith and his people are ruining that zoo. He's a farmer who doesn't know anything about zoos, parks, or anything else that is important to that operation. We need to get him out of there and get someone who is trained in park management."

"Someone like your son Robert, I suppose," said Beneman absently. "I believe I've heard this story before."

Beneman and Bertie Wallace were regulars at the Downtown Athletic Club. They often sat in its plush, paneled rooms sipping brandy and smoking cigars, and a frequent topic of conversation for the mayor and the newspaper publisher was the growing zoo and who should run it. The Mayor just wanted the zoo to be successful. Like any good politician, he recognized the potential for votes from people who appreciated the popular attraction. Bertie Wallace, on the other hand, couldn't have cared less about popular opinion. He was the owner and publisher of the local newspaper. He created public opinion. He liked to control things and he wanted to place his son in charge of the zoo so he could rule it like he ruled so much of the rest of the town. And, of course, there was the issue of money – lots of money. The Federal government was pouring money into local projects all over the nation through its Works Progress Administration, or WPA. The government paid the wages and the community provided the resources. The funds were usually distributed under the guidance of a military or ex-military man.

"There's a new wrinkle to the story, Jasper," said Bertie as he blew a stream of smoke to the ceiling. "A new wrinkle that could bring a lot of money to the community."

Jasper looked up from his newspaper and Bertie knew he had the Mayor's attention.

"Last year," Bertie began, "The federal government distributed over a billion dollars to the states under the watchful eyes of Harry Hopkins, Roosevelt's man at the WPA. Each State and local area has an overseer who is on the payroll and who ensures that the money is spent correctly."

"I know all that."

"A twelve per cent State match is a good deal, and an average to each State should be about twenty million. Our State received thirty five million and we only had to match ten per cent."

"So what?" replied Jasper. He knew that, as well.

"We're doing well because Senator Dobbs supported Roosevelt's New Deal back in thirty-five, and we'll do even better now that my son just got a job in Dobbs' local office."

The Mayor knew that most of the Federal dollars were going to the bigger cities. He was pleased to have received the one hundred fifty thousand dollars for the elephant house, but he wanted more. Other cities were building amphitheaters, swimming pools, and sewer systems. His allotment had been for street paving and the zoo.

"What's his job," asked the Mayor with interest.

"Administrative Assistant," replied the proud father. "He'll be Colonel John Taylor's right-hand man, traveling the State and reporting on projects. He will even be recommending new projects."

Bertie now had the Mayor's full attention. This was the break he had been hoping for. Their community would finally receive some attention.

"So, I guess you don't need the zoo anymore."

"On the contrary. The zoo is where most of the money will go."

"What?" sputtered the Mayor. "Why?"

"Robert's future is here, not as some government flunky. He'll help build the zoo, and then he'll come back and run it. That's the deal."

"But the city needs more than that," Jasper pleaded. "We need infrastructure to support growth – and to support the zoo."

"OK'" said Bertie. "We'll get what we need. Find someone to draw up plans for the zoo.

James Malone woke up with a start. It was too quiet. The ship's engines had stopped for the first time since they had left Capetown two weeks ago and they still had another week before they would arrive in New York harbor. It was odd how the rumble of the engines vibrated the entire ship, but he never noticed it until they stopped. The calm was eerie and a bit worrisome. They were in the middle of the Atlantic, they had been through rough seas, stormy nights, and endless days with no land in sight. He was anxious for landfall, but they would never get there without the engines running. He pulled on his short pants and canvas shoes, and bounded down the stairs to the deck.

"What's wrong?" he asked the captain as he burst into the wheel-house.

"Nothing," replied the bearded man with the clipped German accent. He wore a dirty white shirt and a cigarette dangled from his lips. "We must do repairs. We lubricate bearings, check linkages after storm, then we underway."

James was relieved. From the wheelhouse of the massive freighter, he had a commanding view of the deck in front of him. The Bremerhaven was a German ship with a German crew. They had treated him well because, he assumed, of his cargo – animals for American zoos. The ship rocked gently in the calm waters and he had a fleeting fear that they would not be able to restart the engines and they would be stranded in the middle of the ocean.

The six giraffes were in pens on the deck, three on each side of the hatch cover just in front of the wheelhouse tower. The large hoofed animals and the carnivores were in crates that were lashed to the top of the hatch cover and the more delicate birds and reptiles were below-decks in their crates. This was the first calm day they had had in nearly a week and most of the animals had not eaten in that time. He hoped they would be back on their feed today. He had only lost one animal, a crowned crane that had died when they were still in sight of land. He had worried about what to do with the carcass, but the captain had set him straight. He had it tossed over the side.

Conversations with the captain were awkward and formal. There was not much small talk, so James left the wheelhouse with a nod. He made his way down to the deck where he uncovered the stacks of hay and bags of grain. Most of it was wet, but he could still use it until it began to grow mold. With any luck, that would not be for several days and, by then, he should be near landfall. The morning feed for the hoofed stock was a couple of handfuls of grain which he scooped out of a bucket. The giraffes had a wooden trough that ran along the top edge of their pen. He walked along the elevated hatch cover to dump in the grain.

The other hoofed animals were in wooden crates that had a lift-up sliding door at the front and back ends. Each door had two nails side by side, one in the door and one nail in the crate, with a one-foot long piece of wire tied to each nail. This allowed the doors to slide open about a foot for feeding at the front end and raking out manure at the other. He went down line of crates and shoved a scoop of grain into each crate. He had six zebras, three young eland antelope, and two baby Cape buffalo. He also had some carnivores – two lions, two hyenas, and four caracals – in crates. They were on a different hatch, away from the prey animals, and in metal-lined crates. They received a chunk of horsemeat every few days and he would feed them later that day.

After he had checked and fed everything on the deck. He climbed down the metal stairs to the hold to check the rest of his cargo. The bright, sunny day turned to gloom and the fresh sea air evaporated into a stale mixture of sweat and fuel as he descended into the bowels of the ship. He passed one of the young crew members as he made his way along the narrow corridor.

"Gut morgen," he said, trying out one of the few German phrases he knew.

"Morgen," came the reply.

In the cavernous cargo hold, one section to the right of the door had been walled-off for the animals. One large box with a canvas top held the three remaining crowned cranes. A second large box contained a dazzling assortment of twenty colorful songbirds – bee eaters, weavers, sunbirds, and more. He knew and loved them all because birds were his specialty. Next to the birds was another pile of crates that he was not so fond of – the snakes. These were boxes he would not open because they could last the twenty day voyage without being fed. Though he had not seen them, he knew he had an African rock python in one box, some cobras and black mambas in another, and an assortment of ten or more snakes of unknown identity in the third large box.

After he checked everything and was satisfied that all was well, he turned to clamber out of the claustrophobic bowels of the ship, when the floor gave a lurch and a rumble rattled his chest. His alarm gave way to relief as he realized that the engines had just come to life. They were back on their way to New York.

Bobby set the two buckets into the bottom of the boat and stepped carefully in after them. They had come onto Monkey Island filled with fruits and vegetables and they were leaving with the poop and refuse from yesterday's feeding. The island was home to three capuchin and four spider monkeys, all former pets who had been donated to the zoo. It was one of the nicer animal areas in the zoo because the animals were not caged. They were free to roam the island, climb on its wooden towers, and walk around on its ropes like they were on jungle vines. Keeper access was by a boat connected to a rope that was fastened at each shoreline. The keeper stood in the boat and pulled himself along, hand over hand, in whichever direction he needed to go. Since these species of monkeys could not swim, the system worked pretty well.

"What took you so long over there?"

Bobby looked up startled. He had just arrived on the other shore and had not yet looked up from the rope he was pulling.

"The island was a mess," he replied to Gunther. "How long since it's been cleaned?"

He was in no mood for this pompous German's criticism. He was still shaken by the kid's death on Saturday and he blamed the supervisor for not paying more attention to the danger. He hauled the buckets to shore, tied up the boat, and stood to confront his accuser. They were evenly matched in height, but Bobby outweighed Gunther by about twenty pounds. Bobby had the look of a fighter while Gunther, everyone knew, was a lover. He just liked to talk big.

"Is there a problem here?" Alvin Doyle, the zoo foreman and the superintendent's chief assistant had stopped a few yards away and was sizing up the situation.

There wasn't much about Al Doyle's appearance that commanded respect. He was of average height and build with a mop of reddish-blond hair over a broad freckled face. He was quiet in voice and demeanor and walked with a nervous halting gait. The only thing about his appearance that made people take notice was his prosthetic left arm. It was an articulated contraption that did not look all that real because much of it was actually made from steel and painted a flesh color. The artificial hand was made from a material called empire cloth, which was basically cotton coated with oil, and a leather upper arm piece was used to strap the arm to the shoulder.

Al had grown up around the zoo, was there when it opened, and knew more about animals than anyone who worked there, including the superintendent. But he had come back from the Great War missing more than an arm. He had suffered shell-shock and he could not forget the horrors of the battlefield. He would never view life the same way.

"No problem," said Bobby without taking his eyes off of the German. "We were just discussing the cleaning on Monkey Island."

Gunther did not reply, but he held Bobby's gaze. Al did everything he could to avoid confrontation, so he chose to ignore the obvious animosity. He walked quickly away without another word.

"If you have something to say to me, go ahead," Gunther said.

"Why did you send that kid to take care of an animal he knew nothing about?" Bobby began.

"It was not my idea," Gunther replied. "If you have a problem with his death, you need to speak to someone higher than me."

"Like who?"

"Like Alvin Doyle, or perhaps the Super himself."

"Griffith?" said Bobby with a laugh. "He would never have sent that kid to his death."

"Believe what you will," said Gunther. "But it was not my idea."

Bobby did not like the good looking German, but he believed he was telling the truth. He looked pained by the tragedy that had struck on Saturday. Bobby decided to let it go.

"The island is done, what do you want me to do next?"

The sign over the door said *Carnivores* but everyone called it the Lion House. It had been built ten years earlier and, though it showed its age in the form of rust and dust, it was a large, solid structure that anchored the center of the zoo. Its stone masonry and iron bars has housed a variety of animals over the years. Currently, it held the adult lions, Leo and Leona, and their three cubs. It was also home to a jaguar, a leopard, and two tigers. In a few weeks, the newest residents would arrive – two hyenas.

Tom Chandler was perfectly suited to this area. He was large, like his animals, and the cage floors were raised so he didn't need to bend over to service them. He could simply walk along the service aisle between the public area and the caging, sweeping, hosing, and shoveling poop and refuse into buckets. The cages had a generous slope to the front where water and urine flowed into a trough which led to a drain. If he did need to climb into a cage, there was a rolling step-stair that made it easy on the big man.

Each cage had an indoor and an outdoor area and animals could be safely shifted anywhere in the building through a series of heavy iron sliding gates. The public entered the building at one end, passing through a vestibule which led to an office on one side and a kitchen on the other, and through a second set of doors into the main exhibit hall. The cages were arranged in a row down each side of the building. On the left were the leopard and the lions, and on the right were the jaguar, the tigers, and spaces for the hyenas.

Tom turned to the sound of footsteps echoing down the hall. He knew who it was before he saw him. Alvin was making his morning rounds.

"How are the cubs?" asked Al without preamble.

"Fine. She's taking good care."

They walked to the other end of the building – Al in the public area and Tom on the animal side of the railing – and stopped in front of the last cage. The lioness was lying in a thick bed of hay at the back of the cage under the wooden bench. Three squirming cubs were at her belly as she watched the two men intently. This was her second litter and they expected no problems. She had raised the first two cubs until they were sold to the circus.

"The new hyenas should be in New York next week," Al said. "The train ought to get them here next Thursday or Friday."

"I'm ready for them," said Tom, glancing over Al's shoulder to the empty cage across the hall. "Just let me know when to pick them up."

Al turned to leave and raised his hand in goodbye, and Tom returned to his cleaning. He walked back down the hall to retrieve his hose from the front of the leopard's cage. He felt a little wobbly and knew it was time to return to his office for a break. That's what was on his mind when he absently reached for the hose that lay in the trough just outside the bars of the cage. She was on the bench at the back of the cage, but before he could draw his hand away, she was there. Her paw extended through the space under the bars and one needle-sharp claw caught the fleshy portion of the bottom of his hand. It dug deep and had a good hold, but he instinctively jerked back and tore free, ripping open a small gash. He stumbled back against the guardrail, startled and embarrassed covering the wound with his other hand. The warm blood oozed between his fingers. That should never happen to an experienced zookeeper.

After he regained a little composure, he staggered back to his office, closed the door, and sat at his desk. He opened the drawer to his right and pulled out a bottle of whiskey along with a box of clean rags. He poured some of the whiskey over the wound and wrapped his hand. He then took a long pull and leaned back to feel the hot alcohol sting his throat. This would be the first of many drinks that day as he tried to drown the memories that washed around inside his head – memories of his family and that terrible night of the fire. He was barely aware of the guttural rumble that Leo made before he did one of his roars. It began as a deep cuffing sound, like he was clearing his throat, and rose to a roaring crescendo that could be heard a mile away.

A zoo director who lives on the grounds never has a day off. Even though he had put in a long, stressful weekend dealing with the death of a zookeeper, Calvin Griffith was working at his house on the property. He barely noticed the roar of the lion because he had heard it so many times before, but when the volume increased he knew his front door was opening. He waited in his office expectantly and was not surprised to see Al poke his head around the corner.

"You busy?" he asked.

"Just writing a letter to Matthew's parents." Cal sat back in his chair looking relieved to avoid his task.

"I saw you down by the tree this morning." The copper beech tree Cal had planted when his wife died had grown into quite a specimen. It was over twenty feet tall and the trunk was as big around as he was. Cal could be seen there on many mornings, but especially on those days when he had something on his mind.

Al looked around the dining room that Cal used as an office. He wasn't sure how Cal's wife Bea put up with the mess. The round, oak dining room table hadn't been used for eating in years. The room was strewn with boxes and papers. It smelled of animals.

"When's the new guy coming?" Al asked.

"Should be here in a few weeks. His ship docks in New York the first of next week and he'll need to get everything off-loaded. He'll ride the train here with the hyenas, birds, and snakes."

Cal had met James Malone back in November. He was due to graduate from the University of Chicago with a bachelor's degree in zoology and he wanted a zoo job. When Cal had received the cable from Schultz Exotics offering free animals if he would supply a keeper for the journey from South Africa, he had offered James – even though the only experience he had was as a volunteer at the Chicago's Lincoln Park Zoo. James would be the zoo's first curator and the only person on staff with any scientific training.

"Hello," said a voice as the screen door squeaked open.

"That you Simon?" Cal replied.

Simon Poston slipped his boots off at the door and walked into the room in stocking feet. He was a light-skinned black man who could easily pass for white. That is one reason he had risen to an unusually high position for a Negro of that era – along with the fact that he was smart, resourceful, and experienced in all types of construction. He did have one handicap to overcome. He had a developed a crooked spine as a child that resulted in a hunch-back.

It not only did not affect his work, it seemed to make him stronger. Calvin had used him for odd jobs around the zoo for years, and he had been a construction supervisor when the lion house was built a decade earlier. When the City had needed a superintendent to run the government work projects at the zoo, Simon jumped at the chance when no one else would step forward.

"Forms are set and we're ready to pour concrete at the elephant house," said Simon.

"Did you figure out how to anchor the rails to the walls?" asked Al.

"We've placed steel plates in the wall. We'll bolt the rails to them. That'll be plenty strong enough to hold an elephant."

"And what about the lake?" asked Cal. "When will we start on that?"

"Mule-teams are moving in this afternoon," Simon replied. "They can start digging tomorrow."

The lake was to be a new feature in the zoo. It consisted of digging out a large area and letting the creek that already runs through the park fill it.

"I need you two to come help me stake it out."

Cal shook his head. "Al can do it. I've got to finish this letter."

"I have a guy who says he can carve us a stone elephant," said Simon, changing the subject.

"What?" said Al as he glanced at his boss. "Who's going to pay for that?"

"Federal Art Project," he replied simply. "Its government money that's available to pay out of work artists. This guy is from Poland and looks like he knows what he's doing. He said he'll carve the elephant for free is we'll hire him to do more sculptures around the zoo."

"I guess we can't refuse that offer," said Cal. "Now you two get out of here and let me finish this."

26

"How long are you going to wait?" asked Adam Swindler.

"As long as it takes," replied big Tom. "Why aren't you two in school?" he glanced at the boys leaning on the rail next to him.

Adam looked at Danny Tyler but said nothing. They had skipped school to come to the zoo and had lucked into seeing some new animals arrive. They had watched big Tom direct the workers as they hoisted the heavy, metal-lined, wooden crate into the cage and shove it against the sliding door to the adjoining cage. Tom had tied it in place with a heavy rope and opened the cage door. Then he directed one of the workers – because he was too heavy to do so – to climb onto the crate and lift the door. They had expected an animal to come charging out, but after what seemed an eternity, nothing had happened.

Behind them, leaning back on the railing on the far side of the aisle, stood Calvin, Al, and James Malone. James had arrived by train late yesterday with the animals and they had spent the afternoon transferring them to the zoo and unloading some of them. The young Cape buffalo had gone into one of the hoofed stock stalls. The birds remained in their travel cages in another hoofed stock stall. The snakes were to be transferred into glass-fronted cages here in the lion house as soon as they were completed. The last of the animals they would deal with this day were the hyenas.

"What can you tell me about hyenas?" asked Alvin.

"These are a couple of young brown hyenas, maybe eight months old," James began. "Don't know what sex they are. They are from southern Africa and will get to be about eighty or ninety pounds when they are grown – about the size of a German shepherd. When they come out of the crate, you'll see they have longer front legs and a squat back-end, so they're not fast runners. They generally eat meat that they steal from lions, cheetahs, and other predators. But their most prominent feature is their big head and massive jaws. I'm told they can crush a man's arm with one bite."

Cal was impressed. He had hired James to be his first college-educated curator and the twenty-two year old ornithologist did not disappoint. The slender, bespectacled, young man had traveled to Africa, escorted a ship-load of animals back to America, and was unloading them like he had been doing it all his life. Larger zoos had, he knew, curators of mammals, birds, and reptiles. A smaller zoo had to make do with a general curator, and James seemed perfectly suited for the job. Cal, at 63, was ready to begin the process of turning over the reins to a professional. He knew Al would be around for a while, but Al was not interested in running the zoo. James had already assembled an impressive collection. Now they needed to build them some cages.

"There he is," said one of the boys excitedly. "He's coming out."

With that, the animal ducked back to the safety of the crate.

"You'd better be quiet," said Tom crossly, "Or I'll have to clear you out of here."

The boys said nothing, and after a few minutes, a couple of heads peered out of the crate. They walked out as though they were attached at the hip, staying carefully at the back of the cage. Tom moved quickly to close the sliding gate and he directed the workmen to drag the now-empty crate out of the cage. It smelled awful and he would need to hose it down and apply some bleach. The crowd watched the young animals cower in the back corner of the cage in their bed of straw. They had clearly never seen anything like the scene before them and it would take them some time to adjust.

"Let's go to lunch," Cal said to his two companions. "Our construction manager, Simon, is going to join us and you can meet my wife and my daughter," he continued, addressing James.

It was a short walk to Calvin's residence at the back corner of the property. The old house was small but well-built. Bea had installed a white picket fence to set it apart from the zoo and she had developed a beautiful garden around it. They entered under a trellis of wisteria. To anyone who had to endure the smells of a zoo, it was a fragrant transition. A pair of dogwood trees flanked the walkway, golden forsythia lined the fence, and the lawn was edged with daffodils. James stopped halfway up the sidewalk to marvel at the scene.

"My wife's the gardener," Calvin said proudly.

Before James could reply, two children burst out of the house.

"Hey, Gramps," said the boy as they tore past.

"My grandchildren, James and Sally," said Calvin. "Off to terrorize the zoo."

Bea met them at the door and patted Cal affectionately on his ample stomach. She had aged well, her long, dark hair turning to gray, but otherwise youthful in appearance. Her Cuban ancestry showed in her dark eyes and white teeth. After the introductions, they moved into the large kitchen where a table had been set and where their daughter Raven and her friend Lizzie Harner sat. A knock at the back door meant the final luncheon guest had arrived, Simon Poston. The long table and its miss-matched chairs would comfortably seat six, but today it was set for seven. The lunch was simple with ham, cheese, coarse bread, and fresh vegetables from the garden. If Calvin had wanted to impress his new recruit, he and his wife had certainly succeeded. They had also unknowingly succeeded in impressing Simon and Lizzie, who were seated next to each other.

"So, Mr. Malone," began Raven when they had all been served. "Tell us about your trip to Africa."

"Call me James," he said. He had just taken a bite of food so he paused to chew. "It was the trip of a lifetime for a zoologist. I spent a week touring Southern Africa before I boarded the ship in Capetown. The broker had assembled all the animals and oversaw the loading, so all I had to do was care for the animals until we reached New York."

"How long were you at sea?" asked Simon.

"About three weeks," he replied. "That's when the real fun began. I was seasick, the animals went off feed, and one of the cranes died. I spent my days worried that I would arrive in New

York empty-handed, with everything dead and thrown over the side."

He laughed and everyone joined in. "But it turned out fine. The animals and I all regained our appetites and, except for a storm or two, the journey was pretty uneventful."

"Where are you from?" asked Bea changing the subject.

Before he could answer, a loud knock turned their attention to the back door and to a man who slowly entered the kitchen. He wore rough, dirty clothes and pulled a ragged cap from his head. His beard disguised his appearance so it took a minute before Raven sprang from the table and grabbed him in a fierce embrace.

"Buddy," she exclaimed.

James scarcely knew what to make of the situation. He gathered from the conversations that this scruffy, forty-something man was Calvin's long-lost son, who hadn't been seen in these parts in twenty-five years. He also gathered that Calvin was not happy about his sudden re-appearance, most likely because of his failure to communicate his whereabouts or even whether he was alive in all those years. He was fascinated by Buddy Griffith's life story. His baseball career was cut short by the war, where he spent four years overseas tending teams of horses. After the war, he signed-on with the circus as a horse trainer before shifting his attention to elephants. He recently left the circus for reasons he did not appear ready to discuss, but he claimed to have nearly twenty years experience as an elephant trainer. James was now the curator of a zoo elephant that had recently killed a man. Buddy's sudden appearance was too good to be true. He did not want Cal to drive this opportunity away.

"He's an elephant trainer," James said tentatively. "Maybe we could use him with Bwana."

"Not a chance," Cal was fiercely cutting a slice of ham and did not look up. He had just asked his son to leave and he was followed by Raven and Al. Simon and Lizzie had also asked to be excused and left.

James could see there was no point in arguing, but he had no intention of letting this opportunity slip away.

"I'd better get over to the lion house and help Bill Ross uncrate some snakes," he said more to Bea than Cal. "I thank you for lunch, Mrs. Griffith."

He left the house and turned purposefully toward the lion house, but he was looking around for any sign of Buddy as he walked. He saw Al standing in the doorway to the hoofed stock barn and began to make his way over there by walking around the lion house and sneaking in the other door to the barn.

"Did Cal send you over here?" asked Al defensively.

"No," James replied holding up both hands. "He doesn't know I'm here. We need someone to work with Bwana and I wondered if he might help us"

"I was just asking him," said Al.

"You keep the old man off my back and I'll help," said Buddy lifting a shaking hand to light the cigarette that dangled from his lips. He looked around carefully. "And I'll need somewhere to stay."

"You can stay with me and Buckley," Raven said. "But I don't know how you're going to train an elephant without Pa finding out."

"Leave that to me," said Al. "I'll figure something out."

The snakes were in large cotton bags some individually and others in groups. There was no way of knowing which snakes were in which bags or even what kind of snakes they had. The broker had hired natives to go out into the bush to capture the reptiles and paid them by the snake to bring them to him. James' strategy was to dump the snakes into large boxes, sort them out, and place them into the glass front of cases later.

They had taken over Tom's office and placed three large boxes around the walls. The boxes had hinged lids and were tightly constructed so nothing could escape. James and William Ross had closed the door and sealed all openings before they began unloading.

He knew from the agent that he had a huge python in one box, some venomous cobras and black mambas in another, and an assortment of ten or more snakes of unknown identity in the third box. His plan was to leave the cobras and the mambas for last. They would go in their own boxes. The assortment of snakes would need to be dumped and sorted. He figured they would start with the python, since it was just one snake. He knew it was a big one since the box weighed well over one-hundred pounds. This snake was said to be over ten feet long. They placed the box on a clear spot of the floor and pried open the lid which had been nailed shut for shipment. As William pushed down on the pry-bar and forced up the lid, James peered carefully into the box to see if the snake was secure in the bag. He was astonished to see a head as big as his fist and two beady, black eyes peering back at him. He slammed the lid and sat on it.

"Jesus!" he said with a wild look in his eyes. "This one's not bagged."

William backed up a step. He loved reptiles and amphibians. He had been catching snakes, lizards, and frog all his life. But he had never dealt with anything like a python. He had seen photographs of them swallowing pigs and knew they got big enough to eat a person.

"What do we do?" William asked. He was eyeing the crate that James sat upon.

"Let me think."

James' mind was racing. He was responsible for transferring these deadly animals and he had no idea what to do. Birds were his specialty. He did have the glimmer of an idea, but he needed time to think.

"Let's nail this back down," he said. "We'll wait to uncrate them when their display cases are ready, that way we won't have to handle them twice."

"Fine with me," said a relieved William.

"I'm going to help Jacob with the birds," James said without leaving his perch. "Hammer these nails in so I can get up."

The tool room in the hoofed stock barn seemed like an unlikely place for an office, but it actually worked quite well. Bobby had cleaned it up, moved the tools to the side, and brought in some old chairs and an electric coffee percolator. It was a quiet place to get out of the rooming house and have his morning coffee. Gunther was late most days so the earlier he arrived the better. He especially enjoyed it now that he and Simon had discovered their common interest in current events and politics. Bobby listened to the radio in his rooming house and Simon at his Masonic Lodge. They were an unlikely pair, the out of work businessman and the Negro construction boss, but their enjoyment of politics and Edward R. Murrow kept them interested, even at 6:30 on a Saturday morning.

"The WPA employs millions of people," said Simon, sipping his coffee. "It constructs public buildings and roads; it feeds children and distributes food, clothing, and housing; and it trains people for new jobs. How can that not be a good idea?"

"Because it wastes federal dollars on projects that are not needed or wanted." Bobby replied. "Most of those projects are made-up for political considerations. Roosevelt's building a nationwide voter base with all of us out of work workers."

"Come on," Simon's annoyance began to show, "the paper says that general productivity, business profits, and wages are back to their 1929 levels. Unemployment is still high, but it is lower than it was a few years ago."

"Propaganda," said Bobby. "That's what they want you to believe. The We Poke Along is just buying Roosevelt some time in office"

"I take it you are not a fan of Roosevelt," said James from outside the door.

Bobby and Simon looked up, surprised to see anyone else there that early in the morning.

"I'm here to start feeding the birds," he said. "Mind if I sit in?"

"Not at all," said Bobby. "Care for a cup of coffee?"

"Thanks. So what are you all talking about?"

"We just like to talk about what's going on in the world," said Simon, "We both listen to the radio the night before and argue about politics and such."

"So what do you think about the crisis in Europe?" asked James.

"Scary stuff," Bobby replied. "Hitler is a maniac."

"I hear he's rounding up Jews," said Simon. "I wonder what's going to happen to them?"

"Edward R. Murrow seems to think war is in the air," said James. "They're already at it in Spain."

"I hear we have a new elephant man," said Bobby, changing the subject.

"It appears that way," Simon replied. "But it sure is a strange situation. Calvin's long-lost son appeared at lunch yesterday."

"Sure did," James agreed, shaking his head.

"He spent years with the circus as an elephant handler," James continued. "He's just what we need, but Calvin ran him off."

"Well Calvin better find someone soon," said Bobby. "That elephant is going to kill someone else if he's not careful."

"We haven't lost him yet," said James. "Al is planning to work around Calvin. We may need your help."

"You sure he won't see us?" asked Buddy.

"He's never up this early," said Al. "And even if he is, the kitchen's on the back side of the house."

They stood in the dim, early morning light just outside the circle of rope that contained the elephant. Buddy had a thick stick in his hand that had a metal hook and point embedded in one end. It was about four feet long and he twirled it comfortably as he sized up the beast.

"What's his name?" he asked.

"Bwana."

"How did he kill the guy?"

"Did a head stand on him," said Al. "Then walked away like nothing happened."

Buddy was silent for a moment as he continued to study the elephant, then he suddenly stepped inside the rope.

"Bwana, move up," he commanded loudly.

The elephant lifted his head with surprise.

"Bwana, move up," Buddy said again.

Bwana fanned his ears out, dropped his head, and lunged forward, but Buddy stood his ground and raised his stick. He smacked the elephant between the eyes with all his might. The elephant stopped, but Buddy kept swinging, hitting the elephant repeatedly until it backed up a step. Al was amazed. This ten-thousand pound animal was backing down from a two hundred pound man with a stick.

"Bwana, move up," Buddy repeated.

The elephant did not hesitate this time. He walked forward until he was nearly touching Buddy's chest. Buddy was still for a moment before moving to the elephant's left side just behind the front leg.

"Bwana, go on away," he commanded, using his hook to pull the animal behind the front leg.

The elephant began to walk, though he could only go in a circle, with Buddy keeping step.

"Baseball season starts next week," Buddy said casually to Al as he walked by. "Who do you like this year?"

Willow Creek was flowing at a pretty good rate at the moment, which made Simon's task very difficult. He had been asked to excavate a lake as a new feature for the zoo. He had plenty of WPA manpower, twelve mule-teams, and no heavy equipment. All of which meant he had to devise a pretty ingenious plan.

First, he built a diversion channel to take the creek around the area he wanted to excavate. Then he started digging and moving the earth into an embankment that encircled the new lake. He had men with shovels filling wheelbarrows. He had mule teams pulling steel-toothed rakes to till the soil and other teams pulling scoop-buckets to drag the soil up the sides of the lake. At the end nearest the river he would place an overflow weir above the old creek bed to allow the excess water to flow to the river. He envisioned a nice, wrought iron bridge that would cross the waterfall and complete the promenade walkway that would encircle the lake. He also envisioned himself standing on that bridge looking at the swans swimming in the lake with Elizabeth Harner at his side.

He couldn't stop thinking about their lunch together yesterday. She had looked at him like he was the most special man in the world with those dark eyes. She smelled of lavender and when she smiled the whole room lit up. She was a widow whose husband died eight years ago. She had never remarried, choosing instead to look after her aging father. Simon, on the other hand, had never married. He told himself he was married to his work and had no time for women but, truth be told, he was a little afraid of women and found it easier to avoid them in the first place. He had never even been on a proper date. Now, he was unsure what to do next with Mrs. Harner.

He turned back to the zoo site and looked over towards the elephant house. He was a man of vision who could see things as they might be, and not be restricted by how they were. The zoo had so many possibilities. They could build cages for all the birds and reptiles that were coming in, perhaps even new buildings like they had at the bigger zoos. He hoped this new kid could make things happen.

The walls of the elephant house were finished and the forms were being taken down today. He could see the glowing lights of the welder who was fastening the heavy rails that would serve as the elephant cage. As he began to walk towards the construction site, he was still puzzling over how they would hoist the timbers for the roof with no crane. He had stockpiled the 12 inch by 12 inch wooden beams that would span the top of the building and had a team of men hewing-out the rafters that would hold up the roof itself. This was the kind of challenge he enjoyed turning over in his mind, the kind of challenge that kept him awake at night.

"Hello," said a voice from behind, startling him into a quick stop and turn around.

"Oh, hello," he said. "I didn't hear you coming up."

It was Elizabeth Harner.

27

"What did you think about the Hindenburg disaster?" James asked as he walked in for his morning coffee in the hoofed stock barn. "Did you hear that on the radio last night?"

"We were just talking about that," said Simon.

It was one of the most dramatic moments in radio history. The German airship Hindenburg had burst into flames as it was about to land in Lakehurst, New Jersey and the horror of the incident was conveyed live by a reporter at the scene. The crash killed 36 of the 97 people on board.

"How could that happen?" asked James. "The reporter said is just exploded for no reason."

"They have giant bags inside them that are filled with Hydrogen gas," Simon explains. "It is lighter than air and that's what makes them float. Unfortunately, it is also extremely flammable. Anything could set it off – lightening, a spark, even sabotage."

"I worked on the ground crew for the USS Akron back in '32," Bobby said. "I was there at Camp Kearny when three sailors on the ground crew were carried up by the mooring lines when the she climbed unexpectedly. Two of the men fell to their deaths."

"Amazing airships," mused Simon. "The big ones are nearly 800 feet long, a hundred feet in diameter, and able to go seventy miles in one hour. They can stay in the air for days and fly thousands of miles."

"How do you know all that?" asked James.

"Because he's a genius," Bobby chimed in.

"When are we going to start some new buildings?" Simon asked James. "There's money available for the workers. All you need to do is find the materials."

"I know," James replied. "I want to see if Cal can find an architect to work with us. We need to plan the whole zoo."

"You need a master plan," said Bobby.

James and Simon looked at each other, then at Bobby. His shaggy, graying hair and rumpled, stained clothes disguised the sharp-eyed look of someone who had more to offer than shoveling animal manure. Simon had been sure that Robert Crofton was a professional who was down on his luck or hiding from his past – or both.

"What do you know about master planning?" asked Simon.

Bobby paused. He knew the game was up. "I'm a landscape architect and a civil engineer."

"Wow," said James.

A pause hung in the air as the three struggled with what to say next. James was hoping Calvin could find someone with those very credentials. Simon needed someone to handle the technical aspects of design process. And Bobby, although he knew he could do the job, wasn't sure he wanted it. After a moment, they shifted in unison and rose from their seats.

"I'm going to say something to Cal," said Simon. We need to get this project moving.

"Get what moving?" asked Gunther appearing in the open doorway.

"Nothing," Bobby said sharply. "We're ready to go to work."

Gunther looked carefully at Bobby. He had heard everything and now liked this new guy even less.

"What do mean 'None of these will do'?" said Simon in frustration. "You have ten pieces to choose from. Surely one of them will work."

"They are all flawed," said Arthur Nowitzki. "They must have come from the same seam."

Simon and his sculptor were behind the elephant house looking at pieces of limestone that Nowitzki had ordered for his carving. Each piece was five or six feet square and weighed about a ton. Moving these enormous stones was no easy task and Simon was tired of this fussy man causing him all this bother. He was almost sorry he had brought him onboard.

"Look," said Nowitzki, running his knarled hand over one of the stones. "See this dark brown seam. It runs through the stone. It runs through all the stones. When my chisel hits this, the stone will break along this line."

Simon removed his floppy, soft-brimmed cap and scratched his head. He didn't have time for this. He had to get the elephant house and the lake finished before cold weather sets-in next this fall. He would need to plan new cages for the animals Jimmy Malone had brought back from Africa. There was talk of a new bird house, a new reptile house, and even an amphitheater. And now, with Bobby Crofton's talent brought to light, maybe even a new master plan for the whole zoo. No, he had no time to argue with this opinionated Polish man with the big nose and the wheezing cough.

"I am not getting you any more stones," Simon said finally. "Just use one of these."

"Can't do it," said Nowitzki. "I'd be wasting my time. I'll quit first."

Simon threw up his hands in frustration.

"Then quit," he said, and walked away.

James sat in Cal's office and looked around. He wondered how anyone could function in this mess. If he ever got an office it would be neat and orderly. He'd know where everything was and would be able to retrieve documents in minutes. Cal had to shuffle papers constantly, and still failed to find what he was looking for.

"Whew," said Cal as he walked back into the room. "Had to take a leak."

James smiled. The old man wasn't one to mince words.

"So what's this big secret you and Simon have discovered?" he asked, settling into his chair.

"You know Robert Crofton, the new guy who works in hoofed stock?" asked James.

"Yes," Cal replied. "They call him Bobby. He doesn't look like a 'Bobby' to me. He looks like an out of work professional – a Mr. Robert Crofton."

"And that's just what he is," James replied. "Mr. Robert Crofton, Landscape Architect and Civil Engineer."

They sat in silence for a moment while James let this sink in.

"We need an architect to do our master plan for the zoo," Cal said finally. "Do you think he's interested?"

"I don't know," James rubbed his chin. "He didn't seem too enthused when Simon and I proposed it to him. It's almost like he's afraid to get involved – like he just wants to shovel shit and be left alone."

"Maybe he has something to hide," Cal suggested. "Maybe there's a reason he's out of work."

"There are millions out of work," said James. "The depression affected his industry just like everyone else's. Who hires landscape architects anymore?"

"Maybe you're right," Cal said. "I'll have a word with him. If he agrees, we'll have Simon put him on the Works payroll, but we'll need to find another zoo keeper first. I wonder if he has ever been to another zoo."

"So, Ida Mae Gottshaw," Gunther said sweetly. "How long have you worked in the Mayor's office?"

"Three weeks," she replied. "I was promoted from the typing pool."

"I'll bet you are quite the little typist."

Ida Mae rather liked the attention of this handsome, blond-haired German. She would gladly continue to sit through her lunch time to bask in his admiring gaze. She was not accustomed to this type of interest from a man. She knew she was not terribly attractive, but he did not seem to mind. She opened her mouth to reply, when the Mayor emerged from his office and motioned for Gunther top enter. He slipped a piece of paper into Ida Mae's hand as he passed her desk.

"I have news," he announced when the door was closed.

He was surprised to see Bertram Wallace standing at the window. He must have entered through the side door.

"Griffith may have found an architect to plan the zoo," said Gunther.

The Mayor and the newspaper man looked at each other with surprise.

"How?" asked Wallace, somewhat befuddled. "From where?"

"From the zoo," Gunther said. "He's a zookeeper Griffith hired back in March. He says he's an out of work architect."

"What's his name?" asked Wallace.

"Robert Crofton. They call him Bobby."

Wallace moved to the Mayor's desk and made a note.

"So, what do you want me to do?" Gunther asked.

"Nothing," they said in unison.

"You just keep watching and report back," Mayor Beneman addressed him for the first time.

"You said I would be rewarded."

"You will be rewarded," said Wallace impatiently. "Just keep your eyes and ears open."

"I want to be director of the zoo," said Gunther.

Wallace and Beneman looked at each other in surprise.

"That was never part of the deal," said the mayor. "You wanted money and a steady job at the zoo."

"Well," he said. "I've changed my mind. I want to be the director."

They knew that was not going to happen but told him they would consider his request and ushered him out the door.

"Looks like your son has some competition," said the mayor when Gunther had left.

Wallace continued to stare out the window without replying. He did not feel particularly threatened by these revelations but he did need time to consider his options. He already had a candidate for architect and one for builder, both of whom he knew he could control. And he had already talked to his son about the zoo position. Robert had not been particularly enthused about the prospect because he rather liked his position with Colonel Taylor. But Bertie Wallace would not be deterred.

Calvin walked slowly across the petting area, stepping carefully to avoid the animal droppings. Bobby had looked up when the gate slammed but did not move in his direction. He knew why the boss had come to call.

"Afternoon," Cal said brightly. "Beautiful day."

He looked to the sky, looked around the pen at the sheep and goats, then passed his gaze back to the zookeeper – who did not reply.

"I guess you know why I'm here," he continued.

"I'm not interested," Bobby said finally, avoiding Calvin's gaze. "I am not an architect anymore."

"What do you mean," said Calvin in frustration. "You don't become unqualified when you have professional qualifications."

Bobby raked on, shoveling the goat and sheep droppings into his wheelbarrow without further comment. Cal watched him for a few moments. He sensed a profound sadness in the man, a story untold. But he could see there was no changing his mind, so he turned and picked his way back across the pen.

"Hello."

Gunther jerked his feet off the desk, put down his newspaper, and sat upright. He had not expected to anybody this late in the afternoon, especially the bright female face that appeared coming up the steps to his loft office. It wasn't much of an office but it gave him the privacy that he needed. He had a small desk with a light over it, a comfortable wooden chair, and plenty of hay for bedding down his frequent female visitors.

"Ida Mae?" he asked incredulously.

She had transformed herself from the demure typist in a shapeless dress and hair in bun, into a lovely sexual female. Her long red hair framed a smooth, freckled face and her white blouse and long skirt revealed a spectacular figure. As she moved up the stairs and into the loft he was speechless.

"What are you doing here," he stammered, knowing full well that she was answering his invitation.

"What do you think I am doing here?" she said, as she leaned on his desk.

He stood up put his hands on her waist and kissed her. Without further conversation he led her around a stack of hay bales and into a secluded chamber in which blankets covered a bed of hay. No one was around this late in the evening so he was confident they would not be disturbed. He unbuttoned her blouse, dropped her skirt, and skillfully removed her underwear. She slid her hand up the inside of his leg and unbuttoned his trousers. They both stood there naked for a moment before lying down on the fresh, straw bedding.

28

"I see the Cardinals lost yesterday at Pittsburgh," said Buddy mockingly. "I guess Dizzy Dean had a bad day on the mound."

"Could we just pay attention here?" Al replied. "You're taking Bwana off the chain for the first time. Where are you going to walk him?"

"Relax. I'm going to keep him on hobbles," said Buddy, describing the short length of chain that would link his front legs together. "He can't run away."

"I'm not worried about him running away," said Al. "I'm worried about him hobbling over and crushing someone. Maybe even you."

"You're just mad because Gehrig and DiMaggio combined for seven hits and each hit a home run yesterday," Buddy crowed. "Beat the Athletics in Philly to go twelve and eight on the season."

"I'll put Johnny Mize and Joe Medwick up against your guys any day," Al said. "Besides, we've got thirteen wins to your twelve."

"We'll be happy to see you in the Series. Care to put some money on it?"

"I feel like I should tell Cal what we're up to," said Al.

Buddy held up a length of chain about six feet long and let it untangle. He laid it carefully on the ground and commanded the elephant to 'move up'. Buddy stood unmoving as the beast shuffled obediently to him.

"Bwana Steady," he said.

He touched behind the left front leg with his elephant hook and said 'foot'.

Bwana lifted his foot and waited until the chain was wrapped and secured like a bracelet. 'Alright' was the command to put the foot down. Buddy repeated the process with the other foot and released the long tether. For the first time in months, Bwana was loose and walking around the yard.

"Robert Crofton?" asked the dapper man leaning on the fence.

"Who wants to know?" Bobby replied, leaning on his rake.

The zoo was not yet open and he wondered how this man had found him in the petting zoo. He was a tall, thin, and in his late fifties or early sixties. He wore a nice suit, clean shoes, and a flat-topped straw hat.

"I'm Bertram Wallace," the man said without offering to shake hands. "I understand you have been offered a job designing the new zoo."

Bobby moved closer, eying him carefully.

"I turned that down," he said

The man appeared surprised. He reached inside his coat and pulled out a piece of paper.

"That's good," he appeared to study the document then looked Bobby in the eye. "I've been doing some checking on a Robert Crofton and it appears that you've had a troubled past – a building collapse that killed eleven children, fired for drunkenness, even an armed robbery."

"That's all in the past," Bobby growled. "I've paid my debt to society."

Bobby turned to walk away but Wallace did not move.

"This is my zoo," he said to Bobby's back. "You can keep your pathetic job raking goat shit, but if I hear your name mentioned again I'll have to let the community know about who you really are in my newspaper. Bobby turned to tell the man to beat-it, but he was blinded by the flash and pop of a camera. The news photographer had appeared out of nowhere.

"And the front-page article will be complete with your photo here at the zoo."

Bobby was still fuming mad an hour later as he listened to instructions from Gunther. The female African Cape buffalo was favoring her back, left hoof and they needed to catch her to have a closer look. The two animals were less than a year old, but they were big enough to be a handful for two people.

"Don't we need some more help?" asked Bobby.

"No," Gunther said. "I just want a quick look. If we need to treat it we'll do that later."

They leaned on the gate and looked into the stall. The male had been locked outside and the female clearly knew something was up. She paced at the door to the yard, mooing loudly. The plan, as Gunther explained it, was to push her quickly into a corner before she had time to run, and squeeze her against the wall. Bobby would take the head and Gunther the back end. That way Gunther could hold up the bad leg and have a look. It sounded like a good plan, except for the fact that she weighed over three hundred pounds and had those spikey little horns. Bobby had never done anything like this before. Gunther looked over at his partner.

"Are you OK with this?" he asked.

"Yes," Bobby replied with more confidence than he felt.

"You must grab her quickly and push in close," Gunther instructed, "So she can't get you with those horns. Don't hesitate."

"OK," said Bobby. "Let's do it."

They both stepped inside the pen and Gunther latched it behind them. The buffalo picked up her pacing and mooing, but Gunther moved with a quickness that caught Bobby off-guard. By the time Bobby got to the head, Gunther had grabbed her just in front of the back legs and was pressing her against the wall. The little calf twisted her head and front end into Bobby just as he made contact, bumping him into the middle of the stall.

"Get on her," Gunther yelled between clenched teeth.

Bobby jumped up off the floor and took another run at her, hitting her with his chest on her front shoulder. She barely moved, but he kept pushing.

"She's going down," Gunther said. "Let her go down and stay in close on her back. Watch those horns."

Bobby was too winded to reply but he kept up the pressure until she was lying down and he was on her neck. He could feel Gunther moving around but could not see what he was doing.

"She has a piece of wire stuck in her hoof," he said finally. "I'm going to try to pull it out."

She mooed loudly and thrashed, nearly throwing Bobby off again, but he held on.

"Got it," said Gunther. "We'll let go on the count of three."

"Wait," said Bobby. "Let me get my feet under me."

He shifted his weight and at Gunther's count of three, they both jumped up and scrambled to the gate. Bobby knew he hadn't done well. He didn't expect any kind words of encouragement from Gunther, and he didn't receive any. Gunther just walked away with a grunt. Bobby was sore, he was tired, and he was angry – angry with Gunther for not being more patient, angry with Bertram Wallace for threatening him, and angry with himself for letting both of them get to him. It was time to have a talk with Calvin. Maybe he was not cut out for zoo work.

"The lion house has to be the anchor point," James said pointing to the substantial building on his right. "It's the only building that'll still be here in a hundred years."

He and Calvin were standing in the middle of the zoo pointing and looking at a new map of the zoo that James had drawn up.

"I'd say we put the birdhouse over by the new lake," he pointed to a spot on the map, "right here, and I'd demolish the old alligator pond and build a new reptile house here."

Rushing footsteps caused them to turn and see Bobby Crofton trotting their way. He was looking around, as if he was worried about being seen.

"Sorry to break in," he said catching his breath. "But I need to talk to you. Does your offer to help plan the zoo still stand?"

James and Calvin looked at each other and nodded in unison.

"I need to tell you something," he said. "If you're still interested then I'll take the job."

Robert Crofton, architect, then spun the sad details of his past. His firm had designed a school building that had collapsed in an earthquake in California, killing ten children and their teacher. He blamed himself, even though there was nothing he could have done. He turned to alcohol, had robbed a store to get money, and had served time in jail. Now he was being blackmailed by the publisher of the local newspaper who threatened to expose him and run him out of town. He had come to love the zoo and wanted to contribute to its success, but not as a zookeeper.

"Bertie Wallace is an asshole," Calvin said. "He won't hesitate to follow through with his threats. Are you willing to deal with that?"

Bobby looked around at the zoo grounds. It was a Monday and not many people were visiting, but the property was rich with possibilities. He could imagine a network of intersecting boulevards and tree-lined pathways. The new buildings would be carefully aligned with flowerbeds and gardens in between. The small trees they would plant would someday provide shade and respite for people and animals alike. At that moment he knew what his mission was. He was not willing to give that up for anybody.

"Yes," he said finally. "I am."

Tom Chandler hated cleaning the bears and foxes. Their cages consisted of heavy wire mesh framed in wood, with mesh and rocks around the edges to keep the animals from digging out. He had been told they were the only cages left from when the zoo was originally built – and he could believe it. The wood was rotting and falling down. The wire was rusted through in places and had been patched many times. And the smell was terrible. They had to get a crew in the pens every spring to dig out a foot of soil and shit, and replace it with clean dirt. He stood by the gate while two work crews with shovels and wheelbarrows shoveled out the pen.

"No," he shouted at one of the wheelbarrow drivers, "keep to the side. Don't crowd the bears."

He had instructed the men to give the two black bears a wide berth, pushing their wheelbarrows along the fence line from where they were working toward the gate. The bears were accustomed to the routine and tolerated their presence, as long as the men didn't get too close. The male had been at the zoo for about ten years. He was lying down in the corner with one eye on the action. The female, on the other hand was less tolerant. This was her first year of having these people intrude on her space. The fact that her cage mate was so calm helped keep her calm. But it wouldn't take much, Tom could see, to set her off.

"I ain't scared of no bear," said the skinny shirtless young man as he passed through the gate to empty his load.

Tom did not respond. He imagined the kid being grabbed by a bear and shaken like a rag doll. He'd be scared then.

As the kid re-entered with his empty wheelbarrow, Tom said, "I gotta go take a piss. You guys stay on that side of the pen." He fastened the gate and headed toward his office in the lion house.

Tom closed his office door, strode purposefully to his desk, and sat down hard. He desperately needed a drink, but just as he put the bottle to his lips, he heard a commotion. It sounded like shouts of distress. So he took a long pull on the bottle and hurried out.

"Get'em off me," was the cry coming from the bear pen. It was the skinny, shirtless kid. Tom saw him as he emerged from the lion house. He had climbed the fence and the female bear had a firm hold on his foot. Tom rushed through the gate and grabbed a shovel.

"You three stand here and watch him," Tom shouted pointing to the male bear. The workmen looked at each other as if to decide whether to stay or run for their lives. They were relieved to see Calvin Griffith and James Malone enter the pen and even more relieved when Calvin told them to leave.

"What happened here?" Calvin asked angrily.

"I only left for a second," Tom said.

The three zoo workers crowded around the bear and, as they were trying to decide what to do, she let go and walked away. They helped the young man down and examined his foot. He had two puncture wounds where upper and lower canine teeth had pierced his flesh. Tom and James helped him hobble out of the pen and back to Tom's office. They poured some of Tom's alcohol over the wounds and wrapped his foot. He could walk by putting weight on his heel, so they sent him home.

"I guess we'd better stop work in there for the day," said James. "I'll send the crew over to Simon."

"What were you thinking, leaving those idiots in the bear pen unsupervised?" Calvin was clearly upset.

"I had to take a leak," Tom said weakly. "What was I supposed to do, pee in my pants?"

"I know why you left. I can smell it on your breath. If this happens again, you're through." Calvin slammed the door as he left.

29

The nice thing about being a construction superintendent is that you can construct your own office, and that's just what Simon Poston had done. It was a simple wooden structure that was located on the edge of the property near the hoofed stock barn. It was a pole barn and equipment shed that he had enlarged for construction material storage. He had enclosed one end for an office. One wall of the office was lined with an elevated, angled shelf. It was covered in construction drawings. He had a seldom-used desk tucked into a back corner and a well-used conference table in the middle of the room. That is where he conducted business, and that is where he, Bobby, and James spent early mornings discussing current events over coffee.

"Eighth round by a knock out," crowed Simon the minute Bobby and James walked in.

Joe Louis had gained the world heavyweight title the night before by knocking out James J. Braddock in the eighth round of a title bout in Chicago. Louis, at twenty three, was the youngest fighter ever to win the championship.

"Great," said Bobby sarcastically. "I hope he doesn't turn into another Jack Johnson."

"He won't," said Simon confidently. "He's a gentleman. You'll see."

"Who was Jack Johnson?" asked James as he poured a cup of coffee.

"Another colored fighter," said Bobby. "A heavy weight champ from about twenty years ago who wore flashy clothes, drove fast cars, and consorted with white women – even spent time in jail."

"How's Miss Elizabeth?" asked James, changing the subject.

"Best thing that ever happened to me," replied Simon.

"When are you two going to get hitched?" asked Bobby. "You've been seeing each other for months."

"She's still looking after her Pa and he don't seem to like me much," Simon said. "Seems I'm not black enough for his daughter."

"What does that mean?" asked James. "You're both Negros."

"Colored people," Simon explained, "sometimes judge each other by the color of their skin, just like you whites do. But for us it is not just black and white. It is also shades of darkness. To her Pa, my light skin means I'm part white, even though I'm no more a white man than he is."

"What are you going to do?" James asked.

"I'm going to wait him out. He can't live forever."

"How's the design for the bird house coming?" James asked Bobby, changing the subject again.

"How do you want the glass-fronted cages to open?" Bobby answered the question with a question. "Front or back?"

"Back," James replied. "That way if a bird gets out, it'll be contained in the hallway."

"It will be cheaper and easier to have them open from the front," said Bobby. "Then I can eliminate the back hallway and the back wall of the cage won't need a door."

"The back door won't matter. I'm hiring an artist to paint murals. He'll paint-out the door."

Bobby thought about questioning the need for an artist, but he knew the person would be an out of work artist paid by the W.P.A.

"I can put in more cages if I leave out the back hallway," he tried a new argument.

"How many new cages?"

Bobby knew he had won the argument.

The heat and the lack of rain had made the digging of the lake almost impossible. Simon had wanted to go down another six feet and see if they might hit some ground water, but the crew – and the mules – were exhausted. It sloped down to about fifteen feet at the deep end and that would just have to be enough. As soon as they had the berms and walkways around the edges finished, he would begin the filling process. He needed to move his crews on to the completion of the elephant house and the ground breaking of birds.

"Quite a little project you have going on here."

Simon turned in surprise. He had not heard anybody walk up. "Mr. Wallace," he said in surprise.

Everyone at the zoo knew the newspaper man, and knew what a threat he was to the zoo. Simon had heard of his threats to Bobby, but he had no hidden past that could be exposed. He sized up the dapper man in the straw hat and decided, perhaps a bit too quickly, that he was not afraid of him.

"You know, my son Robert is Colonel John Taylor's right-hand man," Wallace said with a sideways glance. "He oversees all W.P.A. projects in the State. We could have a lot of work for a man with your talents."

Simon did not respond. He was smart enough to see where this conversation was heading.

"I imagine this type of work is hard to find for a Negro," Wallace continued ominously. "I could make sure you were secure. Secure enough to marry that little Negress you've been seeing."

Simon went cold. This pompous asshole was not only threatening him. He knew about Elizabeth Harner. How could he know that?

"What exactly do you want?" asked Simon.

"Control," Bertie Wallace replied simply. "I want to know what is going on, what is planned, and who is planning it. I want you to report to me every week."

"And if I don't?"

"You'll be one unhappy, out-of-work nigger," Wallace snarled as he left.

A twenty pound sledgehammer can wear a man down in a hurry – unless he is working out a deep seated frustration. Simon had been pounding on the cement bottom of the old alligator pool for nearly half an hour and showed no signs of letting up. It was being demolished to make way for one of the new buildings. The cement dust clung to his sweaty skin giving him a ghostly appearance and, since he had sent this crew to other jobs, he pounded alone in the afternoon heat.

It was bad enough being called a nigger by that piece of shit newspaper man. He could even deal with the man putting his job in jeopardy. But to threaten a woman – that was almost more than he could bear. He imagined his strong hands wrapped around Wallace's throat, slowly crushing the life out of him. He imagined Wallace's face in the concrete below his feet. He smashed, and smashed, and smashed.

"What did you want to see me about?" asked Bertram Wallace as he ascended the stairs to Gunther's loft. It was well after lunchtime, but Gunther was still sitting at his desk. Wallace wondered if this guy ever did any work.

"Crofton is designing a new bird house," said Gunther.

Wallace walked around the loft, looking up and down. He peeked behind the wall of hay bales into Gunther's 'bedroom'.

"Quite a set up you have here," he said finally. "Is this where you meet Miss Ida Mae Gottshaw?"

Gunther was stunned. He didn't know how to respond. How did this man know about her?

"A new bird house," Wallace repeated. "And where is this new building going to go?"

"I don't know," Gunther said. "It will be part of a new master plan for the whole zoo. James Malone and Robert Crofton are working on it for Griffith."

Gunther was pleased to see that Wallace had stopped walking around looking so smug. This was clearly news to him. Wallace was trying to let things move ahead, but he didn't want to lose control. He had already dealt with Crofton. Now he would need to see about James Malone. This kid from Chicago was a threat to everything he was trying to do.

The ceiling fans turned lazily in the high ceiling of the lion house with no effect at floor-level. Tom was drenched with sweat as he pushed his meat-covered cart along the aisle. The carnivores were getting calf hind-quarters today and they were eagerly pacing, awaiting their afternoon meal. The barred cage-fronts were designed with a six inch gap at the floor level. This allowed droppings and refuse to be hosed out and meat to be shoved underneath. These leg bones were pretty thick, but if he shoved the narrow end under the bars, the animals would pull them through.

"Cal wants to see you over at the office," Said Al Doyle.

"Shit!" jumped Tom. "Where did you come from?"

"What's wrong with you?" Al asked. "You didn't hear me walk all the way from the other end of the building?"

Tom did not reply. He had not heard a thing, but he was distracted this afternoon. He had been expecting a call from Calvin ever since the bear incident. He was still drinking, and Cal knew it. He had already finished off his pint for the day. Maybe that's why Alvin was able to sneak up on him.

"When?"

"Soon as you're done here," said Al.

Al walked away and Tom did not reply. So, this is how it would end for him at the zoo. He picked up one of the leg bones and pushed it under the bars for the male lion. The powerful animal grabbed the end of it and began to pull it into the cage. Tom pushed to help it along. His hand slipped on a piece of fat and became wedged between the meat and the bars. As he placed his other hand around the bars to pull free, the lion let go of the meat and grabbed his fingers. Tom was too stunned to cry out. He opened his mouth to scream, but no sound emerged. The lion pulled his hand and arm into the cage and as Tom worked his other arm free and pushed on the animal's nose, it grabbed that hand as well. With both of Tom's hands in its mouth, the lion began to pull and chew at the same time. Tom could feel flesh and tendons being cut and bones being crushed. He watched in horror as his blood flowed from the lion's mouth and the animal made deep, guttural sounds. It was the last thought he had before he heard a woman scream and he passed out.

30

"I hate it," said Buddy. "Elephants belong outside walking around, not living in some cage and sleeping in a box."

"This is how it's done in zoos," Al replied. "It's a modern elephant exhibit. It's safe, we can clean the area, and people can see what an elephant looks like. Besides, we'll take him out for walks every day."

Al and Buddy were inside the new elephant barn looking out into what will be Bwana's new home. It was not totally complete, but it was ready to contain an elephant. The inside area behind them measured about thirty feet square, not counting the storage area along the back wall that was separated by a heavy pipe wall. The outdoor yard was two or three times that size. It was surrounded by barriers made of old railroad rails that were welded together.

Buddy just shook his head and walked back inside. "All right," he said finally, "let's bring him over and see how he likes it. Where's Malone?"

James Malone was supposed to be there for the move. He and Al were receiving instruction from Buddy on how to handle an elephant.

"Let's walk back over to Bwana," said Al. "He'll meet us there."

"Too bad about your boy, Dizzy Dean," Buddy said as they walked.

"What are you talking about?" Al asked in surprise.

"You didn't listen to the all-star game last night?"

No," said Al. "I was at a Lodge meeting."

"Dizzy got hit on the toe with a ball hit by Earl Averill. They took him out of the game."

"Great," said Al facetiously. "There goes our season. How did Medwick and Mize do?"

"They did OK," said Buddy, "But it was Gehrig who won it for the American League. He hit a two-run homer in the third after DiMaggio had singled, and he hit a double later in the game. Drove in four of their eight runs."

James was waiting for them as they arrived back at the place where Bwana had been chained for the past several months. He and Buddy did not care much for each other and neither minded letting it show. James was the college-boy who was knowledgeable about animals from reading books, and Buddy was the uneducated circus man whose knowledge came from living life. Buddy moved near the elephant and said something that made the animal move forward and place its head on Buddy's chest, Buddy wrapped an arm around Bwana's trunk as the animal used the tip of its trunk to sniff Buddy's shoes.

"OK," Buddy said turning around and facing James. "Ready to go?"

"What?" James looked surprised.

"You can move Bwana to the barn," Buddy said. "Where's your hook?"

"Are you sure I'm ready?"

"As ready as you'll ever be. Go get your hook. You should have it here anyway," Buddy said sternly. "Never be around an elephant without your hook. It's the only authority he'll recognize and he won't hesitate to take advantage of you if you don't have it."

James ran to a nearby wheelbarrow, grabbed an elephant hook from its pile of tools, and returned like a soldier falling into formation.

"What's your first command?" Buddy quizzed.

"Bwana, move up?" asked James.

"Right," said Buddy. "Just do it like we practiced."

James moved near the elephant and began his commands. "Bwana, move up", brought the animal near. "Bwana, steady," ensured that he would stand still. "Bwana, foot," caused him to raise his foot so James could remove the chain. "Go on away," was the command for them to begin walking, James at the elephant's left shoulder pulling occasionally with his hook.

As they walked, James' mind wandered. He was thinking about the design for the new bird house when he felt the elephant pushing him to the left. As he unconsciously pushed with his right shoulder, the animal pushed back until he felt himself beginning to stumble under the animal's weight. He was about to be crushed, when he heard Buddy yelling "no" as he beat the animal between the eyes with his hook. James watched from one knee as Buddy backed up the animal with repeated blows that seemed more to surprise than hurt the beast. Once he had control, he turned on James.

"What're you doing?" he screamed. James thought Buddy was going to hit him next. "You can't let that animal test you like that. He'll kill you. You've got to keep your wits and be in control. If he senses you're afraid or not paying attention he'll test you every time. You've got to make him believe that you're bigger and stronger than he is. That's all he understands."

"Bwana move up," Buddy commanded. When the animal hesitated and fanned his ears out, Buddy resumed hitting Bwana between the eyes as hard as he could. He then stepped back and gave the command again. This time Bwana responded quickly.

"Now," Buddy said to James, "You do it."

James was scared, but with Buddy and Al looking on, he knew what he had to do. He stepped up and gave the commands just as he had seen Buddy do. The animal responded and they finished their journey. James Malone never had any further problems with Bwana, or any other elephant. He was now an elephant man.

"I hear they're moving the elephant to the new barn this morning," said Bobby.

"Yep," said Simon. "It's finally ready to hold an animal. We still have work to do, but we can work around him."

"I guess you heard about Amelia Earhart and Fred Noonan disappearing in the Pacific?" Simon continued.

"They'll turn up," said Bobby confidently. "They're probably eating coconuts on some tropical island waiting to be rescued."

"What's up, Jimbo?" asked Bobby as James walked in and poured himself a cup of coffee.

James plopped down heavily in his usual chair, took a sip of coffee, and glanced at the two other men without making eye contact. They waited expectantly.

"I've been offered another job," he said finally.

"What?" said Bobby in surprise.

"Where?" asked Simon.

"Lincoln Park Zoo in Chicago," he replied. "Curator of Birds."

"Birds?" asked Bobby. "Just birds? We have more than that to offer here. You'll be Director when Cal retires."

"I know," said James. "But Chicago is home. It's a bigger zoo with higher pay and more prestige."

"So, what are you going to do?" asked Simon.

"I don't know, but don't tell anybody until I figure it out," he looked at his two friends, "especially Calvin."

William Ross stood in front of the cage staring at the lion that had mauled Tom a couple of weeks ago. This was the first day that he was on his own, caring for his snakes, which lined the hallway of the lion house in glass-fronted boxes, and the carnivores. Neither Al nor James was available to assist him, so it was going to be a long day. He would begin with the reptiles. He hated getting near those stinking cats.

The reptile cases were nothing more than tightly constructed, wooden boxes with glass fronts and hinged backs. William had placed sand or dirt in the cage bottoms, and some rocks, sticks, and potted plants to give a natural appearance. It was not an ideal set up because they were in the middle of the hallway and they were difficult to service, but it was only temporary. He was working with James and Bobby Crofton on the design of a new reptile house.

The big African rock python had his own box in the middle. It had turned out to be twelve feet long and it was as docile as a big puppy. William loved working with it. The cobras and mambas were another matter. They were flighty, unpredictable, and smart – if you could consider a snake smart. When they looked at you, they seemed to be thinking about how to do you in.

"Can you tell me where to find Calvin Griffith?" asked a woman.

"He should be over at his office," William replied without looking up.

"Is that the lion that hurt the keeper?" she asked.

William glanced up at the lion cage and at the woman. "Yep."

"I'm looking for a job," she said. "I figure you'll need someone to take that guy's place."

"We don't have any women working here," William said, "but you'll need to talk to Cal about that."

The man standing in the door of his office looked familiar, but Calvin couldn't place him. He was a tall, thin, and well dressed right down to the flat-topped straw hat he held in his hands. Cal stared at the hat for a moment then studied the young man's face. Bertram Wallace, Cal thought. This must be his son.

"Come in," Cal said. "Have a seat."

"I'd like a private word, if you don't mind," the young man said glancing at Al, who sat in the other chair.

"Oh," said Cal somewhat surprised. "This is Alvin Doyle. He's been here with me since the beginning. If you want to talk about the zoo, Al needs to hear it."

The young man glanced at Al again, hesitated, but then went on. "I'm Robert Wallace. I think you know my father."

Cal nodded his head and made eye contact with Al. Anything to do with Bertie Wallace meant trouble.

"My Dad has been scheming to get me to take over this zoo," Robert continued. "He has this idea for raking in government money on projects that we will never do. The problem is, I already have a job I like."

"Just tell him no," Al offered.

"If you know my Dad, you'll know why that won't work. He's determined to do this and no one – not even his own son – will stand in his way."

"You know," said Cal, "you'll both go to jail for this."

"You think I haven't thought about that?" Robert exhaled heavily. "I need somebody to help me stop him."

"What makes you think we can stop him," asked Al. "Why would we care if he goes to jail?"

"He'll take you down with him," said Robert. "He'll ruin the zoo's reputation and you'll never get another dime of Federal funding."

Cal knew he was right. He hated Bertie Wallace, as did most people including, it appeared, his own son. "So, what can we do?"

"I'm not sure, yet," Robert said. "I need to talk to my boss. Colonel Taylor oversees all W.P.A. projects in the State. He's a no-nonsense, ex-military man. He won't like this one bit. I just needed to know where you stand before I stir this up." Robert Wallace rose to leave. "You both had better watch your backs if this gets out. My dad will be furious."

"Mr. Griffith?" said a woman's voice from the doorway.

"I'll be in touch," said Wallace as he squeezed past the woman and left.

"I'm Calvin Griffith," said Cal.

"I'm looking for a job," she said. She was a stout woman of medium height. Her brown hair peeked out of her cap in wisps and her clothing was neat, clean, and worn. She had rough hands and the look of one who was accustomed to hard work.

"Sorry, Miss," said Al, "But we don't have any openings."

"That's not what the guy in the Lion House said," she lied. "He said he needs help to replace the guy who was injured by the lion."

"Sorry," Al repeated.

"It's because I'm a woman," she cut him off, clearly agitated.

"This is not the kind of work for a woman," said Calvin. "It's hard and dangerous. You could get hurt."

By the time Cal stopped talking, he could see she was not going to accept 'no'. She was fuming mad. He found himself thinking that if he was ever going to hire a woman, this tough strong-minded woman might be the one. But in the end, he simple said, "Sorry, Mam," and showed her the door.

Gunther wasn't sure this new guy, Spenser Rodman, was going to work out. He was big, hulking kid who was not long out of his teens. He was slow moving and not too bright, but Gunther was desperate for the help since Bobby Malone moved out of animal care, so he would make it work. He was in a good mood and looking forward to seeing Ida Mae after work, so nothing was going to get him down today.

"How did it go at the petting area?" Gunther asked.

"Fine," Spenser replied. "Those sheep sure do like to run, though."

"I told you not to chase them around," said Gunther, feeling a twinge of anger.

"But they like it," said the keeper.

Gunther paused to regain his composure. "I need you to clean and feed the gazelles. Do you think you can handle that?"

Gunther unlatched the door to the antelope stall and opened it to allow the kid to enter with his wheelbarrow, rake, and shovel.

"Don't take too long," Gunther said as he passed. "I need you to clean the hallway before we're done for the day. I'll throw down some fresh hay from the loft."

Gunther watched as Spenser wheeled his tools through the door from the indoor stall to the outside yard. A good hoofed stock keeper has a kind of animal sense that is difficult to describe, but Gunther knew it when he saw it – and this guy definitely did not have it. He had no awareness of where his animals are and what they're doing. He did not walk along the perimeter of the pen, keeping an eye on their movements, and he did not stop moving when they became agitated, as these three gazelles were inclined to do. In fact, Spenser Rodman walked purposefully out the door and across the middle of the yard directly to the pile of morning hay that needed to be picked up.

The three animals came tearing into the indoor stall and paced nervously. Gunther realized, too late, that his presence at the door was not going to help matters, but when he turned to go one of the gazelles spooked and went tearing out the door. She ran full speed across the outdoor yard and directly into the wire fence. Gunther's heart stopped. He had seen many animals break their necks running into fences and she had certainly hit hard enough to do that. But she was still kicking. Unfortunately, one of her horns had become entangled in the fence and she was thrashing helplessly trying to get free. Gunther watched the scene unfold as if in slow motion. He was sure she would rip her horn off, break a leg, or even break her neck as she struggled. He couldn't risk spooking the others by rushing through the pen, and Spenser was just standing there, a few feet away from the struggling animal, watching her kill herself.

Gunther finally decided he had to do something. The other two gazelles had gone to a darkened corner of the indoor stall, so he slowly pulled the latch and entered the stall. His heart was racing and he badly wanted to run, but he slowly and calmly walked along the wall remaining as far from the frightened animals as possible. They watched him intently, but his experienced demeanor kept them calm. As he arrived at the door to the yard, he quickly pulled the door shut and ran to the struggling animal. He grabbed it around the mid-section and pushed her into the fence as he yelled for help. Spenser finally dropped his rake and came forward.

"Get her horn out of the fence," Gunther grunted. "And hold her head so she doesn't horn me."

"Wow," said Spenser. "Did you see that? She was fast. I wonder why she didn't get hurt?

As soon as her head was free, Gunther took her horns in one hand as he held her around the middle. "Get your tools and go out the front gate," he said.

"You want me to leave you here?" Spenser asked.

"Get the fuck out of here," Gunther screamed.

Spenser stumbled backward and scrambled out of the pen. Gunther turned the animal away from the fence, let her go, and quickly moved out the gate himself. The gazelle ran to the middle of the pen, looked around, and stood calmly.

"You dumb son of a bitch," Gunther seethed. "Why didn't you do something? Why did you just stand there?

"I didn't know what to do," Spenser replied simply.

Gunther was still angry, but he didn't know what else to say. He just wanted to get the day's work done and get this idiot out of here. As they rounded the corner and entered the hallway of the barn, he was surprised to see Ida Mae sitting on the stairs.

"Get this hallway cleaned up and all the tools put away," he said to Spenser.

"What are you doing here?" he smiled warmly at Ida Mae as his anger melted. "You're early."

She stood without smiling and walked upstairs without speaking.

Gunther turned to Spenser as he started up the stairs. "Get to work," he said sharply.

She was standing at his desk and turned as he moved toward her. He slipped his arms around her from behind and cupped her breasts in both hands, but instead of pushing her backside into his groin as she usually did, she pulled away. She was crying.

"I got fired today," she said.

"What? Why?"

"Mayor Beneman said he couldn't take a chance on having a loose woman working in his office. Scandal would be bad for his political campaign.

"How did he know about us?" asked Gunther.

"How do you think?" she replied coldly.

"Wallace," Gunther said. "That son of a bitch."

"That's not all," she said walking away from him with her head down. "My husband has thrown me out."

"How did he find out?" Gunther said in alarm, even though he knew the answer. He was trying to process all of this, trying to think of what to say, when she rushed to him and wrapped him in an embrace.

"Let me come live with you," she begged. "I won't be any trouble. I promise." By now she was sobbing uncontrollably. "If you don't take me in, I'll have to go to my parents in Cleveland."

Gunther thought about what it would be like living with this woman, waking up with her luscious, naked body in his bed every morning. But then he thought about the other women he had been with over the years. He might tire of the same woman day after day. And then there was the prospect of taking over the zoo. It was a dream job and one that Wallace had promised him. If he took up with this woman, it would be in defiance of Wallace and the mayor, and he wasn't about to risk it.

He pulled her arms from around his neck and kissed her on the cheek. "I can't take you in," he said simply. He turned away and said, "You'd better go."

Simon stepped back as the elephant swung his trunk from the ground up, tossing moist dirt his way. Buddy had complained that the latch on the new gate was not going to hold, and Simon could see that he was right. The padlock was secure, but the hasp it was attached to was bent and ready to break.

"What do you suggest?" asked Simon.

"A chain," Buddy replied. "I told you this thing wouldn't work. Or you could try a one-inch bolt through both pipes and drill out the through-bolt for a padlock."

"Alright," Simon said with a sigh. "Let's throw a chain on it for now and I'll work on drilling out the pipes tomorrow."

Bwana seemed to be adjusting to his surroundings, but he was testing every point of weakness. It was the last thing Simon needed this afternoon. He was trying to get out of work so he could get ready for his evening with Lizzie Harner. He had been doing a lot of thinking since his run-in with Bertram Wallace two weeks ago. He was supposed to be reporting to Wallace every week, but he just could not bring himself to betray his friends. He had not told anyone about his encounter, not even Lizzie. He was hoping to ignore the bastard and see what happened.

31

The big snake lay stretched out on the warm grass like some great, mottled log. He had been measured at twelve feet, three and a half inches and he weighed in at just under a hundred pounds. His body was as big around as a man's thigh and he looked large enough to swallow a small child. That was part of the fascination for this crowd that had gathered on the lawn just outside the elephant house on a warm Sunday afternoon. This deadly reptile was not in a cage. He had been carried out of the lion house by four burley men and laid on the ground. He could strike out at any time.

"We'll need two large cages," explained James, "just inside the door. These will be for the feature attractions – the snakes everybody wants to see. One will be for this guy and the other one for the cobras. Giant snakes and deadly snakes."

"How large?" asked Bobby.

He was getting ideas and information for his design of the new reptile house.

"I'd say ten or twelve feet long by six feet wide," said James, looking at William Ross for confirmation. "And all of the cages need to be elevated to three or four feet off the ground. We want people to be at eye level with them, especially children."

"Hey!" hollered William at the crowd, "you three stay back."

A young boy was inching forward with a stick in hand ready to poke the snake, and he was being pushed by two older boys.

"How much bigger will this guy get?" asked Bobby.

"The rock python is Africa's largest snake. He could grow another few feet."

"And what about the cobras?"

"Ah, the cobras," said James. "William. Come tell Mr. Crofton about your cobras."

"The Cape Cobra," William began, "is one of the deadliest snakes in Southern Africa. Cape Cobras grow to an average of around 4 feet. They are nervous and aggressive, and they have a deadly venom. The Cape Cobra is a beautiful looking snake. We have one that is yellow and one that is more of an orange or copper color. When they are agitated, they can rise up and spread their hood. People love to see these guys."

"Let's go inside," said Adam Swindler. He moved away from the crowd and was followed into the lion house by Danny Tyler and Chucky Thompson – two thirteen-year-olds and a nine-year-old looking for mischief on a Sunday afternoon.

"Look at this," said Chucky, reading a sign and trying to impress his friends. "Puff Adder, a venomous, thick, heavily built snake with a large, flattened, triangular head and large nostrils which point vertically upwards."

"Here's a good one," said Danny from down the row of cages. "Black mamba – A large, aggressive, highly venomous snake with a narrow head and smooth scales. The mouth lining is black and it grows to over six feet."

"Cobras," Adam said as he gazed into a large cage at the end of the line. "Did you notice that there are no locks on these cages?"

"The monitor lizards will also need a large cage," William reminded James. "They're small now, but they can grow to five or six feet long."

"That's true," James said to Bobby. "We'll need an assortment of cages for the reptile house. We'll also need a large pool for the alligators. Maybe it could have a glass roof so we can grow tropical plants."

"I need to get big Jake back inside," said William. "I have work to do."

"I'll get Al and Gunther to help us," James said.

"I'll help," said Bobby. "Can the three of us handle it?"

James looked at Bobby, who shrugged his shoulders and nodded yes. William moved to the head of the snake, James walked to the tail, leaving the middle for Bobby. As William grabbed the snake with both hands behind the head, James lifted the tail. Bobby wrapped both hands around the snake's middle and lifted. Its skin was dry and leathery and, though massively heavy, it did not move much. His heart was pounding with excitement as they walked in line back into the building.

"Holy shit!" said William, stopping the procession at the first cage.

Bobby looked at William, then back at James who was also wide eyed. They were looking at the empty reptile cage in front of them – the cage with the open back and the sign that said 'Cape Cobra'.

"Hey," shouted Buddy, running to catch up. "You're the newspaperman, aren't you?"

Bertram Wallace did not stop, but he looked over his shoulder. "Who are you?" he asked.

"Buddy Griffith," he shoved out a dirty hand as they walked side by side. "Elephant man."

Bertie looked at the hand then up at Buddy. It was hot, the zoo was crowded, and he was in a hurry. "What do you want?" he asked crossly without taking Buddy's hand.

"I have information you might be interested in."

"I seriously doubt that," Bertie replied without breaking stride.

Buddy stopped but spoke loud enough to be heard. "So, you already know about your son's secret meetings out here?"

The dapper man in the straw hat stopped and turned. "What the hell are you talking about? He's never been out here without me." He sounded confident, but the fact that he had stopped to face Buddy for the first time told Buddy all he needed to know. Wallace looked at Buddy for a moment, as if weighing his options. "What do you want?" he asked finally.

"Money," Buddy replied simply. "I want out of this shit hole and I need a stake to get me out of here."

"What makes you think you have anything worth buying?"

"The fact that you're listening," said Buddy confidently.

Bertie looked around nervously, not wanting anyone to overhear their conversation. He hadn't known about his son's visits to the zoo, but it made perfect sense. Robert had been avoiding him for weeks and the Colonel's office had not been returning his phone calls. Something was going on, but he was quite sure this scruffy, asshole standing before him wouldn't tell him anything useful. "Piss off," he said finally. "I don't give money to pathetic beggars like you."

Buddy watched him stride confidently away. He was fuming mad. 'I'm no pathetic beggar' he thought. He wished he could club the arrogant bastard into the ground.

William, Bobby, and James had placed the big python back in its cage and were now looking around the floor of the lion house. Having two cobras loose was a new experience and they were not sure how to react. Bobby had moved people out of the building and locked the doors while William and James had picked up snake hooks and began turning over boxes and crates.

"Where would they go?" asked Bobby as he remained safely in the middle of the room. He was not terrified of snakes, but he was not fond of them either.

"Could be anywhere," William replied tensely.

Bobby wandered over to the open cage and looked in the front. "How do you know they're gone?" he asked. "Couldn't they be under this big rock in the cage?"

"No," said William. "They're smart snakes. When that cage opened, they headed for freedom."

"I wonder how they got out?" Bobby asked as he walked to the back of the cage. Since he was into animal cage design, he needed to know how to secure them. "There's no lock on this cage."

"What do you mean, 'no lock'?" asked James, looking up and speaking for the first time.

"No lock," Bobby repeated, flipping the hasp on the open door.

James looked at William.

"I didn't think we needed them," William shrugged. "The building is locked at night and during the day, one of us is always around."

James opened his mouth to blast the stupidity, but was cut off by a shout of alarm. He and William turned toward the cobra cage. Framed through the glass viewing window was Bobby standing at the back looking through the open cage door at a cobra. The snake was, in fact, still in the cage, but it had hooded itself up and stood about two feet from Bobby Crofton, hooded up and eye to eye.

"Don't move," James said calmly. "William."

On hearing his name, William moved quickly to the back of the cage. He pushed Bobby back and slammed the door in one motion. The snake sensed the sudden movement and lunged forward to strike, but it hit the door with a harmless thud.

"You were supposed to be reporting to me," Wallace said angrily.

Simon looked Wallace up and down and returned his gaze to the lake construction before him. They were almost finished. Water was filling the basin and grass was growing at the edges. Sidewalks and railing were all that remained.

"I've been busy," he said. "Besides, there's nothing to report."

"That's not what I've just heard."

Simon stiffened. This was uncomfortable, but he was not afraid. He hadn't risen to his current position by backing up when people push. He remained silent.

"What was my son doing out here?" Wallace continued. "Who was he meeting with?"

"I don't know what you're talking about," Simon lied.

"Listen you son of a bitch," Wallace had turned to face Simon and was pointing a finger. "If you know something you had better tell me."

Simon hated this man as much as he had ever hated anybody. He knew that if he did not cooperate that Wallace would seek revenge, and he knew that from their earlier conversations that it might not be aimed directly at him. Wallace was the type to take it out on someone else, someone dear to his victim. Simon knew, at that moment, that if he did not cooperate with Wallace, the revenge would be on Elizabeth Harner or her father, or both. He love Lizzie and would do anything to protect her, even stop seeing her. He knew that what he was about to do would mean an end to their relationship – but he did it anyway.

Miss Harner and I have stopped seeing each other," he lied. "So, it seems you have nothing more to threaten me with."

"We'll see about that," said Wallace, shaking with rage and walking away.

"We have a snake on the loose," James said.

"We know," Al replied as he and Calvin closed the door to the lion house. "Where have you looked?"

"He's not in the office," William walked down the hallway toward the three men. "I don't think he's in here. We've looked everywhere."

They paused a moment as this sunk in. If the snake was not inside, that meant it was outside. It could be anywhere by now. Calvin rubbed a hand through his hair. He was in charge here and he had no idea what to do. If anyone was hurt by this deadly reptile, he would be held responsible – and rightly so. The silence that filled the room was broken by a loud banging on the door. A crowd of curious bystanders had gathered outside waiting for the lion house to reopen.

"You'd better get out here," said a breathless man through the door that William cracked open.

William looked over his shoulder to see his three bosses rushing to see what was so urgent, and knowing what they were likely to discover. They were horrified to see a woman looking down into her baby stroller, her eyes wide in terror and her hand over her mouth. They approached quietly and peered into the bottom of the stroller, where they were met with a baby smiling back at them, oblivious to the danger that surrounded her. On either side of the blanket she was lying on, they could see the body of the cobra. It was not moving and its head was not visible. All four men moved back a fraction, but it was James who acted. The child was on top of the blankets and the snake's head was not. He reached carefully into the stroller to pull the child to safety, but the mother lunged forward to stop him and bumped the stroller. Cal grabbed her and pulled her away, but it was too late. They all jumped back in horror as the head of the cobra popped up from the stroller, hood spread and ready for trouble.

The mother screamed and the crowd roared in fright as Cal and Alvin tried to move people back.

"Calm down," shouted Cal.

"We need quiet here," said Al. "Please, move back and give us some room to work."

"What are we going to do?" asked William quietly, his large eyes revealing his fright.

James was still for a moment as he studied the snake. Then he looked around at the crowd.

"Go get me that broom," he said to William, pointing to one of the custodians standing nearby.

When William returned he said, "I want you to hold the broom about two feet from the snake's nose and wave it slowly back and forth, like this."

The crowd had gone quiet. James edged around the stroller while William kept the snake occupied. When he was behind the snake, James rubbed his hands on his pants two times and slowly moved toward the stroller, being careful to step lightly and not bump the stroller. When he was in position, he lashed out with his right hand, grabbed the snake behind the head, and pulled it out of the stroller. As he backed away, the mother lunged to her infant and William grabbed the snake's body to keep it from pulling itself free of James' grasp. They walked to the building, where Cal was waiting at the door, and inside to find Alvin with his hand on the cage door. Like a well-rehearsed play, Al opened the cage, William stuffed the snake inside, James threw the head in, jerking his hand out just as Al slammed the door.

The four men stood in the hallway where, barely tem minutes earlier they had been wondering what to do. Now they were breathing heavily as the excitement of what had just happened began to sweep over them.

"Where did you learn how to do that?" asked William.

"I saw snake charmers doing that when I was in Africa," James replied. "Only over there, they use one hand to wave in front of the snake while they grab with the other.

"Well," said William, "I prefer the broom method."

They all had a good laugh.

"I have something to tell you," said Gunther.

Bertram Wallace stalked around the loft, not looking at Gunther. He was still fuming from his discussion with Poston. He didn't like being talked to that way by a one of those people and he especially didn't like hearing about his own son's treachery that way.

"Your son has been out here," Gunther continued. He was surprised that Wallace did not stop pacing, did not even seem surprised. "Did you hear me?"

Wallace finally stopped and looked at Gunther with hatred in his eyes. "I already know that."

Gunther looked surprised, which made Wallace smile. "Is that why you called me here?"

Gunther just nodded.

Wallace was quiet for a moment.

"You're a pathetic little Kraut," he said finally. "You know that?"

He paused for another moment, weighing his next words.

"You'll never run this zoo, not as long as I'm alive. Maybe I'll let Miss Ida Mae run it for me."

Gunther was clearly shocked, so Wallace continued. "That's right. Ida Mae and I are seeing each other now."

"You're lying," said Gunther.

"Oh, am I? If I am, how would I know about that mole on her left breast – right about here?" he said point to a spot on his jacket. He cupped his hands in the air, taunting. "They're about this size, wouldn't you say? And smooth as a baby's butt."

Gunther moved forward in anger, but Wallace stepped back. "Whoa, boy. There are a lot of people out there on a Sunday afternoon."

Gunther stopped. His fists were balled-up at his side and his face was beet-red. "I'll get you for this."

Wallace laughed as he descended the stairs. "Somehow, I doubt that." And he was gone.

32

"Busy weekend ahead," said James. "Are you going to get this done?"

"Not if this rain doesn't let up," Simon replied.

The two men stood at the door to the elephant barn looking out at the water-soaked grounds. It had been raining for three days and, though the rain was still coming down, the sky was showing some signs of clearing.

"I need to get this slab poured and the foundation laid for the hay shed on the side," Simon continued. "Then we'll take the Labor Day weekend off."

"I wonder why there's no water in this hole?" asked James. They looked down into the foundation pit that they had walked over using a plank in order to get inside.

"Don't know," said Simon. "It looks like Willie may have dug a drainage hole. See that disturbed dirt on the side?"

"You two ought to have a look at this," Buddy called from inside the building.

They turned and walked into the hallway adjacent to the elephant stall. Buddy was in the stall with Bwana, a running hose in his left hand. When they were opposite him, he said, "You'll need to come in here to see it."

The wall between the elephant and the keeper aisle consisted of concrete pillars, about four feet apart, with railroad rails place horizontally. The first rail was four feet off the ground and additional rails were placed every three feet up to about ten feet. The elephant was securely contained, but caretakers could duck in and out of the stall with ease. Simon and James ducked into the stall to join Buddy. Bwana stood at the back of the stall. He appeared nervous, even to the inexperienced eye, as he swayed and looked around.

"Bwana was nervous as hell when I came in this morning," Buddy began, "but I didn't think much of it. He gets that way some times. I fed him some carrots and washed the mud off him and he seemed to calm down.

Simon eyed the animal nervously as Buddy continued.

"Then I saw him up here," Buddy pointed to the bars and pillar before them. "He was sniffing this area with his trunk and getting agitated all over again. So I put some hay down at the back of the stall where I had just cleaned, and had a closer look."

Buddy moved closer and pointed to the spot and the two others moved in to see.

"What is it?" asked Simon.

"Looks like blood," said James.

Buddy nodded, "That's what I thought."

A section of the pillar was stained with what appeared to Simon to be mud, although on closer inspection, it was a deep red color in spots. As he peered in he asked, "Where would blood have come from?"

"From Bwana?" James offered as they all looked back at the animal.

"No," Buddy said. "I looked him over real good. There's not a scratch on him."

They all turned back to the stain.

"I just wanted somebody to see it before I hosed it off," Buddy said.

"Go ahead," James said finally. "It's probably just mud anyway."

"We need to get this meeting started," said Colonel Taylor. He flipped his pocket watch closed and stuffed it back into his vest pocket. "It's not like Robert to be late, but I need to get going."

John Taylor was called Colonel because he had retired from the Army as a full-bird Colonel. He ran the State's Federal Works Projects, and was constantly on the road. He was not a big man, but he had a big presence that was aided by the white cowboy hat that he had placed on the knee of his crossed right leg. He was decisive, direct, and demanding. He had already looked around

Mayor Jasper Beneman's office. Now he addressed the Mayor himself.

"My assistant tells me that his father may have been siphoning off some Federal dollars that are supposed to be going into projects in this town." He said. "Do you know anything about this?"

The mayor fidgeted in his chair, looking nervously at his other guests. Calvin and Bobby carefully avoided his gaze. It was an uncomfortable moment for everyone except the Colonel. Silence settled over the room and Cal could hear motorcar traffic outside.

"Bertram Wallace has been threatening my staff," Cal said finally, "and I've had enough. It's about time someone stood up to that bully."

"Who has he threatened?" asked Colonel Taylor.

"Me," said Bobby. All eyes turned to him. "It was back in May," he began, "right after I started working at the zoo. Cal found out I was a Landscape Architect and a Civil Engineer and offered me a job planning the zoo. I turned him down."

"Why?" asked the Colonel.

Bobby explained the unfortunate story of the earthquake, the building collapse, and his descent into alcoholism and crime. "I just wasn't ready to step back into that arena," he said. "I didn't want the responsibility."

"But Wallace threatened to expose you?" asked Colonel Taylor.

Bobby just nodded.

"Then he started working on Simon Poston, my Construction Superintendent," Calvin said. "He is a visionary, a construction genius who happens to be colored. Wallace threatened him a month later. Even threatened the man's girlfriend."

"He's using one of our zookeepers as a spy," Bobby added.

"So, about six or eight weeks ago," Cal continued, "young Robert Wallace comes to see me. He admits that his dad is up to no good – maybe even planning to take over the zoo and get his hands on the Federal Works money. The kid said he was going to talk to you, but he never came back."

"What do you know about this," Colonel Taylor turned to an increasingly uncomfortable looking Mayor.

Mayor Beneman admitted to his involvement with Wallace's schemes, but insisted he was looking out for the good of the community. No crime was committed, no money was stolen, and Wallace's plans never materialized.

"Why was he so interested in the zoo?" the Colonel said to no one in particular.

"Robert is his only son," replied the Mayor. "Until he got the job at your office, it didn't look like he was ever going to amount to anything."

"He's a smart lad," said the Colonel. He just needed someone to listen to him." He paused, looked at the rolled paper under Bobby's arm, and said, "That your zoo plan?" When Bobby pulled it out and nodded in the affirmative, he said, "Let's have a look."

The Mayor cleared space on his desk and Bobby rolled out the master plan of the zoo property that he had been working on for months.

"The zoo sits on nearly fifty acres of property," he explained, "on a bluff overlooking the river. Calvin, James Malone, and I have worked out this plan that calls for new animal buildings here, here, and here." He pointed to various parts of the map that showed in detailed pen and ink drawings, the buildings that would eventually house apes, monkeys, hoofed stock, pachyderms, birds, reptiles, and more. He included a large flight cage for birds and a beautiful garden area overlooking the river. Walkways were lined with trees and the major axis of the zoo was anchored by a large fountain at one end and an impressive copper beech tree at the other.

"There are features of this plan that are a little out of our control," said Cal. "We need the Mayor's permission for a new road below the bluff along the river. This will stabilize the river banks and protect the zoo."

"And we want to widen the road to downtown," Bobby continued, "creating a four-lane boulevard with the streetcar line in the center."

Calvin and Bobby looked at the Mayor, who was clearly pleased, and then at Colonel Taylor, who was still running his index finger over the plan.

"I've seen a lot of plans and heard plenty of schemes since I took this job," he said finally. "But this is one of the best. You'll get your ..."

He was interrupted by the door opening and the entrance of Robert Wallace.

"Sorry I'm late," he announced, clearly flustered.

"Something the matter?" asked the Colonel.

"I was with my mother," he explained. "She's worried because my father didn't come home last night."

"That can't be too unusual," said the Mayor, knowing about Bertie's dalliances, but not wanting to say it out loud.

"No," admitted Robert. "That's what I told my mother. He'll turn up." He looked at the plans on the table and said, "So, what have I missed?"

"Who's the new guy?" Calvin asked.

"Name's Max Winston," James replied. "He worked with Buddy in the circus. Buddy must have called him because he showed up a few days after Gunther disappeared."

Calvin did not reply. James knew that Calvin had finally accepted Buddy's presence at the zoo, but it was an uneasy truce. They seldom spoke. Anyone who was a friend of Buddy's was unlikely to be welcomed by Cal.

"He's a good elephant man," James continued. "And he grew up on a farm, so he knows hoofed stock."

James and Calvin stood under umbrellas in a light drizzle. They were standing in roughly the same position that visitors would stand when the elephant exhibit opened, except they were standing on planks to keep their feet out of the mud. Calvin had just finished telling James about the morning meeting in the Mayor's office.

"If the Colonel approves of our plan," asked James, "when can we get started? How soon will we get the funding?"

"It'll take a while to get approval from Washington," Cal replied. "But he did say he can divert some funding here right away for underground work – infrastructure, he called it."

"Bobby and I want to start with that, anyway," said James. "Now that we have a master plan, we know where to put the water pipes, the sewer lines, and the steam trenches for heat. We can put in walkways, service roads, and a parking lot."

"Is this rain going to set back the opening?" asked Cal.

"Simon and I were talking about that this morning," said James. "He figures about another six weeks of work. The rain may slow him down a bit, but we're still planning on a mid-October opening."

"What is left to do?"

"He is going to pour the slab around the outside of the building – the apron he calls it – today."

"Today?" questioned Cal. "In this weather?"

"That's what he says. He's going to cover it with tarps. If it doesn't rain too hard, it'll be fine. He still needs to build the hay storage building, lay sidewalks, put up public barriers and fences, install signs, and when the rain stops he'll paint the building."

"I wish we'd built it bigger," Cal mused, nodding to the building before them. "People are already asking when we will get another elephant."

"The new guy mentioned that he knows of another elephant," said James. "It's a female Asian."

"Is she with a circus?"

"No," James replied. "Some guy has her. He travels around giving elephant rides. According to Max, the guy is sick and needs to sell her."

"It'd be pretty crowded in there with two elephants," Cal said. "Especially an African and an Asian. Would they even get along?"

"Max says they would."

"You trust this guy?" Cal glanced at James.

"He seems to know his stuff," James replied. "And he seems to like the zoo. He's taken to it better than Buddy ever has."

Cal did not reply. They could see Max and Buddy across the yard and through the door of the barn. They were working the elephant. Max was average height, but that was the only thing average about him. He was broad-chested, with long hair and a full beard, and a booming voice. They could hear him clearly from where they stood giving commands to the elephant.

"I need to go meet Simon over at the site of the bird house," James said, finally. "Want to come?"

"No," Cal replied. "I have some paperwork to do before the weekend. You go ahead." As James walked away he heard Calvin shout, "And tell Simon I'm expecting this elephant house to be open in six weeks."

James liked the smell of the hoofed stock barn at the end of the day. The stalls were freshly bedded and the animals did not yet have that strong odor that would build up after being inside all night. The temporary bird cages that lined the hallway added their own odors, too. It was mainly the smell of over-ripe fruits and vegetables. Calvin had hired another zoo keeper to help with the birds, but he would not begin work until Tuesday, after the Labor Day weekend. So James was left to clean and feed the birds, a task that he actually looked forward to.

He had already done the large birds that were in outdoor pens – the crowned cranes, the blue cranes, and the black-bellied bustards. He had shaken off the rain and was now working his way down the line of cages. He would enter each cage and pick up food and droppings from the floor. Then he would spread some wood shavings, replace their food and water, and move down the line. He did the lilac-breasted rollers, the violet-backed starlings, yellow-billed hornbills, and the gray parrots. There was a large cage outside near the new bird house that held some owls and hawks that only needed to be cleaned once a day in the morning. The blue jays, quail and assorted local birds were also in an outdoor flight cage in the zoo. He'd look in on them before he went home, but he was anxious to get out for the weekend.

The last cage in the hallway housed the group of yellow weaver birds. He had twelve birds that had come back from Africa with him and, and they had started building nests almost as soon as they were released to their cage. The nests were elaborate, pendulous, basket-like structures that hung from the tree branches that he had placed in the cage. He had been providing the birds with long tufts of grass for them to work with, and the results were spectacular.

As he moved along the floor looking for any bits of detritus that needed to be picked up, he heard an unusual set of high-pitched peeps. There were no birds above his head. They had all moved to the other side of the cage to get away from him. The sounds were coming from a nest. Could he have chicks in the nest? It would be a first for the zoo – maybe a first for any zoo. He had to see.

The nest was hanging from a branch about eight feet above his head. He could almost touch it, but he needed to get higher in order to see inside. He looked around for something to stand on, but there was nothing in sight. He tried to visualize the rest of the barn, but no ladders, stools, or boxes came to mind. What he did visualize, however, was a bale of hay just down the hall. He could stack bales and climb on them.

He threw four bales down from the loft and carefully stacked them in the cage. The birds flew in circles, but with nowhere to get away, they finally accepted his presence and settled to watch. He climbed carefully up the bales, holding onto the cage wall for support. When he was on the two-bale step he was head high with the nest. It was his first close look at a weaver nest, and it was a marvel of engineering.

It was larger than he had expected, almost the size of a football. It was suspended from a branch by a few blades of grass, giving it a precarious appearance. And the nest cavity was completely enclosed inside a mat of woven grass. He could definitely hear chicks inside but he could see nothing. The parents enter the nest through an opening at the bottom. They climbed up a kind of tunnel to enter the nest area that contained the chicks.

James carefully lifted the nest and moved the opening nearer to his eye level. He badly wanted to see inside, to see the chicks. Were they feathered or naked? As he moved the nest, he ducked his head and stepped to his right – and right off the bales of hay.

The floor of the hallway in the hoofed stock barn was concrete. The few inches of straw and wood shavings that covered the floor of the cage were not enough to break his fall. He went down nearly head-first and caught himself with both arms, breaking both wrists in the process. The pain shot up his arms and he cried out, but there was no one around to hear. He sat for a moment cradling both arms in his lap and looking around at his predicament. 'What the hell am I going to do now?' he thought.

33

"Mind if I join you boys?" asked Al from the door of Simon's office.

"Not at all," said Simon. "What brings you over here?"

"Just looking for some calm before the storm," he replied, pouring a cup of coffee and finding a seat.

Bobby and James were lounging in Simon's office as they did on most mornings – but this was not most mornings. The elephant house was set to open in a few hours. That was the storm of activity that Al was seeking shelter from. He didn't often join them for coffee but when he did, they knew what the conversation would turn to, especially today.

"So," he began, "who do you boys like in the Series?"

Game four of the World Series would be played later in the day, and the New York Yankees led the New York Giants by three games to none. The Yankees only had to win one more game to take the Series.

"I'm a White Sox fan," said James. "So I'll go with the American League. I say the Yankees will finish it out today.

"It's not looking good for the Nationals," admits Al, "especially with the Iron Horse and Joe D. both hitting around three fifty, but I'm still going with the Giants."

"How are the arms?" Bobby asked James. "Do you have to do anything today?"

"They're fine," he said. "I get the plaster casts off at the end of next week."

"You should've taken that job in Chicago," quipped Simon. "You'd be sittin in some cushy office and not climbing around bird cages."

What job?" Al asked, looking around at the others.

There was an awkward silence as they all realized that James had not told his two bosses about the offer he had turned down last summer.

Now it was James' turn to change the subject. "All I need to do today is show Colonel Taylor around. Will you be able to help me explain the master plan?" he asked Bobby.

"He's already seen it," said Al.

"I know," said Bobby, "but he hasn't seen it on the ground. After he sees the elephant house open, we'll take him past Monkey Island and explain the fountain and pathways. Then we'll show him the bird house construction and the aviary, with Bobby's drawings of what they will look like. We'll take him to the copper beech tree and the garden area, where you can look down on the river and the location of the new River Road. And we will swing by the hoofed stock barns and the site of the reptile house."

"At least you got a nice day for a tour," said Al. "Fifty degrees and sunny. And that copper beech tree is starting to turn. In another week it'll be in full color."

"What's the Colonel like?" asked James.

"He's a no-nonsense, military man," said Bobby. "I imagine he can be a pretty tough customer when he wants to. But he will be with Robert Wallace, and Wallace seems to handle him pretty well. Besides, he really seems to like the zoo. He's a hunter. Probably shot every animal in America."

"I wonder what ever happened to Wallace's dad," said Al. "There was another article about him in the newspaper this morning."

"I hope he's dead," Simon said.

Nobody responded. They all knew the story of how Bertie Wallace had bullied Simon and threatened his lady, Lizzie Harner. Simon had waited weeks to try and mend his relationship with Lizzie, and though he had made progress, she was still wary of a relationship. Nobody in that room mourned the disappearance of Bertram Wallace, whether he was dead or not.

Buddy was glad he had insisted on the large diameter, one-inch water hose. It made washing the elephant so much faster, even though he was not the one doing the washing. That task had fallen to his new assistant. He was nursing a hangover and, truth be told, he was still a little drunk from last night.

"Bwana, steady," Max's voice boomed in the cavernous elephant building. The elephant was shifting his back end, making it difficult to use the scrub brush. Max Winston was new to the zoo, but he was not new to elephant routines. By the time all the dignitaries were in place in a couple of hours, he had to have the yard cleaned, the stall cleaned, and the elephant washed. He had started with the indoor stall and was now working on Bwana. He would save the outdoor yard for last so it would be clean for the visitors and guests. Buddy was not going to be of any use today.

Buddy leaned his head against the wall. He sat on a bucket in the hallway, oblivious to the work that was going on before him. He should have been worried about the boss coming in and finding him slacked-off, but he wasn't. The boss was his Pa, who didn't like him anyway.

Max dipped the scrub brush into the soapy water and scrubbed Bwana's side. The elephant seemed to enjoy the process and moved around, causing Max to shout, "Bwana, steady." Max wanted this to be done properly because he, too, had a surprise to spring today.

When the men left Simon's office, they scattered in different directions. Al went to Calvin's office to get ready for the arrival of the guests. James went to the elephant house to check on preparations. Bobby went out to inspect the zoo grounds in anticipation of his tour with the Colonel. And Simon gathered his drawings to take over the bird house construction site.

"Did you remember to stop all deliveries for this morning?" Simon asked Willie when he arrived at the site.

"Yes, Boss," Willie replied. "But we got concrete and another load of bricks coming after lunch."

Simon surveyed the new construction site. It was different from the elephant area they had just vacated because it was larger and it was brick construction instead of concrete. The building was located between the lion house and the new lake and, though it was still just a series of foundation holes in the ground, the size and layout were becoming obvious.

It was nearly ten thousand square feet of space, not counting the basement, which was under half of the building. James had asked for over twenty cages of various sizes, including a couple of large aviaries. Bobby had taken James' wishes and put them on paper. And now it was up to Simon to make it a reality. They were quite a team, and Simon was proud to be a part of it. Keeping wild and exotic animals in cages was a tricky business and it began with the process of planning, design, and proper construction.

"Why are these foundations so big?" Willie asked.

"The bird cages are going to add a lot of weight," Simon replied without looking up.

"Lord," said Willie. "How many cages they gonna have?"

"Ten on each leg of the 'U' and two big cages to let the birds fly around in."

"So," said Willie after pausing to do some simple math, "they're going to keep thirty birds in here."

"Ha," Simon laughed. "Probably more like three hundred. They want to have birds from all over the world and they will keep many birds together in one cage."

Simon looked at his friend and co-worker. They had been together for many years and made a pretty good team. Simon, the light-skinned negro who was smart enough to do just about anything but for his race, and Willie, the short, muscular, black man who had never been to school a day in his life and could read very little and write not at all.

"It's almost like these zoos are collecting stamps or bottle caps," Simon said. "They seem to want one of every kind of animal they can get their hands on."

"Do they make babies with 'em?"

"Can't do that with one animal," said Simon. "I think they just send someone out to keep catching more."

They stood in silence for a moment before Simon said, "Let's get this site cleaned up. Bobby and Cal are bringing some big-shots around this morning. Stack those bricks and pick up the trash. And tell the men to stay busy. I don't want them sittin around when Cal comes."

"How about the other areas?" asked Willie. "They goin all over the zoo?"

Simon thought for a moment. "I suppose so. Send a crew around the lake and a crew over to the garden area. Let's get everything looking good."

"Get those damn kids out of here," Calvin growled. "Those are the same boys who were here when the snakes got out." He and James were standing at the zoo entrance awaiting the arrival of the Mayor, Colonel Taylor, and Robert Wallace. The boys had ducked behind some parked cars when they spotted the men, a good indication that they were up to no good. James moved in their direction as the Mayor's car pulled into the lot.

Calvin was already in a bad mood following a run-in with Buddy, who appeared to be already drunk at eleven o'clock in the morning. He had to get Alvin to usher him over to the house to keep him out of sight. Now, instead of having Al and James help him greet the dignitaries, he stood there alone rubbing his hands against the cold.

"Morning, gentlemen," said Cal as they exited the car.

"Great day for an opening," boomed the Colonel. "Looks like you have a good crowd." He looked appreciatively at the people gathered around the new elephant area and they strolled that way. James ran up from behind and breathlessly joined them. Calvin did not ask how he resolved the problem with the boys.

"Who is going to cut the ribbon?" asked Cal.

"Well how about the Colonel?" asked the Mayor solicitously.

"No," replied Colonel Taylor. "I don't cut ribbons. That's for local dignitaries. I'll just make a few remarks."

"Looks like it's down to you, Mayor," said Cal.

It was a busy October Saturday and people had come out to see the elephant enter his new home for the first time. For the past few weeks, tarpaulins had screened the area. Today, the tarps had been removed, but the elephant was inside and out of sight. A giant, red ribbon stretched across the doorway.

As they approached the crowd, the Mayor and the Colonel began shaking hands and greeting people. Calvin pulled James aside. "Is everything ready?" Cal asked. "Can that new guy handle this?"

"Relax," said James. "Max will be fine. He's actually better at this than Buddy. Let's get the Mayor back there."

James gathered the Mayor while Calvin got the Colonel and Bob Wallace into position at the podium. Calvin grew suddenly nostalgic as he recalled a similar occasion twenty five years ago, when they opened a brand new zoo. He looked around at those who were there and who had a hand in this great venture – his daughter Raven, his wife Bea, and pushing his way through the crowd, Alvin Doyle. It had been quite an adventure, but he was ready to step aside and let the next generation take over.

"Ladies and Gentlemen," he shouted. "May I have your attention?" he paused and waited for the crowd to calm. "I'd like to introduce the man who makes today possible. A man whose authority reaches all the way to Washington, DC and whose pen signs checks for millions of Federal dollars – Colonel John Taylor." He paused to allow the polite applause to die down. "But before the Colonel provides his remarks, let's cut the ribbon."

Cal gestured toward the elephant stall and there, to everyone's surprise, appeared in the doorway Mayor Jasper Beneman on the back of Bwana the elephant. The Mayor had both hands on the elephant's back and looked terrified, but when the crowds began cheering the politician loosened up. Max guided the elephant calmly saying, "Bwana, move up," as they moved quickly through the door breaking the ribbon. At that moment, the Mayor grabbed his hat, lifted it in the air, and gave the crowd a big smile.

Part 5

34

Tuesday, March 6th, 2012

Chelsea did not mind the smell of the rhino building. In fact, she found it to be almost pleasant, in an intoxicating sort of way. She just wished the odor didn't adhere quite so tenaciously. She had always felt sorry for the elephant crew when they came into the break room. They reeked of elephant urine and feces so badly that no one wanted to sit with them. Now she worked with rhinos, which have a similar smell, and it didn't smell so bad to her. She only noticed it when she got home and she smelled it on her clothes or in her hair. The amazing thing was that the smell climbed onto you even if you never touched anything. Just walking through the elephant or rhino buildings would cause the odor to cling like steam on a bathroom mirror.

Chelsea walked through the small block building on her regular morning rounds, talking in soothing tones and checking Ike and Tina, the male and female African black rhinos. She fed a carrot to each rhino as she checked it for injuries or signs of illness. She noticed the pile of dung in each stall, the color of chocolate milk but firm and very fibrous. The rhinos had the curious habit of defecating in the same spot every day. This made the keeper's job easier, unless the spot was in the water bowl or blocking a doorway. Each rhino had a stall that was twenty five feet square with a ten foot wide keeper aisle separating them. The barrier along the aisle was four inch steel pipe set vertically in the concrete floor to allow an eighteen inch gap. The corrugated, metal roof had four fiberglass panels that were supposed to act as sky lights, but they had darkened with age so the only light when the doors were closed came from a single one hundred watt light bulb that hung over the keeper aisle. It was a long, dark winter for the rhinos, since they seldom went outside after the weather turned cold around Thanksgiving.

After she checked the rhinos, she proceeded to the next building on her string, the African antelope barn. The greater kudu, the impala, and the Thompson's gazelles were nervous animals that would run into the walls of their building if spooked by sudden noises. That is why Chelsea shuffled her feet, fumbled with the lock on the door, and started talking quietly as soon as she entered the building. The routine was the same, count heads, check animals, and look for problems. Next, she would clean the antelope yard, turn them out to the exhibit, and then clean the rhino exhibit. They might get outside later if the sun came out and the weather warmed up. After her morning break she would come back and clean the stalls where the animals had spent the night. She loaded her rake and flat shovel into the wheelbarrow and started outside to the antelope yard.

The exhibit for kudu, impala, and gazelle was a large, grassy, quarter-of-an-acre paddock. An eight foot high chain-link fence enclosed most of the perimeter. The public viewed the antelope across a fifteen foot wide water moat which was deep enough to prevent the animals from wading out. In the distance, the public could also see the lions, appearing to be in the same area as the antelope. Actually a deep, dry moat separated the predators and prey.

Chelsea trudged out into the frigid, morning air pushing her wheelbarrow. Her usual route was to start around the exhibit in a clockwise direction, stopping every few yards to rake animal droppings. The antelope defecated in random locations, so she was forced to clean countless small piles of black, hard pellets. The peanut-sized droppings were produced by the gazelles and the larger grape-sized droppings came from the kudu. The ground was frozen, so the raking was easy. She also needed to rake around the large log and boulder, and pick up yesterday's hay. As she moved around the paddock, she checked fences, looked for obvious parasites in the feces, and inspected the general condition of the exhibit. When she finished cleaning, she placed a half bale of timothy hay in front of the log and a fourth of a bale of alfalfa hay on the boulder, for the kudu. She took one last look around and went to the barn to let the animals outside for the day. The whole process had taken forty-five minutes and she had about an hour do some training with the rhinos before she took her morning break.

As she walked back to the rhino barn, she went over in her mind what she had covered yesterday with Janice. Janice Fredrick had given up her position as Curator of Birds to take the new position of Animal Training and Enrichment Coordinator. It was a bit of a step down, but she had to get out of the bird house and its personnel problems. Training the female black rhino to enter a crate-sized stall and stand still enough to be artificially inseminated was her first big project. She and Chelsea had made tremendous progress. Chelsea smiled as she entered the hallway thinking it was Janice she saw sitting on a bale of hay. But it was not Janice. Her smile faded when she saw Parks Jones stand up.

"Well," he said. "It's about time you came back inside."

She did not reply. She couldn't stand the pompous little man and his constant sexual advances. She attempted to brush past him but he grabbed her arm and spun her back toward him.

"What's your hurry?" he asked.

"I have work to do," she replied. "And keep your hands off me or I'll file a complaint for sexual harassment."

"I know you don't mean that. I've seen the way you look at me"

She opened her mouth to reply but the notion was so absurd that words failed her.

"See," he smirked. "I knew it. I'll be director of this shithole when Laskey quits or dies. I can see great things in your future if you play your cards right."

She moved away, trying to put some distance between them.

"On the other hand," he continued, "I can make your life miserable."

She weighed his words. Mr. Laskey was soon going to retire because of his cancer treatment. When Parks Jones took over, this job was going to become unbearable. She had grown to love the zoo and its contribution to the understanding of animals. The thought of having to resign left her with a sick feeling, but the thought of giving in to this creep made her feel even sicker. She was far enough away from him that, if she swung the shovel she was holding, it would catch him flush on the side of his head. All of these thoughts came in a split second, jumble of fantasy that was broken by the squeak and bang of the hall door opening and Janice Fredricks entering.

"Did I interrupt something?" she asked, stopping in mid-stride.

After a moment of awkward silence and unbroken stare-down, Chelsea said, "No, Mr. Jones was just leaving."

"Think about what I said," he mumbled to her, and he was gone.

"It can't swing in," said Fred Williamson, "there's a pipe in the way."

"All of the cage doors have to swing in," said Billy Scales. "It's a safety feature. If the chimp hits an unlocked door it needs to hit against the door jam, not just swing open for him."

"I know that," Fred replied. "But this one won't do that."

Billy could see he was right, but he didn't like it. He decided to let it go and move on to the reason he had come to the construction site. The welders had taken over the chimp holding area as cage fronts were installed and sliding shift doors were fabricated. It was a complex operation, but Fred had done similar jobs at the zoo, so he was comfortable with their progress – except for one detail.

"Is this blood-pressure sleeve going on all of these cages?" Fred pointed to a metal pipe about six inches in diameter and three feet long leaning against the wall. It had an oblong opening on one side and a metal rod inserted through one end. It was designed, he had been told, for a chimp to place its arm in, grab the metal rod, and either have blood drawn or its blood pressure taken.

"Yes," Billy replied. "Every cage but the gang-cage at the end."

"Do you guys know how heavy this thing is?" Fred grabbed the metal rod and hoisted the pipe a few inches. "Your girl keepers won't be able to lift this thing."

Billy could see he was right. "What should we do?"

"Well," Fred replied, "we could make it lighter, say out of PVC pipe, or we just make a bunch of these and permanently mount them."

"If we permanently mount them we'll have them sticking out in the hallway," said Billy.

"Yep."

"Will the PVC be strong enough?" Billy asked.

"It'll be plenty strong," Fred said. "Want us to make up a sample?"

"Yes," said Billy. "Make one up and we'll let Sonny have a go at it."

"Have you read this?" asked Joanne Newman holding up a blue ring-binder.

"Yes," Don Laskey replied.

They were sitting at the conference table in Don's office. Joanne had asked Don to meet with her prior to the Board meeting. Don hadn't known what she wanted to discuss, until now.

"He's got it all wrong." She said dramatically. "My grandfather created this park, not some mayor. My family created this zoo and he says practically nothing about us."

"I've seen his references, Joanne. He has the paperwork and news articles to back it up."

"Newspapers?" she said getting up to stalk around the room. "Who believes what you read in newspapers?"

"It's all he has to go on. The articles are eye witness accounts from the time. He has to use them."

"He also has eye witness accounts from my family. Why can't he use them?"

"Probably because they're biased."

"No more biased that some publisher writing headlines to sell newspapers," she said shrilly.

Don knew he was in a tough spot. Amos had done his research and could back up most of what he had written. On the other hand, it was a commissioned piece. The Dotsons were paying him for a service. And it was not scientific research. He could ill afford to alienate his largest potential donor by publishing a book of which they did not approve.

"And this thing about Bertram Wallace," she continued. "His connection with the zoo was pretty tenuous. He needs to leave that sordid chapter out."

Joanne was getting more agitated by the minute. The fact that Wallace was the body that had been discovered on the zoo was not widely known yet. He decided to back off.

"All right," he held up both hands in surrender. "I'll talk to Amos. We'll take out the Bertram Wallace stuff and we'll have a closer look at the Dotson involvement in the foundation of the zoo. Will that make you happy?"

"Yes," she said simply. "Yes it will."

"Is there any Old Business to come before the Board?" Joanne asked rhetorically. She knew full-well that there was important Old Business to discuss.

"I have something to come before the Board," said Milt, as rehearsed. "I have a copy of the agreement with the City that we discussed at last month's meeting." He waved some papers as Wilma passed copies around the table. "The City Attorney has drawn it up pretty much as the Mayor originally proposed it. They did not accept our request to extend it for ten years."

"It looks like they didn't accept our request for a steady amount of subsidy, either," said Rod. "They still want to wean us off by year six."

"This zoo will never be totally self-supporting," grumbled Ivan. "That's ridiculous."

"Let's send it back," said Rhonda. "Let's insist on a steady subsidy. If the Mayor wants free admission for City residents and school children he needs to bargain with us. That's a big political chip for his campaign."

Heads nodded and random discussions began around the table until Joanne banged her gavel. "Do we have a general consensus that we will stay on as managers of the Zoo?" she asked.

She made eye contact with each person and confirmed their willingness to continue.

"Milt," she continued, "Will you take this back to the Mayor and the City Attorney. If they will agree to these changes, they have a deal."

35

Chelsea stared at the bear-skin rug that hung on the wall behind Donald Laskey's desk. She wondered if he had killed the bear or if it was a gift. He had a nice office with its book shelves, comfortable furniture, and large window overlooking the zoo. But he seemed to be obsessed with bears. He had bears everywhere.

She had been ushered into his office, only to be interrupted by a call from the City Finance office. She was glad for the break because it gave her time to compose her thoughts and explain why she had requested this audience. She had decided in the nine months that she had worked for him, that she rather liked the zoo's director. He seemed a fair and honest man, though a little stressed and troubled. He never really seemed happy in his job.

"Sorry about that," he said hanging up the phone. "Now, what can I do for you?"

"I am working in rhinos and hoofed stock right now, but I want to talk to you about the new exhibit," she said with more confidence than she felt. "I have some ideas I want to share."

He waved his hands for her to continue.

"Last year at this time, I was in West Africa working on my PhD. We were studying a group of chimps to determine their ability to communicate with other species. Political unrest escalated into open warfare and we had to be pulled out by a team of Navy Seals. When I came to work here, I didn't really approve of zoos, but I was desperate for a job. I never intended to stay, but I guess you could say I am hooked."

The mobile phone on his desk buzzed. He looked at it to see who was calling, decided to ignore it, and motioned for her to continue.

"I would like to complete my studies here at the zoo. This new exhibit with elephants and chimps together is revolutionary. It cries out for scientific study from both the chimp side and the elephant side. I have already begun some baseline studies on the chimps. I'd like to gain access to the elephants to look at their baseline behaviors so I'll know what differences to look for after they are all introduced."

Laskey had been looking out the window as she talked. He knew she had a good head on her shoulders because he had seen her in action. He despised people who put women down because of their gender, but try as he might, he also had those deep seated tendencies to underestimate. It was especially difficult with a woman as beautiful as this one. He wondered how she would get along with Parks Jones.

G. Donald Laskey was what was known in the business as an 'old school' zoo director. Most zoo directors, these days, came from academia or business – a PhD or an MBA. He had neither. He had come up through the ranks, beginning as a zookeeper with a Bachelor's Degree in biology some twenty seven years ago. This young lady sitting before him was the future of the profession. She clearly had much to learn about the administrative side of things, but that would just take a little time. He was a good judge of character, and he saw things in her that you could not teach.

"I also have some ideas on how to ease the introductions," she continued when he did not respond. "I would like to use dogs and horses as surrogates."

"What?" he snapped to attention. Now he was disappointed. This sounded crazy.

"I would use a big, furry, black dog and let the elephants get used to being around it without either being afraid or aggressive. I'd do the same with the chimps, only I would use the biggest draft horse I could find."

He nodded in agreement so she continued. "And I would like to make some suggestions on the layout of the exhibit area."

"I need to go over there anyway," he replied. "Let's go for a walk."

The new elephant and chimpanzee exhibit still looked very much like a construction site with its heavy equipment moving about, its jumbled stacks of steel and cable, and its piles of dirt everywhere. Chelsea wondered how it could possibly be finished in six or seven weeks. The construction superintendent, Lyman Denton, had joined them and Chelsea was a bit intimidated to be walking and talking with these two experienced and important men – the tall smooth zoo director and the short, leathery man in the hard hat.

"Chelsea has some ideas I want to look at," Laskey said simply, after the introductions. "They may set us back a bit, but I don't want to miss any opportunities."

Lyman Denton was, Chelsea decided, a man of few words. They walked in silence to the edge of the lake where the animal space reached the shore.

"I suggest we give the animals access to the lake," Chelsea began.

Denton looked at Laskey for confirmation and said, "We've already put up the posts for the elephant cables along the shoreline."

"But you haven't put up the chimp fence yet," countered Chelsea. "All you need to do is put those two posts out in the lake and string your cables out there."

"What about the chimp fence," Denton asked.

"You won't need it," she replied. "Chimps can't swim."

"They can climb," he argued. "What's to stop them climbing around the fence where it meets the water?"

"We'll electrify it," she said. "They need to learn to stay off the fence."

Denton was running out of arguments, so he paused for a moment. This change would actually save them money and time by eliminating a considerable run of expensive chain-link fence. "OK, what else," he said finally.

They shifted their attention to their right and to the three-acre chimp forest that stood across a thirty yard clearing that would be the elephant walkway. The elephant walkway was a half-mile loop that encircled the wooded area and the elephants would be excluded from the forest by post and cable barriers. The chimps, Chelsea knew, would simply hide in the forest.

"We need a way to get people over or under the elephants and into the forest," she said.

"Over or under?" Denton repeated looking at Laskey again. "What does that mean?"

"It means," she said, "you can build a bridge or a tunnel. A tunnel would be better because a bridge would need to be elephant-proof."

"Building a tunnel would set back the schedule," Denton said, still addressing the zoo director.

"Actually we need two tunnels," Chelsea said. "We need observation areas at both ends of the forest. Maybe you could just put in some giant sewer culverts for tunnels."

"I wish it were that simple," Denton replied with resignation. "Anything else?"

"I would like to put in some feeders and waterers that the chimps and the elephants can operate for each other," Chelsea said.

"What?" both men said in unison.

"How is that going to work?" asked Laskey.

"I'm not sure," she replied. "We don't need it for the opening, but I would like to train the animals to help look after each other. The chimps could operate elephant feeders and waterers that would be set up on timers and the elephants would be trained to do the same for the chimps. They would work off of separate auditory and visual cues and it would be controlled by computer."

"What do these feeders and water devices look like," asked Denton.

"I don't know yet," she admitted. "Do you have someone who could help me with that?"

"Fred Williamson, my site supervisor," he said quickly. "He's a genius when it comes to stuff like that."

"Great," she said. "All we need to do now is run some fiber optic cable around the perimeter and tie it back to the zoo's main server. I have some ideas I'd like to go over with Mr. Williamson."

"He's off today," said Denton. "He'll be back Monday. Now, if you'll excuse me, I have some tunnels to design."

"Let's walk over so you can introduce me to those elephants you've been talking about," said John.

"Love to," said Chelsea.

They had just finished lunch and neither was anxious to leave the other's company. One of the benefits of working on a property that was one hundred years old was that it was a mature and beautiful garden. Shade trees lined the wide pathways and daffodils, crocus, and lilies colored the landscape.

"I've been told to wrap up my zoo case by the end of the month," he said as they walked.

"Have you figured out who killed him," she asked.

"I don't even know how he died," he replied. "I have several suspects, but until we determine a cause of death…," he trailed off.

"OK," she said stopping outside the door to the elephant barn. "Here are the ground rules."

"Ground rules?" he said playfully as he looked around and bent forward to kiss her.

She ducked away. "Not here," she said.

They could hear Tommy Ross inside shouting orders to the elephants. She was still officially a rhino keeper, but after her meeting with the director, this would soon be her new area.

"You need to stay behind the yellow line. That's the distance the elephants can reach."

Tommy's shouts became more insistent so Chelsea turned and rushed inside. She was shocked to see Tommy in the stall with Bebe and he was in trouble. She had backed him into a corner and he was trying to push her away with his bull-hook.

"What are you doing in there?!" shouted Chelsea.

Tommy turned to respond and Bebe seized the opportunity. She lunged toward him and slammed her head into the wall with terrifying force. Tommy ducked and that action, along with the fact that he was in a corner gave him enough space to save his life. Chelsea grabbed the lid off one of the metal garbage cans that held feed for the elephants and flung it into the stall toward the enraged elephant. When she turned to face this new challenge, Tommy Ross scurried out through the bars to safety.

"What the hell were you doing in there?" she said. "You could have been killed."

Tommy did not reply or even look up.

John looked over the scene with mouth agape. The elephant had been going for the man's head and if she had hit him, she would have squashed it. That was the same injury that had been inflicted on Mr. Bertram Wallace, and his body had been discovered outside the old elephant house. Another part of the mystery was solved. Now, if he could just figure out who was responsible.

"I love it," Don Laskey said with an enthusiasm he rarely showed. "Very well done."

He handed the thick manila envelope back to Amos Morris, who appeared particularly unenthusiastic.

"I feel like I rewrote history," Amos said.

"You can back it all up, can't you?" asked Laskey. "You have references for all this."

"Oh, it's all factual," he replied. "I just don't like the way I was forced to interpret those facts."

"Look. I know we put pressure on you to portray things in a certain light, but the Dotsons are our biggest supporters."

They sat in silence for a moment as Amos looked around the director's office.

"Look," Amos said finally. "I am a historian. I document facts and I don't appreciate being asked to alter those facts. The Dotsons had nothing to do with this becoming a zoo. Cyrus deeded the property for use as a city park and his sons had to be evicted. It was the mayor and a superintendent named Griffith who started the zoo."

"But the Dotsons are the future hope of this institution," Don countered.

"Look," Don continued after a pause. "This is confidential, but we are in the final stages of a complex negotiation with the Dotson family and the State Board of Regents. We are looking at a twelve million dollar challenge grant from the family to create the Dotson Institute for Environmental Leadership."

Don described a revolutionary program for adult education that would turn the zoo into a college campus. The Institute would provide four-year degree programs for Biology students, two-year associate degrees in zookeeping and veterinary technology, and vocational training in hospitality industry management. It would be a residential facility, complete with dormitories and on-site and off-site internship programs.

"This business of leaving out Bertram Wallace's criminal activity," Amos continued unimpressed, "well, that's just criminal. I might write another book about that alone."

"You can't do that," Don said quickly.
"I can, too. It's all a matter of public record."

36

Friday, June 8th, 2012

The screams were deafening in the confines of the indoor arena that had been used for introductions. Jack the young chimp was clearly terrified, despite the two weeks of gradual introductions, and the elephant Bebe was not responding well. She fanned her ears and lunged at him as he cowered along the wall. He attempted to grab and bite the end of her trunk, which made her even angrier.

"If anyone was going to get into it, it would be these two," said Chelsea.

"I hope we don't have to use the fire extinguishers on them," said Janice. She was referring to the two, large Carbon Dioxide extinguishers that would spew a cloud of white powder in a loud woosh. Animals generally found them terrifying. Janice Fredricks was the training manager who had been working on the animals introductions over the past few weeks. The other animals had adapted fairly well and had gradually settled into a peaceful coexistence, choosing, for the most part, to remain separate.

Jack began to run along the wall as he looked back screaming. This seemed to prompt Bebe to give chase, trumpeting as she ran. She caught him with the end of her trunk and punched him forward. As he lay sprawled in the dirt, temporarily stunned and silent, she loomed over him. Chelsea and Janice held their breath. Bebe sniffed him with her trunk, lingering over his genitals, and then calmly walked away.

The bird house was packed. Groups of school children were wall to wall and as far as he could see down the hall and around the bend. Parks Jones was initially surprised, until he remembered that the schools were approaching spring break, and this was the time of year that teachers bundled up the children and took them out on field trips. The Guest Services department called it the 'yellow plague' in honor of the sea of school buses that filled the parking lot. Parks decided not to fight his way through the crowd and turned back the way he had come. He walked around the outside of the building and to the back door of the kitchen.

"I wondered how you were going to get in here," Ann Gordon said as he pushed through the door.

"Damn kids," he replied gruffly. "You alone?"

"Yes," she smiled.

He edged closer and placed his hands on her hips. It was easy to see why men found Ann attractive. She had an exotic, almost Oriental look about her with those dark eyes and her short straight, jet-black hair. She was a petite woman with nice curves that Parks found attractive. Ann had lost interest in Janice Frederick's ex-husband when Janice left the bird house. She had moved onto bigger quarry.

"Did you get the stuff?" he said with his arms around her and his head buried in her neck.

"It's downstairs," she replied pulling away. She took his hand and led him to the door to the basement.

"Where is everyone?" he asked as they rushed downstairs to the cot that was kept in the basement.

"Where's the coke," he said zipping down his pants. "I need to get back to my office."

Ann sauntered to her locker and rummaged in her knapsack as she unbuttoned her blouse. She came back and dangled the baggie of white powder in front of him.

Suddenly, they were blinded by light from the top of the stairs where they heard Betty Willis say, "See, I told you they were up to something."

Don Laskey could scarcely believe his eyes as he looked down on the scene below.

"Your boyfriend is here," Sam Kest called to Chelsea in a mocking tone. He had been standing nearest the door and heard the knock.

"How's it going in there?" John asked as Chelsea stepped out into the humid morning air. He bent forward to plant a kiss and she shifted her face to offer her cheek.

"We're still having trouble with a couple of the animals, but overall, pretty well." She stepped away and looked into the distance. "Were you serious about expecting me to quit my job?"

"Only if I get the job in Claxton," he replied. "I thought you wanted to get married."

"I do."

"And we want to start a family?"

"Yes."

"Well," he said waving his hand. "This is not the kind of job for a mother. You'll need to quit when we start having kids anyway."

"What?" she wheeled around to face him. "I can't believe you just said that. That's right out of the dark ages."

"All I mean is that I want you home raising our kids not out here chasing animals."

"John," she had tears in her eyes. "This is not just a job for me. Don't make me choose."

"OK," he said holding his hands up in surrender. "I'm sorry. The real reason I'm here is that they discovered another body out here."

"Here? At the zoo?" she asked.

"Yep. Over where they are building that education center," he replied, glad for the change of subject. "And this one has a pitchfork sticking out of his back."

"Wow," she said as the image sunk in. After a pause she gave him a light kiss and turned toward the door. "We can talk this afternoon. I need to get back inside."

"Everything OK?" asked Janice.

"Yes," said Chelsea. "No. I don't want to talk about it. Let's have our meeting."

The new elephant and chimpanzee complex had been designed with a large conference room that had a wall-to-wall window overlooking the arena. It was the ideal location for their meeting because they could monitor activities while they discussed contingencies for the day ahead. The animals had been together for almost two weeks, but they were still having trouble with a few of them and they would need to be prepared for how they would deal with problems while under public scrutiny. Joining Chelsea and Janice were elephant manager Sam Kest, elephant keeper Sal Martinez, and chimp keeper Billy Scales.

"We're still on for the ten o'clock event," began Chelsea. "Does anybody have any last minute concerns?"

"So, tell me again what we're supposed to do when one of the elephants decides to stomp one of the chimps in front of the TV cameras?" asked Sam. "Since we can't go in to separate them, I guess we just watch."

"We've been through this, Sam" said an exasperated Chelsea. "Every mixed exhibit has some danger associated. The chimps have plenty of escape areas that the elephants can't get to. Besides, if we were going to have problems, we would have already had them."

"You mean like the one we had twenty minutes ago?" he said sarcastically.

Chelsea ignored him and faced Billy.

"Sonny and Simba will be fine," said Billy. "Elke seems interested in Sonny, but the old couple has learned to move out of the way when the elephants are around. Jana is afraid of all of them. It may take a while for her to warm up to this. She'll probably hide all day. As for Jack, I hope this morning got his attention. I can't predict what he might get up to today."

"Sal?" asked Chelsea, choosing to avoid the sulking elephant manager. "What about your girls?"

"Elke will be fine," he replied. "I think she likes all this. A new home and the strange new animals has really perked her up. Sally and Bebe are a different story. If Elke doesn't keep them in line, they will go after the chimps, especially that idiot Jack."

Chelsea looked at Janice for the training manager's comments. Janice had been devising the training program that would give them some semblance of control.

"All we can do at this point," she began, "is follow our protocols. Let's try to keep the animals focused on us while the cameras are rolling. We'll station ourselves around the perimeter with our feed buckets and do the training routines we've been working on. Sam," she looked his way. "Are you onboard?"

She knew he was not and he confirmed that by getting up and walking out without a word.

It was not the first time the male llama had spit on Colin McDermott, but the timing had never been worse. In a few minutes, he and Ellen Stubblefield were to escort Mr. James Malone to the zoo plaza for the one-hundredth anniversary celebration of the founding of the Dotson Park zoo. He wasn't sure why it was called "spit". It was really more like vomit, with its little bits of partially digested hay mixed with a green mucous. Llamas like to let fly with their stomach contents when they are angry or threatened. In this case, Colin was in a hurry and tried to push the animal out of the way in order to finish cleaning his pen. The llama had obviously objected.

Behind the children's zoo barn, Ellen patiently coiled her hose into a neat circle on the floor just the way John Bullard had taught her

"I need to go, Mr. B," Ellen shouted as she finished with the hose.

"Go ahead, Missy," the old zookeeper said. "I'll be down there shortly."

She ran all the way to the main gate where an old man sat parked in a wheelchair next to the ticket booth with a nervous, young ticket-booth worker standing by his side.

"Are you Mr. Malone?" She asked.

"Yes." He confirmed without looking up. "You're late."

"Sorry," Ellen offered.

"We'll show you to the plaza," Colin said as he hurried breathlessly to join them.

Ellen wheeled the chair around and they walked in silence, past a large woman pushing a red stroller, a little girl clutching newly-purchased stuffed giraffe, and a smiling elderly couple strolling arm-in-arm. A sea lion barked in the distance and the old man looked aimlessly around. A heavy, book with a glossy brown cover was nestled on his lap. It was entitled *The Dotson Park Zoo – The First 100 Years*.

"Stop here," the old man ordered.

Colin and Ellen looked at each other. They were in sight of their destination, an open plaza ringed with newly-planted oak trees. It was paved with expensive bricks that had been inscribed with people's names. At one end, water squirted out of the pavement around a bronze black bear. The other end, overlooking the lake, was dominated by a massive beech tree with a twisted, gnarled trunk. The many hearts and initials carved in its trunk indicate that it was the site of many romantic encounters in the past. A low platform had been set up under the tree for the celebration and a colorful banner proclaimed "Dotson Park Zoo Centennial".

Ellen backed the wheelchair off the path, and she and Colin sat on a bench next to the old man. He was looking intently at a black bear that paced in the last cage on lion house row.

"They can come get me when they're ready," said the old man.

The sweet smell of gardenias wafted over them – two teenagers on a bench and an old man in his nineties slumped in a wheelchair.

"We had a cobra escape from that building when I worked here," the old man said.

"Pardon?" asked Colin.

"A cobra," he repeated. "And you won't see anything about that in here," he continued, stabbing a gnarled finger at the book on his lap.

Colin looked at Ellen and rolled his eyes. He hadn't read the book, but he had looked at some of the pictures.

"How do you know?" Ellen asked politely.

"I was here," he said. "Who is that?" he pointed to Chelsea Johns walking past.

"That's Miss Johns," Ellen replied. "She works here."

The old man stared at her for a long time. The kids thought it odd for an old man to be staring so openly at a beautiful woman.

"Mr. Malone," said zoo director Don Laskey as he strode up the pathway. "Good to see you again." He offered his hand, but the old man made no move to take it. "Have these kids been taking good care of you?"

"Is that woman related to Alvin Doyle?" he asked, nodding toward a now-distant Chelsea.

"Who?"

"Al Doyle. He was Calvin Griffith's right-hand man when I came here. She could be his daughter. Same red hair, same round freckled face, and those big green eyes."

Laskey glanced at Chelsea. "I don't think so," he said. "I'm sure she would have said something."

"Who wrote this book?" the old man asked, changing the subject.

"A historian by the name of Amos Morris," Don replied.

As they began to walk, Don explained James Malone's background to his young escorts. He was the curator of the zoo when many of the buildings were constructed in the 1930's and eventually worked his way up to director. He left the Dotson Park Zoo to be director of the zoo in Chicago where he stayed until he retired. He was an author, an educator, and a world famous naturalist. They had invited him back to cut the ribbon on the new elephant and chimpanzee complex and to help announce the founding of the Dotson Institute for Environmental Leadership.

After the ceremony, the crowd had dispersed quickly. It was a hot day and the speeches went on too long, but people seemed impressed with the new exhibit and, judging by the buzz, they were also excited at the announcement of the plans for the Institute. Don was exhausted. He slouched in his metal folding chair as the old man dozed in his wheelchair next to him. They were alone on the grandstand in the shade of the massive Beech tree as workers bustled around them removing the sound system and podium.

"We found two bodies on this property," Don said idly. "One of them just this morning."

The old man's eyes popped open in interest.

"Today's body has a pitchfork in its back. You wouldn't know anything about either of them," Don turned to James, "would you?"

"Any idea who they were?" James asked.

"Not the pitchfork guy. The other one was Bertram Wallace," replied Don. "That one must have occurred during your time."

"Wallace was a son of a bitch," said James with sudden venom. "He got what he deserved."

"How did he die?"

The old man sat for a moment. The fact that he hesitated told Don that James knew and was deciding whether to open up after all these years.

"Wallace was blackmailing practically everyone out here," James began without looking at Don. "We all hated him and would have killed him if we'd had the chance. It was Buddy Griffith that had the pleasure. Buddy lured Wallace to the elephant house one evening. I think it was the night before the exhibit opened. He knocked Wallace unconscious and let Bwana finish the job."

"Bwana?"

"The bull elephant. Somehow Buddy stood Wallace up against the bars of the cage and got Bwana so squash his head like a pumpkin."

They were silent for a moment. James closed his eyes, seeming relieved to have finally told his story. Don knew he would need to tell Detective Stokes but knew there was nothing to be done when everybody involved was long-dead. As his gaze swung idly to his left he saw Chelsea arguing with Sam Kest. He watched with interest as the young woman shook her finger at the hard-boiled elephant keeper and strode confidently away. As she walked in his direction, he caught her eye and motioned her over.

"Is he all right?" she nodded toward James Malone and drew a chair quietly to face them.

No answer was needed as they both turned to watch his steady breathing.

"I fired Parks Jones a little while ago," Don said quietly, still looking at the old man.

"Good," Chelsea replied simply.

"He would have been a disaster for this place," Don continued. "This zoo has a long history and is deserves the best." After a pause, he asked "Would you be interested in the job?"

Chelsea was shocked. She was sitting in a chair with her back to the plaza, facing the two men and the exhibit behind them. Her break up with John had filled her with an empty melancholy but she knew she had made the right decision. This zoo had been here for a hundred years. It was founded by people who were long forgotten and built by people like James Malone who, she had discovered, was her age when he started at the zoo in 1937.

She was about to say yes when her thoughts were interrupted by one of the chimps emerging from the forest below her. It was Jack and he was on a collision course with Bebe the elephant. They were both moving toward feeding stations in opposite directions, but their paths were about to cross. Chelsea held her breath, bracing for the encounter that was about to happen. Jack looked up startled and rose up for a better look. Bebe also stopped, and then walked toward the chimp in her path. Jack stood his ground and as the elephant drew near, she sniffed his genitals.

Billy Scales was nearby but outside the barrier and powerless to act.

Chelsea sat up in her chair in astonishment and Don turned to see what had captured her attention. Suddenly, as if choreographed, Bebe grabbed jack around his middle with her trunk and threw him up on her back. He sat for a moment in surprise before settling down to enjoy the ride. Bebe ambled down the path with the chimp on her back.

Billy turned toward Chelsea and held up his fist in salute. She saluted back and returned her attention to Don. She imagined herself in a business suit walking the grounds as the zoo's first female director. Then she thought about the research project she would implement to complete the requirements for her PhD in Zoology. Doctor Chelsea Johns would have a nice ring to it.

"I don't know," she said hesitantly. "If I take this job, I'll never complete my Doctorate. There is so much to learn about these animals."

"What about this," Don said as he turned back from watching the animal encounter. "My health is pretty good right now. What if I stay on and keep the seat warm for you? You'll be my Deputy Director while you complete your degree. When you finish…" He left the rest unsaid and held out his hand.

She looked at the elephants and chimps in the distance then at the old man next to Don. "I'd be honored," she said finally. She shook his hand and a new era in the story of the Dotson Park Zoo began in the shade of that ancient Beech tree.

####